MUD WAR

MUD WAR

DWARVISH DIRTY DOZEN™ SERIES BOOK ONE

AARON D. SCHNEIDER
MICHAEL ANDERLE

This book is a work of fiction. All of the characters, organizations, and events portrayed in this novel are either products of the author's imagination or are used fictitiously. Sometimes both.

Copyright © 2022 LMBPN Publishing
Cover Art by Jake @ J Caleb Design
http://jcalebdesign.com / jcalebdesign@gmail.com
Cover copyright © LMBPN Publishing
A Michael Anderle Production

LMBPN Publishing supports the right to free expression and the value of copyright. The purpose of copyright is to encourage writers and artists to produce the creative works that enrich our culture.

The distribution of this book without permission is a theft of the author's intellectual property. If you would like permission to use material from the book (other than for review purposes), please contact support@lmbpn.com. Thank you for your support of the author's rights.

LMBPN Publishing
PMB 196, 2540 South Maryland Pkwy
Las Vegas, NV 89109

Version 1.00, June 2022
ebook ISBN: 979-8-88541-432-6
Paperback ISBN: 979-8-88541-433-3

THE MUD WAR TEAM

Thanks to our Beta Team:

Mary Morris, Kelly O'Donnell, John Ashmore, Rachel Beckford, Larry Omans

Thanks to our JIT Team:

Zacc Pelter
Jeff Goode
Jackey Hankard-Brodie
Dorothy Lloyd
Diane L. Smith
Dave Hicks
Peter Manis
Christopher Gilliard
Debra Hogan
Paul Westman

If we've missed anyone, please let us know!

Editor
SkyFyre Editing Team

This book is dedicated to every craftsman whose strong and steady hands have shaped my world and my life, those who make things, mend things, and are in so many ways the epitome of what I would wish to be. But most of all, this is to one of the finest and most tireless craftsmen and servant-leaders I've had the privilege to know—this is dedicated to my father-in-law Brian. I'm sure you'll probably never have time to read my silly scribblings, but this book is for you, sir. It comes with my sincerest thanks for the man and example you've been and continue to be.

— Aaron

*To Family, Friends and
Those Who Love
to Read.
May We All Enjoy Grace
to Live the Life We Are
Called.*

— Michael

ACKNOWLEDGMENTS

I'd like to take a second to acknowledge that this book, along with being part of the efforts of many people besides myself, would not have been possible without the continued patience of family and friends who tolerate my groanings and mutterings of deadlines one moment and then hold nothing against me when I descend into my cave and plunk away.

I am sure it gets tiresome being the wife/child/brother/companion of an author, but your patience and steady encouragement are like air. I often take them for granted, but without them, I'd quickly cease to be. So thank you many times over.

Hopefully, this book is worth some of what you've had to put up with.

— Aaron

I was born one morning,
It was drizzlin' rain.
Fightin' and trouble are my middle name

16 Tons, Tennessee Ernie Ford

Out of the night that covers me,
Black as the Pit from pole to pole,
I thank whatever gods may be

Invictus, William Ernest Henley

When midnight mists are creeping,
And all the land is sleeping,
Around me tread the mighty dead,
And slowly pass away.
Lo, warriors, saints, and sages,
From out the vanished ages,
With solemn pace and reverend face
Appear and pass away.
The blaze of noonday splendour,
The twilight soft and tender,
May charm the eye: yet they shall die,
Shall die and pass away.
But here, in Dreamland's centre,

No spoiler's hand may enter,
These visions fair, this radiance rare,
Shall never pass away.
I see the shadows falling,
The forms of old recalling;
Around me tread the mighty dead,
And slowly pass away.

Dreamland, Charles Lutwidge Dodgson

SOUTHERN YSGAND VALE MAP

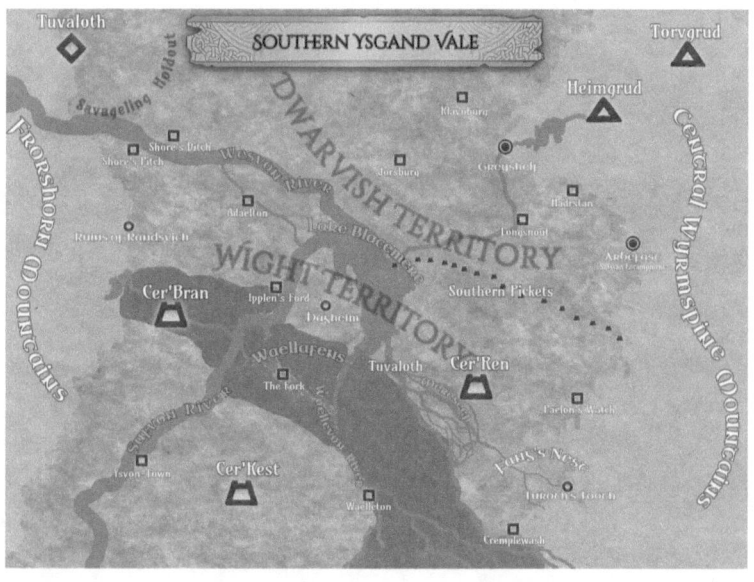

LEXICON

Military Ranks

— Enlisted —

Dwan - The base rank of the Holt'Dwan and also a term that generally refers to a dwarf serving as a soldier

Fordwan - A line officer, typically promoted from veteran dwan

Ascedwan - A dwarf soldier who has developed a useful skill (cooking, herbology, engineering, musical instrument, etc.), marking them out for additional pay/responsibility

— Commissioned Officer —

Schildwan - quartermaster of a division
Tweldwan - commander of a division
— Command Staff —
Kuadwan - command staff, responsible for logistical matters
Lardwan - command staff, responsible for communication and intelligence

Vindwan - command staff, responsible for tactical direction

Ondwan - command staff, supreme commander of the Holt'Dwan

— Informal Positions —

Cubldwan - An unofficial position, represents when a soldier is selected to work under a superior officer, usually either a tweldwan or one of the command staff

Military Terminology

Adyrclaf - a class of theropod typically used as a mount by the svartalf

Blotferow - a class of trained and specially bred pigs that is suitable for use in battle

Duabuw - standard-issue crossbow of the dwarven army

Holt'Dwan - A dwarven army, typically composed of between 8 to 12 divisions

Magsax - standard-issue sword of the dwarven army

Worcsvine - a class of trained and specially bred pigs that are suitable for draft work

Slurs

Badger - Derived from drawing a comparison between the animals and dwarfs

Clacker/Creaker/Rattler/Shuffler - slur for the ambulatory undead who serve in the wight army. Given for the sounds they make

Grem - Derived from drawing comparisons between mythical gremlins and goblins

Longshanks - Can be used for any people group taller than dwarfs, but typically used for humans

Myrkling - Derived from the Dwarvish word for dark/dangerous forest (myrkvaul) and denotes an elf of svartalf or dark elf lineage

Savageling - slur for the wosealf or wild elves of the Ysgand Vale

Wheezer - slur for a wight after the sound of the undead voices

PROLOGUE

Torbjorn looked around the room to make certain everyone was in position before contemplating the stale-smelling drink before him.

"We ready to do this?" Raelon sniffed.

The dwarvish commander picked up the beer as he gave a bare nod.

"Showtime." The younger dwarf grunted as he glanced to make certain the barkeep wasn't distracted. It would have been a shame to waste the performance.

"How do you tell the difference between human beer and human piss?"

Torbjorn groaned and gave a shake of his dark, shaggy head. He grimaced through the first swallow of the watery ale. He swiped off the thin film that clung to his mustache with a thick, scar-gnarled hand, then threw it away with a contemptuous flick. It landed upon boards scored with runes to keep them clean and polished.

"This one again?" he grumbled into his cup, wincing at the thought of the sour ale being an offering to his people's inscription upon the floor.

It's about the Wheezer magistrate, he told himself. *Nothing else.*

After all, Raelon was just doing what he was best at, though admittedly, this was not his best work.

"Huh?" the bartender rumbled from behind a bar that had been crudely raised to accommodate a new kind of clientele some years ago.

The dwarf sitting on Torbjorn's right raised his snout from sniffing uncertainly at the contents of his cup.

"I said," Raelon began after clearing his throat, "how do you tell the difference between human beer and human piss?"

Torbjorn had heard the joke before. That didn't spoil a good joke, mind you, but since it wasn't a *good* joke, the repetition grated. The publican who'd served Torbjorn and his companion said ale was both human and standing right in front of them, but that was neither here nor there.

"You really want to finish that one, *friend?*" the barman asked with enough of a snarl in the last word to make it like a threat.

The dwarf sitting beside Torbjorn performed a far more exaggerated pantomime of revulsion as he took a swig from his own jack of ale.

"Ugh! *Oskilget!*" Raelon growled, the words rattling in the back of his throat like bile. He looked at the glowering proprietor, beer-filled vessel held up. "I'd much rather finish the joke than whatever *this* is."

The first part of the publican's answer was to draw a heavy club from under the bar, and the next was to nod at a pair of rough-hewn men at a table behind where Torbjorn and Raelon sat. The stout men loomed behind the dwarfs, menacing rumbles and sharp sniffs announcing their presence. Well, further announcing their presence, if the crinkle in Torbjorn's nose was any evidence.

"All right, then," the barkeep continued, his voice almost gentle. "How *do* you tell the difference between human beer and human piss?"

Torbjorn sighed as he idly scratched the welted scar on his cheek.

Smiling from ear to ear, Raelon spoke loud enough for the entire tavern to hear him.

"If the barkeep is washing his hands, you know it's beer!" The dwarf guffawed as the publican's already red face purpled. From around the room came angry mumbles. The patrons were huddled about tables that had likewise had ramshackle additions to elevate them to be comfortable for humans.

"Get it?" Raelon called, acting like the participation of patrons added them to his audience. Rather than deterring him, the barkeep's hard-eyed silence made him laugh all the harder. He dumped the offending ale upon the floor.

Torbjorn forced himself not to wince as more of the swill splashed the boards, which had been hewn by dwarvish settlers less than a decade ago.

The wight, he reminded himself. *The wight's what matters.*

Baritone laughter rolled across the bar even as the barkeep's cudgel came down with a sharp smack on the wood.

"That's it!" the human snarled with such vehemence that his jowls shook. "Both of you, out! Damned uppity badgers!"

Neither dwarf seemed to mind the slur. The pair behind the duo moved forward, hands curling into claws to snare clothes, hair, or beards. They were inches from snaring the dwarfs in front of them when the unnoticed dwarf vaulted onto the table behind them, scattering mugs and platters. The pair of bully boys had just enough time to realize that something was amiss before an iron grip seized their lank hair. Their heads met with a meaty smack, which was followed by the *thuds* of their bodies hitting the floor.

A quarter of a second after they landed, Raelon slapped down a hand to pin the bartender's cudgel in place. His other hand swung an ale-streaming tankard toward the man's shocked, blotchy face. The publican tumbled backward, fondling his mashed lips and cracked jaw tenderly. Raelon used the momentum of the swing to propel him onto the bar, where he paused, cudgel in his hairy fists.

Standing wide-legged on the table and the bar respectively, the dwarfs, clearly siblings despite the different shades of their hair, exchanged wicked smiles. The larger of the two, a hulking dwarf with bright red hair and beard, crossed his muscle-knotted arms over his huge chest. His brother gripped the snatched club. Across the bar, angry eyes swung in their direction.

"Impeccable timing as always, Waelon," Torbjorn offered with a nod as he turned halfway around to acknowledge the powerfully thewed dwarf. The serene dwarf, leader by sheer presence if nothing else, had not even bothered to shift in his seat through the explosive turn of events. As before, he stared with pensive concern at the drink in his hand.

"Yes, sir." Waelon grunted. "Satisfactory for our purposes, sir?"

Torbjorn raised his eyes to the cudgel-bearing dwarf on the bar in front of him.

"Has anyone made to fetch the magistrate yet, Raelon?"

Raelon, who'd been busy meeting every human face with a frightful scowl, took a moment to respond.

"What? Oh!" the younger dwarf muttered before straightening a little. "No, sir. Not yet."

Torbjorn slowly set his tankard down and shook his head.

"That simply will not do," he muttered, bracing one hand on the bar. "Waelon, if you would, please."

"Of course, sir." The big dwarf raised his voice to address the seething patrons. "Well, are you peach-faced, spindly-legged, piss drinkers going to do something about it, or are you scared of a few badgers?"

Like a spark set to tinder, the words ignited the seething patrons. The scene in the pub became distinctly more chaotic.

Waelon's fists pumped like pistons, pulping faces that came within reach of his table. Raelon swept the hardwood club in arcs about the bar. Snarling and cursing patrons leapt clear of the whistling bludgeon. Only a few moved too slowly to escape its sting, but there was soon more than enough room for Torbjorn to climb onto the bar, dragging his chair with him. Once stationed beside Raelon, chair in hand, Torbjorn got two hard swings out of the furnishing before being forced to snap a chair leg off in each hand. Thus equipped, he leapt back into the fray, dealing out hefty smacks with the stout legs to every hand, shoulder, and head in reach.

"Think I saw a few go for the door, sir," Raelon growled as he danced back from clutching mitts before dealing a solid thump across the head of an attacker. "Won't be long now."

Torbjorn brought both chair legs up to check a swung stool, catching the furniture with one and the wrist of the unfortunate enemy with the other. The wet snap of bone heralded the fall of both stool and wielder to the floor.

"Very good," the dwarf leader declared, then planted his foot in the face of a lunging assailant. "I was hoping to get this business finished as quickly as possible."

"Quick and hard," Raelon crowed as he held the cudgel lengthwise to chuck a pair of humans off him. "Just the way we like it. Eh, Waelon?"

In answer, the fiery-haired dwarf gave a tectonic bellow, then hurtled off the table into a knot of men. Like saplings trying to bear the brunt of a landslide, they bowed and quickly snapped. Not content with the ruin he'd wrought in his descent, Waelon snatched the nearest wretch and hauled him up to use as a living battering ram against his fellows. The sight was as terrifying as it was comical. The men screamed in shock as they were bludgeoned with their unfortunate compatriot.

After Waelon pitched his impromptu weapon aside, he bellowed at the faces around him, "Who's next?"

Those faces didn't press forward, and after Raelon clubbed the last arm reaching over the bar, an uncertain silence fell. The dwarvish trio's ferocity was not easily matched, and the patron's initial rush had been thoroughly rebuffed. No one was keen to be the next to be corrected, like those who lay on the floor broken, bleeding, and toothless.

The hate still simmered in their flushed, sweaty faces, but they were peasants and thus forced to be pragmatic. Rough, certainly, but only prone to violence when the odds were distinctly in their favor. What had just ensued had drastically altered the calculation. In the face of such arithmetic, obviously not their strong suit, the humans stood glaring above the soft groans of the wounded.

It was easy to hear the doors swing open and the thump and scrape of several pairs of heavy boots.

"What's all this, then?" growled a mustachioed man whose knee-length gambeson and sable tabard matched those of the four men at his shoulder. The only thing that clearly distinguished him was the heavy copper chain that was about his neck.

"What the kak?" Raelon spat. "Where's the damned wheezer?"

"Dwan up," Torbjorn snapped, and even the irrepressible Raelon bowed his chin at the rebuke.

"Wheezer, eh?" The man with the mustache chortled deep in his throat. "That's who you came to see?"

The walrus-lipped man, who was obviously the bailiff of this heel-clinger of a town, eyed the trio of dwarfs and nodded at his men. The guards spread out across the room, repositioning to corral their quarry as well as giving each other enough room to brandish their short spears. The human patrons, their fear gone after the sudden appearance of armed guards, sneered at the beleaguered brawlers.

"If you come quietly, you'll get to meet the magistrate," the bailiff told the dwarfs as he raised one hand to idly toy with the chain on his breast. "I doubt it will be a pleasant conversation, but you'll still be breathing when you get there."

A low rumble sounded in Waelon's chest, and even with weapons in hand, the guards shuffled back a step.

"Come any closer, and you'll be riding that pigsticker," Raelon warned as his brother leaned forward menacingly.

"Come now," the bailiff called, doing a remarkable job of keeping his composure. "You're outnumbered and outarmed. The worst you can expect from this is to pay damages and spend some time in the stocks."

Reassured by their leader's level voice, the guards continued their advance with iron spearheads held level with dwarvish hearts.

"If you resist, though," the bailiff added, an ugly smile beneath his mustache, "you'll be lucky if one of you is left alive to stand trial."

The spear points shuffled closer, and, despite his imposing glower, Waelon slid a foot back toward the bar. Raelon and Torbjorn pressed closer together. It was a testament to the dwarvish brothers that neither looked at Torbjorn but kept their eyes on the advancing enemy.

"I suppose there's nothing for it." Torbjorn sighed, rolled his shoulders, and shook the tension out through his arms. The nicked and bloodied chair legs wobbled in his thick hands, then the dwarf tightened his grip and looked the bailiff in the eye with a stony expression.

"*Gefarer!*" he bellowed in a battle shout, and two more dwarfs sprang from their hiding places in the shadowy corners of the bar.

One, who was nearly as tall as Waelon and even wider, crashed into the rightmost wing of the guards like a blond boulder. He had a round shield gripped in each meaty fist. The other, a dwarfess of pale complexion who was lithe by her race's standards, darted toward the bailiff, whirling a loaded sling about her head. The first man in the path of the towheaded dwarf went bum over brains in short order while the next slammed into his next compatriot. From the newly created breathing room, the stout dwarf pitched a shield to Waelon before retrieving a broad-bladed sword off his belt.

The bailiff hardly had time to appreciate the sudden change in situation before the she-dwarf snapped his shin with a merciless blow from the sling. The man fell with a scream that was drowned out a moment later by a quintet of deep dwarven voices raised in a war cry.

"*BAD BADGERS!*" the dwarfs roared as they surged toward the remaining guards.

With Waelon and the blond dwarf leading the way, iron sparked on iron as spearheads met boss and rim, but nothing slowed the advance. Waelon snatched an over-extended spear from the hands of one guard and beat its former wielder about the head with the shaft until bone and wood gave sympathetic cracks. Beside him, the golden-headed dwarf drove up under a thrust and hacked into an exposed knee. The guard fell back with a choked gasp, spoiling the thrust of his compatriot. Raelon and Torbjorn descended in a storm of crushing blows.

In a matter of seconds, the dwarfs had gone from cornered to on the attack to victorious. The patrons of the bar stared in shock. The guard with the ruined knee and the bailiff with the shattered shin broke the silence with piteous and grating utterances forced through clenched teeth.

Waelon looked at his commanding officer, shortened spear in hand, as Torbjorn rose from his victim. Torbjorn nodded at the guard, whose blood was still pumping from his partially severed leg. Waelon gave a grunt of acknowledgment and moved to comply. The spear bit deep and the man gasped, then there were only the bailiff's moans.

Torbjorn dropped the chair legs as he stepped toward the bailiff, who lay rocking upon the floor. His shin went off at a sharp, stomach-turning angle, but Torbjorn ignored that as he hooked his fingers around the copper chain.

"T-take it," the man whined. Sweat poured down his face even as he paled with pain. "P-please, just don't—"

"Kill you?" Torbjorn mused softly as he examined the chain. "No, I'm afraid you don't need to worry about me."

The bailiff blinked, his pain-addled mind still able to sense that something was off in the dwarf's response. However, a lifetime of toadying to the powerful had trained him well for this moment. His hands pawed fawningly at Torbjorn's sleeve.

"Oh, th-thank you," he began, trying to catch the dwarf's attention to assure his coming flattery would have an impact. The dwarf's dark eyes were locked on the burnished copper.

"You should all get out of here while you can," Torbjorn declared, his voice raised to address the patrons who remained whole and conscious. "Things may take a turn for the worse."

The silence continued for a moment, then chairs and stools scooted, and bowed heads and shuffling feet made their way to the door. The bailiff tried to catch the eyes of those who shambled past him, but all of them kept their gazes averted. It was a silent testimony to their tutelage under the bailiff and his patron that they did it with such quiet obedience. They'd learned to look the other way, so why not now?

The dwarf leader's voice drew the bailiff's attention to the chain being held before his eyes.

"Can it hear you now?" Torbjorn asked when he spied the faintest tracery of a corrosion like verdigris between the links.

"W-what?" The bailiff coughed, swallowing the pleas and promises he'd been about to utter. The game had changed once more.

"Your master, the magistrate," Torbjorn muttered, eyes narrowing as the veins of corrosion slithered and squirmed across the copper wrapped around his knuckles. "Does he always hear you, or do you have to reach out to him?"

A dread far deeper than physical pain warped the bailiff's features as he saw something in the dwarf's expression.

"No," he sobbed. "Please, just go."

Torbjorn frowned as he looked at the bailiff's face for the first time since gripping the chain. The dwarf read the man's expression, then, with a weary sigh, reached toward the man's shattered shin with his bloody free hand.

"What's your name, lad?" the dwarf asked, his voice even and unhurried.

The bailiff gave a soft, gargling whine as he felt the heavy hand settle near raw, splintered bone.

"Ch-ch-chorden," he heaved between hitching breaths. "Please, I-I'm begging you, just—"

"Chorden, listen to me," Torbjorn instructed, his voice flat and hard. "I want you to call him."

Chorden, the bailiff of Ipplen's Ford for nearly a decade, had done what was being asked of him only twice in his tenure. Each time, he'd sworn an oath afterward, telling himself it wasn't worth it, and he'd rather be dead than do so again. Neither time had been as desperate as this incident, but even so, he hesitated.

"Anything," he panted. "Anything but tha—"

Torbjorn's hand clamped on the messy fracture in Chorden's leg and slowly twisted. The noises the bailiff made couldn't be called screams, but the sharp, shrill bleats made the other dwarfs look away, brows lowered and eyes dark.

"Call him, Chorden," Torbjorn instructed, his voice flat and dispassionate, his face stony. "Call him, and it's over."

The bailiff gagged on spittle as he gave a choking, gasping nod. Torbjorn's hand released the grating spurs of bone, and the man's body seemed to deflate.

"All right, all right," Chorden wheezed. "Just a moment."

The bailiff's eyes were pinched shut, so he didn't see the pained disgust on Torbjorn's face as he peered at the blood on his hands.

"Hurry it up," Torbjorn growled in a thickening voice as he

dragged his hand over the thigh of his trousers to get rid of the clinging liquid.

It took the bailiff of Ipplen's Ford, which had been dwarvish homesteads and was now wight territory, several moments to gather himself. When he spoke, it was with practiced words that were foreign to his tongue. The words, which were supposed to sound like chiming bells, sounded like the thuds of a hammer upon a stubborn horseshoe, yet, for all their crudity, the alien words resonated with the chain about Chorden's neck. There was the slightest rustling clink as the chain shifted. Torbjorn felt the metal links grow icy-cold.

The verdigris flashed stabbing symbols that the dwarf's mind utterly rejected.

Torbjorn released the links, and they constricted about Chorden's throat like a noose. The bailiff gave a snarled cough in the back of his throat, and when the air left his mouth, it steamed. A fell light shone in Chorden's eyes, a chill brightness like stars piercing the darkness with an illumination that gave no warmth and no hope.

"What is the meaning of this?"

The question came in the bailiff's voice, but he could never have mustered the magistrate's superior tone.

"Your pet's broken," Torbjorn drawled. "And your little fief is about to be put to the torch. How does that sound, Wheezer?"

Chorden's bluish lips peeled back from his teeth with a cruel, alien expression.

"Sounds like you are dead, dwarf," the magistrate replied. "When I am done with you, I will send your shambling husk back as a warning to the other *tozelchaun*."

"Come and get us, then," the dwarvish leader declared. The strange light faded from Chorden's eyes, and he sank to the ground, limp.

Outside, there was a sudden shift in the wind that set the

frame of the building to creaking like old bones. A chill didn't creep into the air so much as scuttle in with unseemly haste.

"The dead move quick," Waelon rumbled as he took a wedge-headed axe from the belt of the blond dwarf.

"Just one more secret to puzzle out," the pale dwarf stated in a soft whisper as she came over to Chorden's recumbent form. The strings of the sling made a crude garrote.

Torbjorn waved her off.

"Muri, no," he ordered, the words soft on the ear but ringing with an authority that made the she-dwarf step back quickly. She squinted incredulously at the troop's leader as she unwound the cords from around her fists, but she said nothing.

"Anybody know how to handle a wheezer that doesn't involve field artillery?" Raelon asked as he hefted a spear. His eyes were on the door, where an icy fog had begun to pool.

"We hit it until it stops moving," the massive blond dwarf offered. "And then we hit it more."

Everyone's eyes swung to the leader, who shrugged.

"You have a better idea?" Torbjorn asked, tugging a long knife from Chorden's belt. He winced when he heard the man give an unconscious whimper. He did his best not to look at the messy shin while retrieving a chair leg, but his belly was uneasy.

The dwarfs in the public house said nothing, just took their places as the fog continued to slither across the floor in frosty tendrils. They formed a blunt wedge with Torbjorn at the fore, the two shield-wielding dwarfs at his shoulder, and Raelon and the gray dwarfess behind them.

"Anyone want to say anything worth remembering before we do this?" Torbjorn asked, his hands firmly gripping the cudgel and the knife's hilt.

Silence.

Just beyond the door, something stirred the fog, which continued crawling across the floor toward the dwarfs. It began to thicken as though taunting those within that it might consume them along with the dead and insensate.

"Didn't think so." Torbjorn grunted. "Pleased to be serving with you, as always."

The door shuddered, then burst apart in a storm of frosted splinters, and the Magistrate of Ipplen Falls strode in. He was met by bellows from five throats.

"BAD BADGERS!"

CHAPTER ONE

"Now remember, you are a coward," Tomza muttered under her breath as they were marched through camp. "No doubt, no debate. Do you hear me? A coward."

Ober winced at the force in his older sister's whispered instructions, but secretly, he chafed at the idea of being thought a coward. He might have been cursed—damned, even—but this latest indignity was almost too much for him to bear.

"If I'm going to die—" he growled, but Tomza's words cut as quick and sharp as her surgeon's blades.

"If they were going to execute either of us, they would have done it already," the dwarfess stated as she eyed the armored guards who were escorting them. One pair was two steps ahead, another two steps behind. All were careful to keep their distance lest their clans' honor be soiled by proximity. The other dwans they passed in the camp stayed even farther away, and not just to avoid being in the little procession's way. Removing the stain of coming in direct contact with one of the *dwooshoth*, or disgraced dwarfs, would require, at minimum, a priest of the cavern and a compensatory sacrifice, investments of time, money, and effort that no soldier could be bothered to undertake.

"So, where are we going?" Ober asked, the unknown robbing him of the brash courage he'd mustered for his execution. "What are they going to do with us?"

"Send us to the Deeping, I expect," Tomza replied, her voice full of grim determination. "If we're lucky, we'll be sent to the same shaft."

Ober looked at his sister and saw, as he always did, that she was trying very hard to seem strong and sure when she was anything but.

"The Deeping?" he murmured, struggling to keep his voice from rising with dismay. "But Tomza, that'll…"

He couldn't think of how to finish the sentence without it coming out as a cry of despair, so he swallowed the unformed words and tried not to choke. The lump stuck in his throat, and he gave a low grunt that came out sounding like a sob.

Ober looked up to see a dwarf veteran, probably a fordwan—a line officer—staring at him with hard eyes. The soldier was scarred all over and had a pipe clenched in his teeth. As though in answer to the sob, the fordwan removed the pipe with one grizzled, war-gnarled hand to spit in disgust. The thick sputum struck the packed dirt of the camp path a half-dozen steps from where the condemned sibling walked. Even the hoary old battler wasn't going to risk his iron-clad honor by standing near them.

"Hush, now," Tomza soothed, the softness in her tone showing she understood his feelings. "No matter what happens, we're going to try to stick together."

Ober nodded as he gazed at the rows of tents and the bustling army of dwarfs going about their soldierly duties. He wasn't certain what answers he would find among the tall evergreens that surrounded the camp, but he was unsure of what else to do. The world seemed to be shrinking around him until even the sky, which had seemed so terrifyingly vast when he'd first seen it, looked ready to collapse and shrink and be impaled on the stabbing tops of the trees.

How had it come to this?

"W-we c-could tell th-them," he began, his voice betraying him. The very thought of confession churned anxiety and something...else inside him.

"No!" Tomza hissed, one hand gripping his manacled wrist so their irons clanked together. "Don't even think it."

"Enough of that," barked the guard behind them. Tomza's hand was gone in an instant.

"Sorry," she muttered distractedly over her shoulder, then she spied the palisade that formed the commander's field bastion. They had minutes, maybe less, before their fate was decided. She leaned toward her brother as far as she dared under the watchful eyes of their escorts.

"No matter what happens, don't confess," she insisted, then added for the last time, "Stick to the story: you are a coward."

Lardwan Klaus of Gevin couldn't bring himself to look at Torbjorn for the first several minutes of their meeting. It wasn't that the injuries were too horrific or that the former tweldwan was reduced to wearing such shoddy clothing. Those things were part of being a soldier, a dwan in the glorious Holt'Dwan. Blood and sweat and smeared dirt and stained clothes were the expectation, and after the campaign in the Ysgand Vale began, there had been blood and dirt a-plenty. They'd fought the petty kingdoms of men and elves first, then the wheezers. There hadn't been a war like this since the days of the Ancients, when godbeasts and titans had walked the world.

Klaus and Torbjorn had served together in this war, clawing their way up from brash and stupid dwan while fighting what turned out to be minor skirmishes in the mountain passes. Finally, they became fordwans in the valley proper, getting their first taste of real war. After that, their lives took different paths.

Klaus' had made him a lardwan, fourth in command of the Holt'Dwan, with icons of achievement across his breast. Torbjorn sat with shoddily bandaged wounds, the sign of his clan burned from his cheek. What might Klaus have done differently so his old friend would not have found himself here?

That was why he couldn't look at Torbjorn. He wouldn't insult his friend by letting him see the guilt in his eyes, the weight of regrets which did neither any good.

Klaus looked out from his command tent at the well-ordered dwarven camp that marched in orderly ranks down the valley side as Torbjorn finished his terse debriefing.

"So there you have it. Two dead for one wheezer and nearly a half month of hunting," Torbjorn grunted as his fingers played across the goblet whose contents he refused to drink. "At this rate, we'll have the war won in a few more centuries if our luck holds out and they don't figure out our strategy."

The lardwan drank from his own goblet, trying to enjoy the sharp spice of the mulled liquor. His friend's bleak mood seemed to snatch the savor from his mouth.

"A wight magistrate is more than any has managed without a full Holt'Dwan behind them." Klaus sniffed as he frowned condemningly at his drink. "You can't pretend it doesn't matter."

A cold bark of laughter was wrenched out from Torbjorn, stifled by a pain in his messily bandaged head.

"Can't I?" the fallen tweldwan snorted, one hand plucking at the taut bandages. "Isn't that the point of being shabr'dwan? To be thrown into one pointless and hopeless fight after another until you die a...well, not a hero, but not the outcast you were."

Klaus threw back the rest of his drink, sucking his teeth as it burned down his throat, and finally turned to face his old friend.

"Do you expect me to feel bad for you?" the lardwan said, one bushy eyebrow raised. His auburn beard twitched as he smiled wryly. "To join you in your groaning at the unfairness of the Wyrd and its fickle fortunes?"

Torbjorn looked up and stared into his friend's face before giving a soft chuckle. His arms crossed over his thick chest.

"You really are an ass sometimes," the condemned dwarf grumbled as he rocked back in his chair. His back gave several sympathetic pops.

"How do you think I got all these?" Klaus asked, one hand slapping his chest to make the icons clink together. "It's pretty much a requirement."

Both knew it wasn't a joke, but they laughed softly together all the same.

"Unofficially, I'm sorry about the dwan you lost," the lardwan continued. He moved to the table beside Torbjorn's elbow, where several maps were laid. "But that means we'll have a much easier time moving into the westward stretch. The humans get finicky about their levies when their overlords aren't there to crack the whip. When the Sixth heads in, they shouldn't have a problem scooping them out. Is there a suitable building there they can use as a temporary command post?"

Torbjorn grunted but refused to look at the map. Klaus' hand hovered over the blot marking Ipplen's Ford.

"Suitable by whose standards? I'm sure there's a pig hovel somewhere in that midden heap of a town."

Something in his old friend's words struck Klaus' mind and he looked at Torbjorn, who suddenly found the view outside the open tent enthralling.

"Don't tell me you did it again?"

Torbjorn refused to look at the lardwan as he gave his perfunctory denial.

"I have no idea what you are talking about."

Klaus felt an angry retort forming, but he swallowed it as he snatched up Torbjorn's neglected cup and drained it in one angry draft. He slammed the goblet down hard enough that the map rippled as though the illustrated Vale was experiencing a catastrophic earthquake.

"Just tell me there are some buildings still standing," Klaus pleaded as his teeth ground together.

Torbjorn's shoulders rose in a helpless shrug that provoked another wince.

"Like I said, all their hovels look the same," he grumbled. "I imagine they managed to put the fire out quick enough to spare some of the outer buildings, though whether those are actual buildings or just livestock enclosures, I didn't hang around to find out."

It was Klaus' turn to raise a hand to his head.

"Why was there a fire?"

"Raelon's idea." Torbjorn sniffed, his dark eyes narrowing. "Wheezer had already sold Muri, and things weren't looking good."

"I appreciate the difficulty," the lardwan, ignoring the wry smirk that drew from Torbjorn. "But next time, Raelon should come up with an idea that doesn't involve burning down the town we are trying to conquer."

"Won't have to worry about that anymore." The fallen tweldwan sighed, his face growing stony. "Raelon tackled the wheezer into the blaze. Died with three feet of wight-iron in his chest and his beard on fire."

"Damn," Klaus muttered, his head shaking as his icons gave a chorus of soft clicks. "That was a *dwan*."

Torbjorn's expression refused to change, but his head rose as the momentum of history and culture drew the platitude from his tight throat.

"That was a *dwan*."

Into the descending silence came the tromp of boots and the clink of plate-harness, then one of the lardwan's honor guards obstructed the view of the camp with his armored bulk.

"Lardwan, the prisoners are here," the guard declared. His armor gave a slight rattle as he came to attention just outside of the tent.

"Good," Klaus declared, thankful for something else to occupy their attention. "Have them brought to the tent."

The dwarf nodded and smartly turned around to beckon the little entourage forward.

"Prisoners?" Torbjorn asked, a scowl creeping across his face. "I hope you're not planning on having me conduct interrogations in this state."

"No, of course not," the lardwan muttered as he began to gather the maps that had been laid across the table. "Besides, we both know you hate that sort of thing."

Something bitter and melancholy squirmed behind Torbjorn's eyes, but his old friend was too busy clearing the table to notice.

"I certainly do."

"No, these prisoners would better be called reinforcements," Klaus called over his shoulder as he stored the maps in an iron-bound trunk. "Two of them, I believe, which should see you back to…"

"To half-strength." Torbjorn grunted as he forced himself to his feet as he spied the guards herding a dwarf and a dwarfess up the slope toward the open tent door. "Seems I can't keep them alive long enough for a full complement. Where do you want me standing when you put on this show?"

Klaus snagged the chair Torbjorn was sitting in and checked to make sure his friend hadn't leaked any blood on it before sitting down in it behind the table.

"Right there, looking as grim as usual, will work just fine," the lardwan directed as he settled in and squared his shoulders. "Hopefully, these two will last you a good long while."

"Not likely," Torbjorn muttered as he eyed the pair shuffling toward the tent. "What are they here for?"

"Cowardice," Klaus explained idly as he leaned precariously to one side to snatch some parchment documents from a table, along with one other item hidden amid the leaves.

Torbjorn swore fiercely, the profanity denigrating Klaus' familial line back three generations.

"I don't take cowards," he summarized bluntly.

"I believe the humans have a proverb about beggars and their options," Klaus mused as he sorted the papers and smiled at the sour look he knew was on his friend's face. "Let's just let it play out and see what you think."

"Carry on with your little show, then," Torbjorn groused as the shackled pair stepped into the tent with the rattling of chains.

Both looked to be very young, barely out of their thirtieth winter, if that. They had the ruddy tanned skin on their faces and arms that said they were Vale-born, and even if Klaus hadn't read the reports beforehand, he would have known they were siblings. They had the same thick brown hair with a hint of red, the same broad faces and rounded noses. The same gray and currently fear-widened eyes, though the girl was doing a better job of putting on a brave face. They avoided looking directly at either of the dwarfs in the tent.

"Dwan Ober and Ascendwan Tomza of Clan Jaln," the lardwan pronounced as though their very names were an offense to his tongue. "You have been brought here under the weighty crime of cowardice in battle, which resulted in the death of your fellow dwan. Do you deny it?"

The dwarfess Tomza shook her head but the lad, Ober, stared straight ahead. The muscles in his jaw worked beneath his youthful beard.

"I said, do you deny it?" Klaus repeated sharply, and Tomza winced. Ober's nostrils flared, and his cheeks colored.

"No, sir," they replied miserably.

"This report makes it very clear," Klaus began, looking down his crooked nose at them while gesturing at the sheet before him. "Your patrol was set upon by a batch of the heathen elves that still trouble us in the western Vale, and rather than stand beside your dwan-in-arms, you both hid beneath a fallen tree. As a result, the rest of the patrol fought and died valiantly against the blade-eared barbarians while you remained unscathed."

Klaus paused for effect and to see if he could hear Ober's teeth cracking. The boy looked as though his teeth were grinding hard enough to process ore.

"You were eventually found amidst the slaughter by the relief force that was regrettably too late to save or even avenge your worthy companions. The elves had fled in fear of counterattack after the fierce fight your dwan-in-arms gave them, yet both of you cowered in your holes with bolts unfired and blades clean of blood."

Tomza seemed intent on studying the ground beneath her feet, though every so often, she stole a subtle and frightened glance at her brother.

"Do you contest this account delivered to me by your tweldwan?"

Their muttered "no, sirs" came quickly enough that Klaus knew his theatrics were having the desired effect.

"Do you know what the penalty is for such a shameful act?"

Tomza nodded, and Ober managed to force the words through his locked jaws.

"The Deeping, sir," he hissed. "Down into the Begathpytt."

"I'm glad you know its name." Klaus leaned forward, pitching his voice lower and softer. "The First Pit. The true abyss. The place where the titans bored a hole in Eduna's body to cast away the unworthy and forbidden things of this world."

Ober and Tomza recoiled at the mention of the dread place as every childhood tale bubbled up with painful clarity.

"There you will go, the unworthy scraping at the bones of the world to drag out the slivers of forbidden treasure. Away from hearth, home, and even the thought of light, you will scratch away at Malgar's carcass for baelgeld until your eyes fail, your limbs tremble, and the Deeping claims what is left of your pathetic existence and justice is done. That is your—"

"No."

The words were not shouted or snarled or bellowed, but the force of Ober's declaration was enough to pause Klaus' well-rehearsed narration.

"What did you say?"

"No, Lardwan," Ober repeated. "That will not be justice. My sister does not deserve that. It was my—"

"Ober, no!" Tomza shouted, making up for a lack of force with sheer volume. "You can't save me from this. We both shamed our clan, and now—"

"I do not deserve even the Deeping," Ober pressed, his words rushed as though he feared the strength of his declaration was leaving him. "Offer me to Grimmoth, sir. Lay me on the Traitor Stone, and c-cut my heart from m-my chest. B-b-burn it—"

"Ober, please!" Tomza begged, lurching toward her brother. Her guard hauled on her chains.

"Just let my sister go, sir," Ober continued. "It is not her fault. It's mine. I—"

"Enough!" Klaus bellowed. He sat staring at the siblings, who now stood shaking and panting.

The lardwan shook his head and slumped in his chair, then looked at Torbjorn. The fallen tweldwan's eyes seemed to be scouring every inch of the pair's faces, one after the other.

"Well." Klaus sighed, suppressing the bemused chuckle that played at the back of his throat. "These two turned out to be more interesting than I expected. Are you sure you still want them?"

Torbjorn didn't answer, but he stepped toward Ober until he was mere inches from the younger dwarf's face. There was little difference in height, but Ober's frame still possessed a hint of the youthful sveltness young dwarf males lost when they reached full maturity. Dark, flinty eyes met watery gray, but neither flinched.

"Do you want to die, lad?" Torbjorn asked, his rough, rasping voice free of challenge or concern.

Ober held Torbjorn's gaze, refusing to be cowed. Something strange yet painfully familiar swam in the saturnine pools of the young dwarf's orbs.

"No, sir," Ober replied at last, the words heavy on his tongue. "But I'll do what I have to."

Torbjorn held the stare for a moment longer and nodded before turning back to his friend.

"I don't know what he did," Torbjorn announced, one finger pointed at Ober, "but this one is no coward."

"Wait, what?" Tomza began, but Torbjorn was already stumping back toward the table.

"I'll take them both," the outcast commander pronounced, rapping his knuckles on the surface smartly as he held out his other hand. "Now, give me that key."

Klaus couldn't hold back a smile as he retrieved the polished steel key he'd tucked into the reports on the table. With a soft chuckle, he tossed it into his friend's battle-marred hand.

"You really are an ass sometimes," Torbjorn repeated. He unlocked Ober's manacles.

"I-I don't understand, sir," Ober stammered, shock and something pitifully like hope spreading across his face.

"Don't get too excited, lad," Torbjorn warned as he stepped toward the gaping dwarfess. "You're going to be one of the Bad Badgers."

"You mean we're not going to the Deeping?" Tomza asked, her voice so soft she sounded like a child.

"No," Torbjorn replied with a sad smile. "But I'm not sure this will be much better."

The siblings exchanged looks that suggested they doubted very much if that was possible before turning back to Torbjorn. Their plaintive hopeful faces, so freshly liberated from the shadow cast by the Begathpytt, almost took the heart out of Torbjorn.

Torbjorn clenched his jaw and gave a sniff before turning to the lardwan, who had a satisfied smile on his face.

"Am I clear to settle these two in, Klaus?" Torbjorn asked, rallying at the thrill he got from watching the guards squirm at the familiarity in his question. They'd taken everything from him, and that was as close to freedom as he could hope for now. He might as well enjoy it.

"I suppose, but come back as soon as you can." The lardwan nodded before patting the parchment before him. "Your invaluable services will soon be required elsewhere."

"Aye." Torbjorn sighed and turned to his new recruits. "The damned have no feast days. You'll learn that soon enough. Come on, then."

Torbjorn led the pair out of the tent. The guard gave them a wide berth.

CHAPTER TWO

"So, do you two know what it means to be shabr'dwan?" Torbjorn asked as they descended the slope through the discreet and precise lanes of the camp.

Ober and Tomza, still reeling from the sudden change in fortune they'd just experienced, said nothing.

"You Vale-born spoke dwarvish well enough a moment ago," Torbjorn growled over his shoulder as he trudged toward the edge of the camp. "Are you stupid as well as cowards?"

The sting of the insult brought the pair's attention to him.

Tomza was the first to respond. "No, we aren't, sir," she said, the shock leaving with each word. "And I thought you said we weren't cowards?"

"Wrong," Torbjorn corrected. "I said your brother wasn't a coward. I didn't say a thing about you, lass."

A tweldwan doling out instructions to his fordwans shuffled out of Torbjorn's path with unseemly haste when he spotted the glowering dwarf headed his way. Ober and Tomza scuttled past in Torbjorn's wake, seeing the disgust they'd experienced as shamed cowards mixed with what might be genuine fear. Both were too surprised to appreciate the sight of retreating superiors as they hurried to keep up with their new commander's relentless pace.

"Just so we don't start off on the wrong foot, I could be wrong about you too, lad," the big dwarf rumbled. "After all, I would not be commanding you sorry lot if I was immune to making mistakes."

Ahead loomed the fortified gate that was common to all serious dwarven encampments. One of the dwan standing watch atop it must have spotted Torbjorn coming since two dwarfs sprang to work the winch to drag the heavy hewn-log gate open enough for them to pass through. Ober and Tomza could almost feel the dwarfs holding their breath as they passed by.

"I suppose I shouldn't be surprised that a couple of Vale-born wouldn't have the proper education to know what the shabr'dwan are," Torbjorn spat as they passed through the gate to the alpine slope that hemmed the camp with evergreen trees. "I suppose that's also why you still seem to think it was mercy that made the lardwan hand you over to me."

Despite the dwarf's words, Ober and Tomza perked up at the sight and smell of the trees, which were reminders of their home in the southern stretch of the Vale. Tomza seemed content to bask in silence as she walked, appreciating with renewed fervor the wooden giants whose shadows she'd feared she would never walk under again, but Ober's curiosity was piqued.

"So, what did make the lardwan hand us over, sir?" he asked, one hand slipping under Tomza's arm to keep her moving. "And what are the shabr'dwan?"

Torbjorn, stepping toward a path between the looming pines, looked over his shoulder. Seeing the transported look on Tomza's face, turned to the siblings.

"Is she all right?"

Ober looked helplessly at his sister and the frowning dwarf and gave a limp nod.

"She just really likes trees, sir," Ober muttered, then gave Tomza's arm a tug. "Isn't that right?"

Tomza tore her gaze away with obvious reluctance, but her eyes readily focused on Torbjorn.

"Yes, very much, sir."

Torbjorn gazed at the two and shook his bandaged head defeatedly.

"I've got a bad feeling about you two," he grumbled, scratching the raised scar on his cheek before pressing his knuckles into his eyes. "But it looks like I'm stuck with you for now."

"Shabr'dwan, sir?" Ober suggested gently.

"Right." Torbjorn grunted as his knuckles ground his orbs into their sockets. "In the proud tradition of the Holt'Dwan, dishonor and disgrace cannot be tolerated, but also in the tradition of our ancestors, restitution must be made. We can't do what the elves or humans do. You kak the bunk with that lot, and they just cut your throat and dangle you from a tree or pole as an example to others. Barbaric, but you have to appreciate the simplicity. Would simplify things."

Considering that the simplification would have had Ober and Tomza dangling with slashed throats, neither seemed eager to agree. Torbjorn didn't seem to care as he squinted at a nearby tree as though sizing it up for corpse duty.

"Anyway, that's why most get sent to the Deeping, but in times of need, another option exists. Thus the shabr'dwan, a group of disgraced warriors who will do anything to get the job done. We do what needs to be done, no matter what it takes."

Torbjorn eyed Ober, and the corner of his mouth cocked up in a crooked smile.

"Sound familiar?"

Ober frowned but nodded. The commander seemed to be satisfied with that and turned back to continue toward their destination. A few steps further, a thatched roof was visible between the trees, and they heard the burbling of a stream.

"You're here to fight and die for the Holt'Dwan," Torbjorn continued. "Sounds familiar, I'm sure, but now you get to do it without regard to honor and decency since as far as your superiors are concerned, you're not entitled to either. All you have is your life and whatever skills make you useful to the mission. Speaking of which, you're ascedwan, correct?"

"Yes, sir," Tomza answered, nodding though he didn't look at her. "I'm proficient in herblore and culinary matters."

"Herblore?" Torbjorn mused with obvious eagerness. "Please tell me that includes battle medicine?"

The gruff dwarf didn't see the look that passed between the siblings before Tomza answered.

"Yes, sir," she replied, adding quickly: "But I'm not a full battle barber. My schildwan recommended me to learn the knife and needlework, but that was before…"

The dwarfess lapsed into a silence that the soft sounds of the wind through the pines gladly filled.

"Hmmm, I see." Torbjorn grunted, then pointed at his bandaged head. "Still better than we've had for a while if you haven't noticed. This is Gromic's work. He's as hard a dwarf as you could want, but I wouldn't trust him to wrap the nameday gift of a soul I actually liked."

Tomza looked at Ober, who shrugged before giving a permissive nod.

"I could see to it before you have to meet with the lardwan again, sir," she offered. "That is, if you'd like me to, sir."

"Might be a good idea." They rounded a bend in the path and reached a knot of venerable trees. "I'm not sure he didn't press part of my skull back in on itself."

The path quickly widened to a glade large enough to accommodate the crumbling mill that squatted over the gurgling stream, though the wheel of said mill had been removed and left to lean drunkenly against a tree. A slab-shouldered dwarf with a fiery red beard stood with his back to them, hurling axes from his hard hands into the stout wood of the millwheel's frame.

"That there's Waelon." Torbjorn waved his hand. "He's working through some things at the moment, so I'd give him space."

The last axe, sunk up to its haft, hadn't finished quivering when the hulking dwarf stomped over and ripped it and its companions from the wheel. He stomped back to where he'd stood before and started throwing again. The muddy track worn into the turf suggested Waelon had been at this for some time.

Trying not to wince with each angry impact, the pair followed Torbjorn around the side of the mill to where a gap-toothed fence enclosed the packed-earth clearing that served as the camp of the shabr'dwan. Tents, not nearly as ordered as those in the fortified hub a bowshot away, were strewn around a central fire pit. The widest dwarf the siblings had ever seen was hunched over a bubbling pot whose contents he stirred with a stout stick. His round face was red, and his long blond beard glistened with a mix of sweat and condensing steam. His massive form sat upon a sturdy crate that gamely supported his weight, though every slight shift drew grinding squeaks of protest.

"Gromic," Torbjorn called, drawing the pot-stirrer from his ministrations. "What's cooking?"

Gromic scowled as though the very thought of food angered him, which Ober and Tomza found unlikely.

"Laundry, sir," the dwarf explained in a basso that one felt as much as heard. "Haeda hasn't come back with the rashers yet. Probably trying to get someone to wager with her for the best bits, the twit."

Gromic's eyes went back to the boiling pot, and he drew out a drooping lump of fabric before pressing it back down into the simmering morass.

Torbjorn cleared his throat forcefully and inclined his head toward the pair standing behind him. Gromic blinked, realized the bad impression he was making, and rose ponderously to his feet.

"So, this new meat to fill the gaps left by Mori and—" Gromic shot a quick look in the direction of axes biting into timber before continuing. "That is, taking Mori and Raelon's places in the company?"

Torbjorn nodded, then motioned the siblings forward.

"This is former Dwan Ober and Ascedwan Tomza, both of…" Torbjorn's voice drifted, and again his hand rose to his head. "What clan was it again?"

Ober gave Tomza a concerned look as his herbwise sister stepped forward, squinting at Torbjorn's bandages.

"Jaln, sir," she replied, her eyes narrowing as she studied her commander's clear discomfort with a critical eye. "Perhaps I could take a look at that now, sir?"

Torbjorn nodded, and Gromic released the stick he'd been using on the laundry and hauled over the crate he'd been sitting on. Torbjorn sank gratefully onto the doubtful assembly of planks and motioned for Tomza to begin. The dwarfess threw a quick look at her brother, who mouthed the word "Careful" at her as she began to start the process of delicately unwinding the bandages.

"These certainly were tight," Tomza breathed as she did her best to worry the edges of the blood-stained bandages free. "Seems all the blood has soaked through the packing."

"Packing?" Gromic asked.

Tomza's eyes widened as she grasped the meaning behind his confusion. After she managed to peel the blood-crusted strips of cloth away, Tomza swore. Ober looked over and winced. The ragged wound gaping through the hair on the side of Torbjorn's head was deep enough to see the blade-notched bone glinting in the dappled sunlight beneath the looming pine trees. As Tomza cautiously probed about the wound, she found a troubling amount of movement beneath her gentle fingers. The commander snarled curses that even three years in the Sixth hadn't taught her.

"This requires attention, sir, and the lardwan is going to have to wait," Tomza told him as she stepped away. "This should have seen some knife and needlework, but I can see you taken care of until you can meet with a real barber."

"Fair enough," Torbjorn agreed, not bothering to correct her assumption they had any hope of a battle barber. "Already making yourself useful on your first day. Remember that you don't earn medals in the shabr'dwan for exceptional service, but if you want to show off, I won't complain."

CHAPTER THREE

It took the better part of the afternoon and some helpful dashes of profanity to scrounge the necessary supplies and get Torbjorn sorted. The last of Gromic's hidden stash of liquor fortified him to head back into the central camp.

"Well done, Tomza." The commander ran his fingers lightly across the wrapping around his head. "You might have made a fine battle barber if things had worked out differently."

"Thank you, sir," Tomza replied dutifully, trying not to let her face show how much the last words struck at her heart. The glow of escaping the Deeping and the return to the trees was fading, and she was starting to feel the sharp edges of her new fate.

Ober, sensing his sister's retreating spirit, stepped forward.

"What's our instructions while you're at camp, sir?" Ober asked, hoping his tone implied eagerness.

Torbjorn left off appreciating the smooth lines of his new bandage and squinted at the reddening sky, then at the trail that led back to camp.

"Haeda's still not back," he mused, brushing his scarred cheek as he frowned. "That's unlikely to bode well."

"Want us to fetch 'er, sir?" Gromic asked as he set about

hanging the now-cooled laundry on a line between two tent poles.

"Hold off until evening," Torbjorn replied, his scowl deepening. "Hopefully, I'll see some sign of her on my way up, and I can shoo her back to camp."

Torbjorn set off, his steps stronger and more determined.

"Gromic, you've got the run of camp until I'm back," he called back. "See that our fresh meat gets settled as much as they can until Haeda rolls in."

"Aye, sir," Gromic shouted, then turned to cast a critical eye over the pair. "In short order."

"Make sure Waelon at least drinks something," the commander added over his shoulder. "You know how he gets."

At these words, Ober and Tomza realized that the steady impacts of thrown axes had not stopped. The sound had sunk into the ambiance of the wind and the brook, and only Torbjorn's reminder made them realize it was not a natural phenomenon.

With that, the leader of the shabr'dwan vanished down the path. Gromic had what passed for a sly expression on his broad features. "You've got questions, no doubt." The big dwarf grunted as he crossed his arms. "Go ahead and ask 'em."

That was true, but faced with so open an invitation, neither sibling seemed to be able to choose one to articulate first.

When no questions emerged, Gromic wagged his head from side to side.

"Nothing?" he pressed, "You mean to tell me a couple of Valeborn, wet-behind-the-ears whelps have nothing to ask about?"

"What do we call the commander?" Ober asked. He was not certain if that was the most important question, but it seemed better than standing there mutely.

"Sir, mostly. Torbjorn or Commander Torbjorn when you really need his attention," Gromic replied as he adjusted the wide belt that was putting forth a valiant effort to keep his pants up.

"I think what Ober means is, what is his rank?" Tomza

explained, turning toward where Waelon's ax-throwing continued unabated. "This whole thing has happened so fast that we haven't heard what his rank is, and he wears no icon."

"Fair enough." The expansive dwarf nodded. "Simple answer is he doesn't have one. Same as you lot don't."

Ober and Tomza blinked. "I don't understand," Tomza said, working hard to sound reasonable though frustration crept into her voice. "You can't mean there are no ranks here?"

Gromic chuckled until he saw their earnest faces waiting expectantly.

"That might be the official word since we're not worthy of such things," Gromic rumbled, his beady blue eyes darting toward the main camp. "But in this camp and in the field, there is one officer, Torbjorn, and what he says goes."

Ober frowned as he tried to adjust to the concept. As a dwarf, especially one serving in the Holt'Dwan, hierarchy and its strong, familiar lines of authority were what he used to make sense of the world. Admittedly, things had become increasingly disrupted, but the idea of serving under a commander with no real rank felt like a hammer blow to his brittle understanding of the world and his place in it.

"If he doesn't have a rank," the young dwarf began, his mouth strolling a few paces ahead of his brain, "what's to stop me or anyone else fro—"

Gromic's fist struck Ober square in the jaw. His head snapped to one side as he pitched onto his knees. His vision was alight with spectral starbursts as the world rocked crazily around him.

"*That's* what stopping you, lad," Gromic elucidated in a voice so flat and hard you could have hammered iron on it. "That and maybe a bit of this."

Tomza cried out and moved forward, but Gromic was faster than was reasonable for one so large, and his booted heel thudded into Ober's chest. The young dwarf felt as much as heard the gristly crunch as he was knocked flat, and he had trouble breathing after he landed. Worse, he felt something ripple through his skin, sinew, and bones, ready and willing to twist and change.

"Stop it!" Tomza shrieked and lunged forward, catching Gromic across the nose with a sharp hook.

The big dwarf snarled as tears sprang into his eyes and blood spurted from his nose, and his arm swept out blindly. Tomza, hardly a novice pugilist, raised an arm to deflect the blow, but she underestimated its weight and power. An instant later, she was on the ground beside her brother.

"Looks like we've got some lively ones," the big dwarf growled, blood streaking his mustache as his hands balled into knobby cudgels.

Tomza saw the tension in Ober's face as every muscle on his body stood out. His gaze turned plaintively toward her as gray turned to black, flecked in red at the edges. "Please!" she cried, lurching onto her knees to shield her brother. "He just didn't understand!"

Gromic paused, looming over her like a hillock of meat and bone. Blood from his nose continued to run freely, smearing his thick lips as he dragged a hand across his mouth.

"We're sorry," Tomza continued, seizing on the momentary pause. "It's just been so strange today. So scary. First we thought we were going to the Deeping, and then Commander Torbjorn unshackles us and says to follow. We're still trying to figure it out."

Gromic glared at her, and Tomza tried not to turn to make certain Ober was keeping it together. Things hovered on a knife's edge for several eternal seconds, then Gromic's fists uncurled. She must have been holding her breath because she gave a relieved gasp when they did, provoking a concerned look from the broad dwarf.

"Are you hurt?" Gromic asked, one hand stretching toward her.

"No," Tomza declared quickly, shrinking from his touch and continuing to cover her brother. "I'm fine."

Gromic's concern melted into hurt, and regret stamped his broad features as his hands fell limply at his sides. "I'm sorry. I... Well, being what we are, I took it as..."

The big dwarf's voice trailed off. He was suddenly unable to look at Tomza or her brother, who still lay sprawled behind her.

"I-I understand," Tomza managed and tried to stall for time, one hand groping surreptitiously behind her to find her brother's hand. "Sounded bad, I'm sure."

She nearly gasped again as her fingers met thick bristles. She could feel the tension trembling through every fiber of her brother. With all she had in her, she willed him to keep control.

"Is...eh, is the lad all right?" Gromic mumbled, still unwilling to let his eyes leave the ground. "I didn't... Well, that is, I didn't intend to hit him so hard."

Tomza's breath caught in her throat as she felt the stiff hairs retreat and her brother's hands unclenched.

"I'm fine," Ober declared in a thick voice as he slowly got to his feet. "Fist like a hammer, but I'll live."

Tomza forced herself to take a steadying breath before standing.

The siblings return to vertical relaxed Gromic, and he looked them both over. He still avoided meeting their eyes until he was satisfied there had been no lasting harm done. Ober's jaw was purpling and his breathing was shallow and sharp, but he stood squarely on his own two feet. Other than some fresh dirt on her clothes, Tomza looked none the worse for wear.

"What's going on?" growled a voice that couldn't have been gentler if it had come from a rock grinder.

Tomza and Ober swiveled to see Waelon at the corner of the mill, an axe in each fist. They stood very still, neither wanting to give the unsettling dwarf a reason to unleash the whirling barrage he was clearly so adept at. It was hard to be sure, but they seemed to be standing at precisely the distance he'd measured out from the ax-notched millwheel.

"No problem," Gromic called back a touch too quickly to be natural. "Nothing to worry about."

Ober and Tomza both noted something in Gromic's voice as he spoke, though it was hard to tell whether it was fear or shame.

"I heard shouting," Waelon rasped as the failing light stained the smiling blades of the axes a gory hue. "And either you've taken up cross-dressing again, or you've got blood all over your mouth."

Gromic gave a good-natured chuff, then, seeing the raised eyebrows of the brother and sister, shook his head quickly, blood spattering with the motion.

"H-he doesn't mean that. I just...just..." Gromic stammered, scowling past them at the ax-bearing dwarf. "You know it was one time, and it was only for the mission."

"Whatever you say, Grelinda." Waelon leveled an axe at Ober, then Tomza. "What are *they* doing here?"

Gromic was silent for a moment, at a loss for words. Then, glad not to have to explain Grelinda, he stepped forward and slapped his meaty hands on the siblings' shoulders. They nearly lost their footing as Gromic shook each in turn.

"This is Ober, and this is Tomza," he declared. "New recruits. Torbjorn just brought in. Why don't you come over and say hello, eh?"

Waelon's stiffened, and the siblings felt Gromic's grip tighten as the muscles in his shoulders coiled. Whether he meant to hurl them out of harm's way or into the path of an oncoming ax, neither was certain, but they stood mute and unsure as fresh tension crackled in the air.

"Rather milk an ogre," the fiery-haired dwarf replied, turning. "Not that either would do me any good."

Gromic waited until Waelon was a few steps into his withdrawal before releasing Ober and Tomza, along with the breath he'd been holding. The smells of boiled meat, cheap liquor, and blood fouled the air with the exhalation.

"Don't take it personal." Gromic sighed and took a step from the pair, which was greatly appreciated. "Probably for the best at the moment. Waelon ain't the friendliest, and Raelon goin' home hasn't helped things one bit."

"Going home?" Tomza asked, having made sure Waelon had left. "You mean we can eventually return to our clan?"

Gromic winced when he saw hopeful sparks kindling in the young dwarfs' eyes. "Eh, not while you're breathin', lass," he explained with an apologetic sigh. "Word gets sent to your clan so they can carve your name on the dwan stone—assuming you die fighting, of course. That's as close as any of us are going to get to—"

The creak and rattle of a wagon drew Gromic up short. He paused to ensure his senses weren't deceived before he allowed a wide smile to stretch his red-smeared mouth. "That'll be Haeda, the ol' sow-thrasher." He pressed his bulk between the siblings and made for the wide hole in the fence that led to the path.

"Come along," he called over his shoulder. "The quicker we help her unload, the quicker we can get supper started."

Ober and Tomza, who had not eaten since the day before and even then, only a dry crust and a cold scrap of bacon, didn't need to be told twice. As they hurried after Gromic, their stomachs rumbled and murmured in anticipation. Up ahead, the sound of the wagon's protesting wheels was joined by the soft puffing grunts of the team of worcsvines drawing the flatbed wagon. It appeared a moment later.

Even in the gathering gloom, it was plain to see that the only thing upon the wagon was a hunched dwarvish figure bent nearly double around a lantern in its lap.

"Haeda! You kak-headed degenerate," Gromic bellowed. "You gambled away all our supplies, didn't you?"

The crouching figure gave a soft series of clicks, and the draft pigs drew the wagon level with Gromic as they shuffled to a stop.

"Might've been tempted to," came a husky voice from beneath a dirt-stained hood. "But I never saw no supplies, Gromic. Honest."

Despite their unfamiliarity with the speaker and rapidly diminishing light, neither Ober nor Tomza could miss the uncertain way the driver held her body or the unnatural thickness in her speech. Gromic headed for the wagon, his eyes searching the dwarfess.

"By the Bones," he swore as he drew the hood back from her bowed head. "Haeda, what happened?"

It was difficult for the siblings to imagine what she really looked like when the lantern light revealed a battered mess of swollen flesh. It was only a face in that there were signs of where the necessary orifices were. The bruised mass twisted crookedly as the driver attempted a smile.

"Seems someone else laid claim to 'em," Haeda explained, one bloodshot green eye glinting in its swollen socket. "Said they were for proper dwan, not scum like us."

"Bastards," Gromic snarled. "Do they think we can eat stones and wear pine needles?"

"I don't think they much care," Haeda mused with a low laugh that turned into a hiss. "Or that's the impression their boots gave my face."

"Who took 'em?"

The four dwarfs turned toward the mill to see Waelon standing with an axe shoved into his belt above each hip.

"Waelon, look, it's not all that bad," Haeda began, but a low ripping growl from the back of Waelon's throat stilled the equivocation.

"*Who took 'em?*" he repeated. The great muscles across his shoulders knotted, and his dark eyes flashed with silent fire.

CHAPTER FOUR

"I see you're already benefiting from my fortunate find."

"I suppose you expect me to be grateful." Torbjorn snorted as he entered the tent, ignoring the less-than-friendly glares of Klaus' honor guard.

"Expect no, never," Klaus chuckled as he gestured for his old friend to join him. "But I'm not going to pretend it wouldn't be nice."

Torbjorn settled into a chair across from Klaus at the table they'd used earlier, only now, instead of maps, a spread of hearty food on the surface. The shabr'dwan commander ran his fingers across the bandages swaddling his head as he drew in the smell of roast pork seasoned with dill and fresh mash rolls. There was even some crocked butter and a small, uncapped jar of darkberry preserve, the sweet fragrance mingling with the savory scent of the meat.

Torbjorn took a deep breath to settle his eager stomach and his stoked ire. He knew exactly what this was.

"Standard fare for the lardwan, eh?" he remarked dryly as he fought the urge to ball his hands into fists.

"Just some spare odds and ends," Lardwan replied as he drew

a long carving knife across the haunch of pork. "I think most of it was from when the ondwan met with the svartling princep. Those blade-ears are such finicky eaters."

Torbjorn snorted at the weak lie but didn't bother to challenge it. Even amongst the senior officers of the Holt'Dwan, this was fine food. It had been carefully prepared by a culinary ascedwan whose only job was to see that very upper echelons of the army were well cared for or made a good impression on an important guest. That or to bribe a dwarf into doing something most unwise, especially in conjunction with the spiced liquor in their goblets.

"At least the plumskins," the shabr'dwan muttered. "You remember when we were still using those savageling scouts?"

Klaus paused after placing a hefty slice of pork on Torbjorn's plate, and his expression curdled as he went about carving off a healthy portion for himself.

"You always do this when I try to serve you a nice meal," the lardwan complained as the well-honed knife passed through flesh to click irritably on the plate. "Bring up some story that threatens to spoil the whole thing."

Torbjorn chuckled as he took up a mash roll and applied a lavish smear of butter.

"I don't know what you are talking about." He sighed absently and tore off a large bite, which he chewed for a moment before swallowing it with the help of the contents of his goblet. "Anyway, I was talking about how we used to have those savagelings roaming about, supposedly giving us information about the terrain and enemy positions. You know, scouting. Weren't too bad in a fight either, especially fighting tribes they had a feud with. No real battle line or discipline, of course, but they fought like demons—every milk-skinned, ink-stained one of them. Like that time in Randsvich Ridge. You remember Randsvich Ridge, don't you?"

Klaus didn't bother to answer. He had deposited his share of the pork on his plate, but as Torbjorn told the story, the lardwan made no effort to partake. Instead, he frowned at the steaming pink cut and took another drink or three as memories played behind his eyes.

"Randsvich Ridge," the shabr'dwan commander murmured. "Just before the wheezers rose and we all learned how wrong we were. We thought it was going to be the last big battle in the Ysgand. Thinking of that now makes me want to laugh until I get sick all over my boots."

Klaus raised his goblet to his lips and discovered it was empty. Eyes still fixed on the cooling hunk of flesh in front of him, he groped for the jug to refill his cup.

"I was still a tweldwan then, and not just any tweldwan, but the tweldwan of the Sablestone Guard," Torbjorn intoned as he sawed off a bite-sized piece of pork. "We were the spike driven by the hammer of the Holt'Dwan that day, storming the ridge by wading straight through heavy opposition. As we marched along that narrow defile, there were more arrows, bolts, and spears from the coalition than I think had been hurled at us during the entire campaign put together. It was like rain from hell pattering off us, but you don't bring out the Sablestones to crack soft nuts, right?"

Klaus' cup was again empty against his tingling lips, but what little restraint he was holding onto kept him from reaching for more drink. He supposed this was penance for what he was going to ask. He wanted to curse his old friend for the memory, but what would come after for Torbjorn was as mad as it was vital. He needed to let the disgraced tweldwan have his say.

"We tore through their battle line easy enough," Torbjorn declared around a mouthful of pork. "But I never once saw an enemy who could hold their earth when the Sablestones got up some speed and their hearts were in it, and with this looking like the last battle, we were hungry as wolves. So hungry we couldn't understand what we saw when we routed the line and carried on to Randsvich. Do you remember what we found there? You weren't a lardwan yet, but you were his first cubldwan, so you had to see it, being his eyes and ears near the front like you were."

"I remember." Klaus swallowed. "I also remember what happened after that."

"Oh, then you remember that it wasn't full of the last great host, but rather their families." The shabr'dwan chuckled, but the sound failed to touch his cold expression. "Silly buggers thought we were heading to Cer'Bran for resupply, so they were squatting in the marshes waiting to ambush us while the might of the Holt'Dwan descended on their wives and children. Even when I issued the order to hold, you remember what happened? Ondwan Glastuc signaled the charge. I still wonder if those horns were heard by those poor wretches in the marshes."

Klaus shook his head, though whether it was to dismiss the question or the phantoms behind his eyes remained a mystery. "Why are we talking about this?" He swallowed heavily, letting the goblet slip from his fingers.

"Well, partly because we were talking about finicky elf appetites." Torbjorn shrugged with a nonchalance that was not present in his coldly burning eyes. "I remember that as our bolts tore through elders and children, I watched some of our savageling scouts set on mothers running with babe in arms or clinging to their skirts."

"Torbjorn..." Klaus breathed thinly, his face paling. "Please!"

"I suppose you could call it finicky to only pluck out hearts and livers," Torbjorn continued, his plate forgotten. "They weren't nearly as choosey about the bites they took out the young ones. That was after they bashed their wee heads to bits."

Klaus, his skin waxen and his lips clinging to his teeth like wet parchment, finally looked into his old friend's eyes.

"Then you killed them." That had been a day of blood and screams. "I remember, Torbjorn. I remember it all."

"Damn right I did!" Torbjorn gave with a jagged laugh as tears glistened unshed in his eyes. "But not just those heathen animals. You remember when I put my blade into four fordwans that Lardwan Hrolfen, your superior, sent to restrain me? You remember when I caved in Hrolfen's head with my fists?"

Klaus heaved a sigh and sank into his chair, one broad hand pressed to his eyes.

"I had some of his blood in my beard," the lardwan muttered without bothering to uncover his face. "I remember it flying off your gauntlets to splash on my cheeks. I said I remembered it all, Torbjorn."

Torbjorn's mouth curdled into an ugly, bitter smile.

"I don't think you do," the shabr'dwan hissed as his smile became a grimace. "Not all of it. Otherwise, you might know the other part of why I brought this up."

Klaus let his hand slide down to rest on the arm of his chair.

"What's the other part, then?"

"That night after Randsvich Ridge, each of us was called to the ondwan's tent one at a time," Torbjorn growled as his hands swept over the well-appointed table. "You must have seen it before I did because I was the last one brought into him. He had a table set just like this. Fine food, not fancy enough to seem too lavish, but better than anything we'd eaten for months. So he sets me at that table and tells me that I've had a trying day and the whole business was bad, and probably not least of which being because Lardwan Hrolfen trusted in false reports from those savageling scouts he favored. I hadn't swallowed my first bite before I knew what was coming and what he wanted."

Klaus' expression darkened, and he saw his error.

"I'm sorry, Torbjorn," Klaus choked, his gorge rising in his throat. "I didn't mean it to be like this. I just…"

Klaus wasn't sure how to explain it. The words refused to leave his tongue. He'd told himself he was softening the blow, that this final meal was a penitentiary sacrament for what would come next. Yet, staring at it, he saw now what Torbjorn did.

"You're not wrong," Klaus admitted.

It was Torbjorn's turn to sink into his chair, listless and spent.

"Well," the disgraced tweldwan drawled, "with all that out of the way, tell me, old friend, what atrocity am I to be a party to now?"

CHAPTER FIVE

"You know how to use one of these?"

Ober, perhaps caught up with the infectious fury that radiated from Waelon or just appreciating a vent for the emotions of this peculiar day, grinned as he worked the lever on the crossbow. Three quick pumps and the wound steel string cocked with a distinct click a quarter-second before he heard the soft clunk of a bolt falling into place from the boxed magazine. The young dwan set the stock against his shoulder, careful to keep the weapon pointed to the bed of the wagon he was standing on as he had been trained to do what seemed like a lifetime ago but was merely months.

Waelon's teeth flashed in his red beard as the swaying lantern light turned his face into a fearsome mask.

"You might do yet, meat," the big dwarf growled appreciatively before turning to Tomza. "All right, dirtless, your turn."

"I still think we shouldn't do this," Haeda called from the driver's bench as Tomza performed a similar display to her brother's with the duabuw she'd been given. "There's just too many ways this can go wrong."

Gromic, who filled the rest of the bench, put a reassuring arm around the dwarfess' shoulders.

"They can't do this to one of ours and get away with it," he rumbled sincerely, and his stomach expressed its sympathies. "They can't expect us to eat stones."

"As much as you weigh, stones can't be out of the question." Waelon poked a hard finger at the expansive dwarf's side. "But you're not wrong. This is about getting what's ours."

Haeda frowned, and the siblings caught Gromic trying to discourage her from saying more with a sharp shake of his head. The dwarfess either didn't see the gesture through her one good eye or decided to ignore it.

"You sure this isn't about something else?" she asked quickly, as though fearing her nerve would run out before she'd voiced the question.

Waelon was just about to dismount from the wagon. He froze and turned toward Haeda, his face flat and cold.

"What is that supposed to mean?"

Gromic gave a long-suffering groan as he turned about on the bench to face the wagon bed, his thick body tensing for whatever came next.

"You know exactly what that's supposed to mean," Haeda pressed, a pugnacious scowl forcing its way through the swollen, bruise-blotched flesh. "You lost your brother, and now you want to make an armed raid for some cloaks and rations. Doesn't seem this is really about salted meat and wool."

The siblings sensed the thickening tension in the air and got a sudden urge to look around the night-quieted camp. No one had paid them much attention after Waelon had bullied his way through the gate. The few who had noticed their sow-drawn vehicle had let their eyes slide away as though an unspoken understanding insured a healthy degree of disinterest in the collection of disgraced dwarfs. Ober and Tomza couldn't say they were comfortable with the new arrangement, but it was preferable to open disgust and disdain, at least for the moment.

"I didn't lose my brother," Waelon retorted, lips peeled back from his teeth. "I didn't forget where I put him, and he didn't just wander off like some worcsvines I forgot to tie up."

"Waelon," Gromic warned stiffly. "Easy now."

"Raelon's not going to come strolling back into camp with some funny story," Waelon continued as though Gromic hadn't even spoken. "And I'm not going to find him sitting in some cave or pit, just waiting for someone to come and drag him out."

"Waelon, you know that's not what I meant," Haeda whinged, clearly regretting her accusation. "I'm just saying."

"You just said I lost my brother, and I'm telling you he's not lost. He's dead," the big dwarf snapped. "Just like this isn't a raid, it's a bloody reclamation. Those supplies are ours, and those whore-born rats have no claim to them. I'm going to get back what is ours."

Haeda gave an irritated huff but didn't say anything more as Waelon thumped to the ground from the wagon.

"You two stay here with her," Gromic ordered as he heaved himself off the bench. "Hopefully, we can snatch the crates up without anyone the wiser, but be ready to make a good showing if we come back with company."

Ober nodded, but Tomza piped up as she looked with narrowed eyes between the rows of tents. "You mean you want us to shoot them?" she asked, her feet shifting as though the very suggestion made her unsteady. "As in, shoot to kill?"

Gromic's eyes widened as he looked up at her. Haeda muttered a string of profanity under her breath.

"What? No!" the hulking dwarf spluttered. "Just...you know, point the crossbow at them and uh, look...look intimidating. Remember you're shabr'dwan now—dwarfs on the edge without a conscience."

"Except we don't get to shoot anybody," Ober murmured in

his sister's ear, but apparently not quietly enough since Gromic gave him a scowl.

"Listen up, bumstreak," Gromic snapped. "Just try to look scary while keeping your finger off the trigger, all right?"

Ober nodded, but Gromic didn't wait to see it. He galumphed after Waelon. Ober and Tomza looked at each other and then at Haeda, who sat hunched next to her lantern, head hung low. Whether that was from discomfort or an attempt to seem innocuous was anyone's guess. Ober nudged Tomza with his elbow, not the smartest move considering they were holding cocked and loaded crossbows, then he bobbed his head toward Haeda. Tomza narrowed her eyes and shook her head, but her brother nodded emphatically. Tomza rolled her eyes, then shuffled a half a step forward.

"So, uh, Haeda," Tomza began. Haeda raised a hand that brought the younger dwarfess up short.

"If you plan on shooting me and taking the wagon," the battered driver ventured miserably. "At least have the decency to put the bolts through my head or my heart. Bones and Stones know it's a miserable thing to die of a bolt in the guts."

Ober's and Tomza's eyes widened, and they stared at the bent back in silence for a moment. Neither had even considered an escape attempt, no matter how ill-advised, even after they'd been given weapons with which to attempt it. Perhaps that was as much a testament to dwarvish culture as to their characters, but neither knew what to say to that. Their mouths opened and closed a few times.

"We, uh, we wouldn't ever do something like that," Ober announced with as much confidence as he could muster.

"Really?" Haeda groused, half-turning to give him a level look with her undamaged eye. "You were just complaining because you didn't get a chance to shoot any dwan during a robbery."

"But you heard Waelon say this isn't a robbery," Ober protested, the duabuw feeling ungainly as his hands began to sweat. "And I wasn't saying I wanted to shoot anyone. I was just, uh, I—"

"My brother sometimes does his thinking out loud, is all," Tomza explained, coming to her brother's rescue with a sidelong "shut-it" look. "No, I was actually going to offer to mix something to bring down the swelling and ease the pain of your injuries."

It was Haeda's turn to be struck silent, but there was suspicion in her quietness. The dwarfess' eye roved over Tomza like she was food of questionable provenance and quality. With a grunt and a hiss of pain, Haeda shuffled stiffly on the bench and turned toward the pair.

"You know herblore?" Haeda asked, and a lopsided spread over her face. "I suppose that explains why Torbjorn picked you."

Tomza thought about explaining that the commander had chosen them without knowing that about her, but it did not seem worth pointing out at this juncture.

"She treated the commander's head injury," Ober offered with an eager nod. "And I think it's fair to say he's feeling a lot better."

Haeda chuckled, but it was a sharp, cutting sound.

"Considering he had that oaf Gromic bandaging him, I'm not sure that says much about her skills," the driver observed wryly. "But I suppose it couldn't hurt to have you give it a go. Not sure it could hurt more, and if you bungle it, there's a better than good chance that one of the lads will gut you on the spot."

The siblings chuckled at what they hoped was humor, but when their efforts met stony silence, they decided it wasn't a joke. They gave up and watched for Waelon and Gromic as Haeda continued to stare at them with one glittering eye.

"I suppose you'll need to range about the woods outside the camp," the driver offered at last. "To collect the correct ingredients to help little ol' me."

Tomza nodded, though she could feel the sneered accusation in the dwarf's sour tone.

"And I suppose you'll need that weapon in case there's savagelings or clackers about, eh?" Haeda pressed. "Can't very well have you and me wandering about in the dark unarmed, could we?"

Tomza felt the prick of the insinuation, but she flashed a sickly-sweet smile at the older dwarfess.

"I suppose you weren't there, but you don't have to worry about me," Tomza replied with a feigned quiver in her voice. "Being a coward got me here, so I wouldn't have the spine to shoot little ol' you in the back. Especially not in the big, dark, scary woods."

Ober braced himself for a scathing rejoinder, but to his surprise, the driver gave an amused snort.

"Ha, that's a good one." Haeda chortled and wagged her finger. "I know better than most that Torbjorn wouldn't have taken you if you were a proven coward. Not worth the trouble, you see."

"Afraid you're wrong, ol' gel." Tomza attempted to imitate Haeda's thick northern accent. "Me and my brother were denounced as cowards before your...well, I suppose *our* commander inducted us into this merry band."

Curiosity shone in the dwarfess' eye as she looked from brother to sister. Her lumpy jaw worked as though she were chewing her thoughts before she could say them. She'd just spat one over the bench onto the ground when a deep-throated shout and a splintering crash sounded from the direction Waelon and Gromic had tromped off in.

"Merry band, indeed." The driver grunted as she took up the reins of the wagon and gave a soft whistle that had the sows on their feet with remarkable alacrity. "Well, me bonnie pair of cravens, let's hope you've got the nerve for a good show. Sounds like we're going to need it."

CHAPTER SIX

"To be honest, I thought it would be worse."

The lie came off Torbjorn's lips easily as he tucked the folded map into his pocket. The directions stored over his heart, he tucked into the food with renewed vigor, eager for something to distract his body if not his mind. True, it was cold now, but it was still good, and he was very hungry.

"Well, it's bad enough." Klaus sniffed as he prodded at his cold food, his appetite elusive. "It's not quite sticking your head into a drake's mouth, but damned if you can't count the bugger's teeth."

Torbjorn bobbed his head but otherwise didn't bother to pause in his gustation.

Klaus watched his old friend alternate between tearing off chunks of cold meat and mouthfuls of mash roll, wishing there was more he could say. None of this was as it should have been, but "should have been" was a trap for fools, and he had no time for such things.

As foul as this business was, it should not have been the most pressing thing on his mind. The logistical concerns brought to him by the kuadwan were in danger of bringing the Sufstan Holt'Dwan to a grinding halt, but he'd learned since inheriting this position from his predecessor that there was always another crisis and impending disaster. Tackle one and you'd be faced with another, so you had to make time for the things that mattered since waiting for an opportunity was just one more fool's errand.

For the moment, he was going to make time for an old friend who'd been too honorable and noble for the lesser souls he served under, present company included.

"So, what do you make of the pair of mysteries I handed over to you today?" Klaus asked, forcing himself to be present in more than just body. "Not that you wanted additional complications, but if nothing else, a pair of Vale-born, one with some medical training, has to be worth something."

Torbjorn's brow knitted thoughtfully as he slathered a dollop of darkberry preserve on the last of his pork. It, in turn, was wrapped in a new mash roll. The shabr'dwan gave the sandwich a pensive look as though an answer might be found within its confines before filling his mouth with a sizable bite.

"Not sure," Torbjorn admitted around a mouthful of food before taking a swallow of distilled spirits. "I'm fair certain that lad has a secret. His sister is trying to keep it from getting him killed, but what that secret is, I'm not certain. It could be the other way around, and he is drawing the attention to keep her safe. Hell, both could be playing me for a fool, but I'm willing to bet my life that isn't the case."

Torbjorn held out his goblet for a refill and Klaus obliged, a ghost of a smile finally creeping onto his lips.

"I suppose I've seen you wager your life on far flimsier propositions," the lardwan mused. He left his hand on the jug as he entertained filling his cup again. "Do you remember the time you climbed down those frozen falls outside of Naelfint? You know, when we were fordwans under Worric, and our patrols had to fetch that fool of a ranger who'd hunkered down there before the freeze set in and couldn't get out?"

Torbjorn nodded again, pausing before taking another bite to slap his left leg.

"Still hurts when the weather changes," he declared proudly. "Though 'climbed' is generous. I believe I was less than a quarter of the way down before my climb turned into a slide and then a dive. I hit those rocks hard enough that I can still hear my bones breaking."

The shabr'dwan mimed a shudder, but his broad smile undermined the effect.

"If only you'd landed on your head." Klaus chuckled. "You'd have left a decent-sized crack in the icy stone, but it would have spared ol' Frierd your bellyaching and could only have improved your looks."

Torbjorn snorted into his drink.

"No matter what he said, Frierd liked me, if for no other reason than I gave those old needleworking fingers something to do besides tugging at that beak of a nose and scratching that barrel of a backside."

Klaus filled his goblet so he and Torbjorn could toast the memory of the old ascedwan who'd patched them both up more times than they cared to remember.

"Och, bring 'em wit der brains and balls, or half of one or t'other, and I can put 'em back together," Torbjorn quoted, doing a passable imitation of Frierd's thick brogue before surrendering to a fit of laughter. "Ha! That ol' curmudgeon must've traded one of his danglers for baelgeld needles because, by rights, we all should have been on a wagon headed back to the mountains with some of the nasty scrapes he patched us back together from."

"Though not always how we were before he got hold of us," Klaus complained as he ran a finger down the crooked slope of his nose. "I still think that ol' Tub of Guts put this back crooked to spite me for dicing him out of his granpappy's belt buckle."

Torbjorn looked up from the ruins of his meal with a frown.

"You ended up giving it back to him, didn't you?" he asked as he worried at the remainder of the pork on the dish between them. "I swore we buried him with it."

"Oh, I gave it to him long before he took that spear to the back," the lardwan muttered as he allowed his mind to wander. "Speaking of tubs of guts from the old days, how is Gromic?"

Torbjorn's hesitation made Klaus sit up straighter.

"Oh, kak. I didn't miss his clan papers, did I?" the lardwan asked quickly. The liquor threatened to come back up his throat.

"No, no. Gromic's too stubborn and too big to die," Torbjorn assured his old friend as he swirled the quarter cup of liquor left in his goblet. "I just realized that Gromic's the only one that lasted this long. All the rest of 'em, the original Bad Badgers, have had their clan papers sent back home."

The corner of Klaus' mouth rose at the mention of the slur, but he didn't comment. Torbjorn had given his contingent of shabr'dwan the name, and the lardwan had no business complaining. The Holt'Dwan could hardly complain about a disreputable name for a batch of soldiers they treated as beneath scorn.

"At least you still have him with you," Klaus said, contemplating another goblet full until he felt how light the jug in his hand was. "It must be some comfort that despite everything, he's made it this far."

"I suppose." Torbjorn slurped up the last of the spirits and set the goblet down. "Made it this far just to meet this."

The shabr'dwan patted his pocket. Klaus found it hard to look at his old friend, but he forced himself to. It might well be the last chance he had to do so.

Neither could find much to say, so they let food and thoughts digest until the stillness was interrupted by the clank and rattle of war harness rushing toward the tent.

"What now?" Klaus muttered. He was halfway to his feet when one of his honor guard threw back the tent door.

"Fight in the Eighth's camp, Lardwan," the dwarf declared,

obviously in a rush but not so much that he couldn't scowl at Torbjorn.

"That sounds like a problem for their fordwan," Klaus remarked, leaning more heavily on the table than he would have liked. "Or am I now the watchmaster as well as the lardwan?"

"Apologies, sir," the honor guard replied and nodded emphatically at Torbjorn. "The fight is between members of the Eighth and the shabr'dwan, sir."

Torbjorn stood sharply, swearing as his chair tumbled to the floor behind him. "A bad beginning to a worse business, eh?" he growled as he made for the tent door.

The honor guard scrambled crablike out of the way. Klaus mopped at his face with a hand before calling after his old friend, "Might you require my assistance to sort this out?"

"Only if you don't want it sorted without a few corpses from the Eighth appearing."

CHAPTER SEVEN

"Not bad enough that you're honorless scum, but now you're stealing like a pack of skulking grems."

Waelon laughed at the jibe as he checked the area around him.

Two dwarfs had stepped up on his right-hand side, but so far, the left was vacant. If Haeda could bring the wagon around sharply, there was a good chance they could barrel through on that side. Of course, there was also the chance that they might run down a dwan who was stupid enough to try to stop their retreat, and that kept Haeda from snapping the sows into action. That and the eyes full of hate she was throwing at the leering fordwan who was leading this impromptu gathering of the Eighth.

"Funny *you're* talking about grems," Waelon roared, the blood racing in his veins as Haeda's glare stoked his anger even higher. "Only a dung-snuffling, maggot-crawling grem would need a band of fellow rat-faced kak-snackers to rob and abuse one dwarfess."

The fordwan, a brawny dwarf with a scar-seamed face and paired service brands on one cheek, hawked and then spat on the ground as the near-dozen dwan around him growled low curses.

However, not one of them charged to avenge the stinging insult, not with the new meat leveling cocked duabuws at them. The dwan from the Eighth must have known they could overwhelm the shabr'dwan before they got off more than two shots apiece, but at this range, that was a guarantee of four dead dwans. No one, not even the fordwan, seemed interested in being the first to die.

"We didn't rob anyone since those can't be yours," the fordwan drawled, then nodded at the stack of crates Waelon and Gromic had thrown onto the wagon bed. "Go ahead and look at what's stamped on 'em if you don't believe me."

"Well, I don't see Leaky Scumsack stamped on a thing, so they can't be yours," Gromic called from Waelon's shoulder. "Suppose we'll go find the proper owner ourselves if you don't mind."

Gromic nodded at Haeda to bring the wagon around but checked the movement as the fordwan shuffled left. Waelon held his breath and hoped the new recruits held their fire. He wouldn't mind seeing a few of these bastards return to the Stone, but all of them would die bloody if someone started a fight. He'd long ago reckoned that was where he was headed, but he wasn't sure he wanted it to happen here and now, no matter how angry he was.

"Those crates are stamped with the sign of the Sufstan Holt'Dwan," the fordwan hollered in a voice pitched to draw reinforcements. "That means everything in them is for dwans. Since not one of you filth-streaks has proven worthy of that name, what's in those crates can't be yours."

The shabr'dwan stood in sullen silence, anger and shame strangling their angry retorts.

"What happened to your little friend's face was just a failure to understand that." The fordwan sneered. "Maybe if you hand everything over, including those duabuw you have no right to be holding, we'll let you go without having to teach you all the same lesson."

The fordwan turned to his following, which had acquired more angry faces and guttural promises of violence.

"Though maybe we should refresh the rutter," the ringleader crowed to ugly laughs as he threw a wink toward Haeda's spiteful eye. "Seems she didn't learn her lesson after all."

Waelon growled, and Gromic advanced toward the fordwan with a thunderous bellow.

"I've got a lesson right here, you son of a—"

"*Onstaeles Dwan!*"

The words sounded like a thunderclap. The gathered dwans were stunned into silence, except for Gromic. He gave a frustrated snarl as he shuffled back to the wagon with all haste. Once there, he motioned for the befuddled siblings to lower their weapons, then stood waiting with Waelon.

Torbjorn stepped from the camp lane to the open ground between the wagon and the mob of dwans, bandaged head high and dark eyes flashing. The fordwan fought to keep his proud air, but a chill had come into the air, robbing him of his surety. More than one dwan beside him shivered and refused to meet the shabr'dwan commander's eyes as his gaze swept the gathering.

"Gromic, explain," Torbjorn directed without bothering to look at the stout dwarf.

"Your dogs slipped their leash," the fordwan interjected before Gromic could answer. "They were under the impression that those crates were theirs, and like the curs they are, they tried skulking in to steal them when they thought we weren't looking."

"I see," Torbjorn remarked softly, his eyes boring into the fordwan. "Gromic, did you take anything not slated for us according to the kuadwan's list?"

"No, sir," Gromic replied with a rancorous thrust of his chin at the ringleader. "Not a thing."

"I already explained—" the fordwan began, but Torbjorn was already moving toward the sneering dwarf.

"Oh, I heard every word, Fordwan," the shabr'dwan enunciated with precision as he advanced. "My dwarfs are not dwans, so these can't be their crates. Impeccable logic, and exactly what I would expect from a shining example of the Eighth's finest."

The gathering of dwarfs seethed as Torbjorn came to stand inches from the fordwan's face, but none dared make a move. Seasoned campaigners all, not one hadn't heard the stories about Torbjorn Kinslayer.

"But since you are so very clever, I'd like to propose another logical conclusion," the commander continued, his voice barely more than a whisper. "No cur or grem-born filth-streak could ever stand toe to toe with a true dwan, could they?"

Something skittish and uncomfortable raced behind the fordwan's eyes. The game had changed, and he wasn't sure how it had happened.

"Eh, no, of course not," he managed stiffly, his arms crossing over his broad chest. "If it was a fair fight, of course."

"Oh, of course," Torbjorn agreed, his volume rising to a conversational tone. "You would not expect that from a murderous bugger like me, but you see that ugly one with the red hair?"

The ringleader's gaze darted to Waelon, who gave him a hard, lopsided grin.

"He's not a Kinslayer, so you don't have to worry about him drawing a blade in an honest fistfight."

Steel glinted in the lantern light, and the fordwan held his breath as something cold tickled his throat. The dwans at his side seemed entranced, like children at a magic show wondering where the knife had come from.

"Torbjorn," came Klaus' voice over the rattle of his armored honor guard. "Everything under control?"

The blade didn't withdraw. Torbjorn grinned into the fordwan's face. Then it was gone, and the shabr'dwan commander stepped back.

"Absolutely, Lardwan," Torbjorn called as he strolled to the midpoint between the wagon and the gathering of the Eighth. "Just organizing a little inter-Holt competition."

As Torbjorn spoke, he began to gouge a trough in the packed earth with the back of his heel.

"Competition?" Klaus inquired. He and his entourage stopped a few paces from where Torbjorn worked, an armor-plated buffer between the opposing forces.

"Yes, Lardwan." Torbjorn grunted as he stepped back to assess his efforts. "More of an exhibition, brought on by this fordwan's rational deductions."

The lardwan looked from his friend to the nervous-looking fordwan, then heaved a sigh.

"Carry on."

"Thank you, sir!" Torbjorn exclaimed. He motioned to Waelon as he turned back to the bemused fordwan. "Come on, now. Step up, Fordwan. We don't have all night."

The fordwan frowned, but when the lardwan nodded for him to proceed, the dwarf came to stand before the line etched in the ground.

"This will be as fair a fight as you could hope for," Torbjorn explained. "Standard toe to toe, and you both keep a foot on the line as you trade blows. A strapping dwan like you shouldn't have a problem dispatching this cur, especially as you're getting the first swing."

The fordwan blinked and looked from Torbjorn to Waelon.

"What?"

"You heard me, Fordwan," Torbjorn coaxed like a tutor with a trepidatious pupil. "You get to prove that you, an esteemed veteran of the glorious Eighth, are a dwan, while this dwarf is nothing but a vile grem-tickler. Hit the dwarf as hard as you can."

The fordwan narrowed his eyes, certain he was missing something, but his more eager, or dimwitted, followers, gave shouts of encouragement.

"Make him choke on his teeth, Deorgar!"

"Flatten 'im, Fordwan!"

"Come on, Deorgar, split his skull!"

Buoyed by the cheers of his comrades, Fordwan Deorgar of the Eighth broke into an ugly grin before drawing back one muscle-knotted arm and hurling one big fist into Waelon's grinning face. The punch landed with an audible pop, and the fordwan's followers fell silent.

According to the rules of the venerable contest of toe to toe, it was permissible for the recipient of a blow to protect themselves in two ways. A competitor could attempt to avoid the blow through head movement, leaning back, or ducking as long as one foot remained on the line. A competitor could also attempt to rob the blow of its full effect, typically by leaning forward or crowding the punch while bracing for the blow.

Waelon attempted neither of those strategies.

The blow crashed into his smirking face, and he took the full force without flinching. If not for the blood welling from his still-smirking lips, there would be no sign that Deorgar had thrown a punch.

Waelon's eyes didn't leave the fordwan's as his grin widened.

"Another," he growled, the sound welling up from deep in his chest.

Deorgar stared at the shabr'dwan and then looked at Torbjorn, whose cold expression offered no comfort.

"You heard him, Fordwan," Torbjorn intoned flatly. "He's giving you another blow. I suggest you take it."

Some of the simpler dwans behind him took up their cheers again.

The fordwan licked his lips, sucked in a breath, and threw another haymaker.

Waelon's smirk didn't budge, although more of his blood smeared his attacker's knuckles.

"One more," the fiery-bearded dwarf replied to Torbjorn's inquiring gaze.

"You heard the dwarf, Fordwan," Torbjorn stated with icy calm. "One more blow. I suggest you make it a good one."

No one cheered for the third punch, and it was just as well. The dreadful realization of his situation dawned on Deorgar, and that fear made his third blow an unsure and sloppy affair. Red-stained knuckles scudded across Waelon's brow, having little effect except to leave red streaks across the skin.

"My turn." Waelon grinned, and his arm snapped forward in a stiff jab that caught the wincing Fordwan cleanly in the jaw.

Deorgar wobbled as sympathetic groans arose from the dwans behind him, but Torbjorn's hand steadied him before he could shake it off.

"Come on now, Fordwan," Torbjorn cajoled, withdrawing his hand from the dwarf's elbow. "Our little thought exercise is going to fall apart if you don't hurry up and knock this ugly wretch flat."

Fear and desperation congealed in Deorgar's eyes, and without further exhortation, he threw his whole body into another trio of heavy punches. Waelon, despite his opponent's shameful behavior, took them all just like the others—with no fear and no obvious effect.

Fordwan Deorgar lurched back, breathing heavily. Waelon waited for the nod from Torbjorn.

The shabr'dwan, having caught the cunning glint in the fordwan's eye, answered with an uppercut as the dwarf curled forward to choke the oncoming punch. Deorgar's head snapped around, and he landed on his back as his compatriots hissed and murmured among themselves.

"Oh, come on," Torbjorn chided, seizing the fordwan and dragging him back to his feet. "This can't be happening, Fordwan. Show this inbred mongrel who you are! Strike, dwan, strike!"

Deorgar's head rolled toward Waelon's grinning face, and whether born of ill-advised determination or addled misfortune, he managed to launch a limp swing. It bounced harmlessly off his opponent's head.

Waelon's right hook left Deorgar on the ground, slurping breaths through a pulped nose.

"This can't be," Torbjorn fretted with mock concern as he hovered over the felled fordwan. "Maybe he's just luring you into a false sense of security. How many blows does he owe you now, Waelon?"

The big dwarf pivoted one foot forward while the other remained on the line as he knelt over Deorgar.

"Four, sir."

"Carry on, then," Torbjorn waved as he turned to the assembled dwans of the Eighth, who looked on with paling faces. "I'm sure he's just waiting for the perfect opportunity to prove his infallible logic."

Waelon's fist drove into Deorgar's face two more times, producing a pained sob with the first impact and only a choked wheeze from the second. Waelon, eyes burning and fist dripping, drew back for another when Klaus' voice rang out.

"That's enough," the lardwan warned, but Waelon didn't withdraw until Torbjorn nodded at the wagon.

The shabr'dwan commander turned toward the gathered dwarfs of the Eighth with a frosty glare.

"I suppose, logically, your fordwan can't be dwan either. Doesn't bode well for the rest of you."

CHAPTER EIGHT

"I'm beginning to wonder about our current situation."

Ober nodded but made no response. The siblings sat upon the back of the wagon as it rolled back to the dilapidated mill.

At first, Tomza thought that was because he was still processing what had happened in the Holt'Dwan camp, but then she saw the trembling tension in his arms. She tried to tell herself that this was just nerves from the standoff that had left her feeling lightheaded, but as she squinted at his hands, she saw the gradual darkening across the backs.

"Ober," she murmured, scooting over after she checked that the others weren't paying any attention. Thankfully, the rumble of the vehicle on the forest path and the throaty grunts of the worcsvines made it easy to keep their conversation private.

"I know," her brother growled through clamped jaws.

Tomza put a hand on Ober's shivering arm and his head snapped toward her, glistening like pitch in the dark. There was no threat in his rigid expression, but the violence of the movement made her draw back.

"Y-y-you've got to hold on," Tomza faltered, tearing her eyes away from her brother's unnerving stare to check once more that they remained unobserved by the others onboard the wagon. "As soon as I get a chance, I'll get into the woods and get what you need, but until then, you have to keep it in check."

"Sure," Ober hissed through clenched teeth. "No problem."

"I know it's hard," his sister consoled as she leaned close. "But this close to camp, they'll find out, and then—"

A sound that was a mix of a bestial growl and the rumor of thunder came from deep in Ober's chest, and Tomza winced. She shot a look over her shoulder and nearly collapsed with relief. Waelon and Torbjorn, leaning against the crates of supplies, were both looking pointedly into the darkness, while Gromic and Haeda on the bench looked suspiciously at the sky.

Tomza let her frightened eyes do the beseeching for her.

"I know," Ober choked out in a thickening voice. After a monumental effort, his eyes closed, and he let out a long, low breath. When next he looked at her, his eyes had returned to the glittering gray that matched hers.

"You need to hurry," he croaked, his voice raw and haggard. "Otherwise, I'll have to…to try something else."

Tomza saw his hand move shakily across the duabuw as though he were practicing the movement.

"No," she intoned with utter certainty. "Not that."

Ober's gaze was heavy. "If they find out, they'll probably kill you on principle," the young dwarf pronounced as though reading from a judicial scroll. "The tainted blood can have no place among the people."

It was Tomza's turn to growl, though this proved far less impressive, and the wagon's locomotion easily swallowed the sound.

"This has nothing to do with blood," she spat, pinning Ober with her fierce gaze. "It's all to do with that…that *place* and Fordwan Wrolth not listening! This isn't your fault, so stop trying to make it be. It doesn't help."

Ober's throat bobbed as they rounded the bend and saw the shabr'dwans' camp.

"Why me?" he asked with a shuddering breath. "Why did it choose me?"

Tomza, her mind racing as they rumbled across the last stretch to the fenced yard, set a firm hand on her brother's shoulder and pressed comfort and strength into the touch.

"I don't know," she confessed, bending forward to rest her head against his. "But that isn't the answer. Bones, it didn't even work when Wrolth tried it, right?"

Ober shook his head, staring down at the crossbow in his hands.

"He went for the head," the dwarf mused as the wagon lurched to a stop. "I'm thinking if I put one through...through the heart, maybe..."

"No," Tomza muttered, trying to draw his eyes back to her. "Not that way, no matter what."

The wagon bed bobbed and bounced as heavy forms descended from it.

"You Valelings asleep back there?" Torbjorn called from the head of the wagon.

"Looks like we wore 'em out wif all de excitement," Waelon lisped through his mashed lips. "Look awfully cute, don't dey?"

"Adorable," Torbjorn remarked dryly, then turned to the hulking dwarf descending from the bench. "Gromic, sort the darlings out, would you? My head's acting up again."

Gromic's head bobbed, but before he could bawl out a proper dressing down, Tomza sprang to her feet on the wagon bed and darted forward.

"Sir!" she cried sharply enough to make Torbjorn cringe. "Commander Torbjorn, wait!"

Torbjorn scowled at the young dwarfess.

"Good to see you up and about," he remarked wryly. "Is there something you need?"

"Besides a lesson in respect," Haeda spat from where she reclined on the bench. "Telling the commander to wait. Stones and Bones!"

The comment battered some of the urgency out of Tomza, and her eyes darted between the driver and the commander uncertainly.

"It's been a full day for everyone," Torbjorn told the sour dwarfess clutching the wagon's reins, then motioned for Tomza to continue. "Let's just get it over with."

Tomza nodded and swallowed her doubts after one last glance at Haeda.

"If your head is hurting again, the dressing needs to be changed. I'll need some more herbs."

Torbjorn frowned but nodded at the darkness coiling between the trees.

"Well, I imagine that will have to wait until first light," the shabr'dwan commander replied. "I think I'll—"

"With a lantern or a torch, I could gather them in short order," the young dwarfess continued, ignoring Haeda's sharp look. "If proper healing is to occur, especially without a battle barber, it is very important to keep the wound clean and medicated to encourage recovery. Also, with your permission, I'd like to collect some herbs that will help Haeda and Waelon recover from their injuries. This would add little time since most of what I would need grows near where the plants for your treatment are found."

Torbjorn's brows furrowed under the bandages around his crown. Waelon shook his head with enough force to make his blood-crusted lips wag and flap.

"I'm fine, zur," Waelon assured, but his lips split anew, and a fresh red stream began to trickle into his beard. "Honest."

"We all know you aren't getting any prettier." Gromic huffed and nodded at the dwarfess on the wagon bench. "But Haeda's battered bad enough that she can only see out of one eye. If we've got to break camp soon, it'd be a good idea to get her on the mend. That and your head, of course, sir."

Torbjorn looked at Haeda. The older dwarfess seemed intent on scrutinizing Tomza, who stood upon the wagon like a breathless contestant on a stage. Finally, Torbjorn nodded, then winced at the movement, one hand rising to his head.

"Fair enough," he grumbled, turning toward Gromic. "Send her and Haeda off to pick flowers while you three get our hard-won prizes sorted. I'm going to lay down before I fall down."

"Yes, sir," the broad dwarf replied, then barked at those on the wagon, "You all heard him. Fresh Meat One is off with Haeda. Fresh Meat Two, put that duabuw down and start handing those crates off."

As Ober stiffly rose to his feet to comply, Tomza dismounted the wagon. Before the younger dwarfess could take a step toward the trees, the driver held out the hand that was not gripping the lantern.

"Hand that over," she demanded, her bruise-covered chin jabbing at the crossbow in Tomza's hands. "Quick now. Torbjorn's waiting."

"But if you're holding the lantern, you'll only have one shot," Tomza muttered bemusedly. She held out the weapon, though. "You can't work the lever with just one hand, can you?"

Haeda snatched the duabuw, managing it with surprising coordination and control despite having only one hand. Tomza noticed the finger hovering alongside the trigger guard, and the weapon was pointing at her.

"I'll manage." Haeda nodded at the wooded slope as her eye glittered wickedly. "And if I've got to shoot something out there, I imagine I'll only need one shot."

CHAPTER NINE

Torbjorn observed his dwarfs. He was freshly fed, cloaked, bandaged, and smeared with herbal concoctions as sharp in the nose as they were aromatic.

"Well, you lot are in a sorry state," he acknowledged, looking skyward for a celestial reprieve. "I don't suppose it's going to get any better, either."

The early morning sun painted the sky over the mountain's shoulder in shades of pink. On their side of the slope, it would be many hours before the sunlight touched more than the treetops, but Gromic had enlivened the campfire and set a kettle of stout stainleaf to brewing. The first serving was steaming in Torbjorn's wooden mug as he gave up looking for divine intervention.

"I suppose we work with what the Wyrd gives us." The commander sighed as he took a scalding swallow of the enlivening beverage. "But Bones and Stones, it does seem like we've pissed in some godling's ear, every last one of us."

The three veteran shabr'dwans exchanged concerned looks, but none dared say a thing until Torbjorn explained his peculiar mood. The newly initiated siblings did their best to read the situation while remaining very still lest they draw any attention. The duabuw wasn't the only thing they'd learned their way around in their short time in the Holt'Dwan.

"All right, enough pouting," Torbjorn muttered, clearly talking to himself as he forced down another mouthful. "Might as well get it over with."

Torbjorn dragged a thumb across his seared cheek and turned back to the motley assembly, meeting each eye in turn as he spoke.

"We're headed back into wheezer territory, and I mean yesterday." He pressed down the kick in his chest as he saw his veterans swallowing angry, horrified rebuttals. "I would have preferred we get as close to a good night's sleep as we could before setting off, but the best we can manage after our interesting night is no more than four hours' rest. Then we've got to be off. This whole business is time-sensitive, so we've got to move as quick and light as we can at least partway through rough terrain."

Haeda, whose face was already looking markedly better despite being thickly daubed by a deep ochre paste, straightened as her eyes, both of them, roved toward the team of sows rooting beneath the pines.

"We can take the worcsvines with us part of the way," Torbjorn offered, preempting the dwarfess' question. "But you'll be turning them loose somewhere along Turoth's Tooth. I suppose they'll be as well there as they would be here."

"And there's far less chance of the bastards from the Eighth filching them," Waelon added, picking idly at the mask of vegetable matter coating his face.

Gromic gave a grunt of agreement but looked with obvious care at Haeda. She was staring forlornly at her beloved worcsvines.

"You won't have to worry about the Eighth either way," Torbjorn put in. "The Holt'Dwan's moving in two days' time. Orders are probably being doled out this morning to runners from the ondwan's tent as we speak."

Every dwarf who was listening leaned closer eagerly at the proclamation, none more keenly than the three veterans.

"Where are they headed, sir?" Gromic asked as five sets of whetted stares followed the commander's every move. "Pressing south at last? To Fang's Nest? Findorellien?"

Torbjorn looked into his mug as though the answer was floating in the dregs before pitching the contents into the fire to hiss.

"The ondwan's moving the Holt'Dwan to Grayshelf," he told them. "To meet up with the Eststan Holt'Dwan and parts of the Hartstan Holt'Dwan to strategize and fortify for the winter."

There was no swallowing their angry protestations. Gromic blinked rapidly, looking near tears as a long curse slid from his mouth. Haeda's eyes glittered with a disgust that matched the profanities bubbling up from deep in her throat. Waelon said nothing, but his face twitched and spasmed with oaths that wouldn't quite pass his lips.

"Grayshelf?" Tomza groaned as her shoulders sagged. "That's thirty miles in the wrong direction."

"More, since they're going uphill as well," Ober remarked glumly, gnawing on the prepared root his sister had slipped him on the sly. "Looks like Sufstan gives ground yet again."

"And all the while," the dwarfess whispered, "humans reap our fields and squat in our homes."

Her brother nodded but said nothing else as he felt the soothing juices of the root slide down his throat. His relief outweighed the old pain for the moment, but like any deep wound, he knew he would feel it again sooner or later.

Torbjorn tossed his empty mug from hand to hand as he waited for the angry muttering to die down. He knew what it meant to all of them. To his veterans, it was proof that their pain and sacrifices had amounted to nothing since Ipplen's Ford would not see the Holt'Dwan's banners sailing over it anytime soon. For the new recruits, both Vale-born, it meant the

Holt'Dwan was one step further from taking back the homes they'd been driven out of when the wights arose nearly a decade ago.

They all had good reasons to be angry, and he knew things were only going to get worse, so he gave them space to vent. They'd have no time for such things as they beat their way across the Vale toward as miserable a destination as they could imagine.

Whether it was Gromic's incredulous snort or Haeda's bitter laugh that served as the impromptu signal, the sounds of ire died away, and all eyes returned to the shabr'dwan commander.

"Not one of you is wrong for being mad. Hell, for feeling betrayed," he commiserated, refusing to do any less than meet each eye in turn. "But that doesn't change what our orders are. We're headed through Wheezerland to Fang Nest to Turoth's Tooth, then on up from there."

The veterans groaned, and the siblings looked less than enthused. That was no small distance to be covered at speed, even by hearty dwarvish soldiers.

"What comes after the going up?" Haeda asked. Her eyes narrowed when Torbjorn hesitated.

The most well-traveled of the lot, even compared to Waelon, the dwarfess was relied upon for knowing the various locations within the Ysgand Vale and how best to get there. Since Torbjorn hadn't spoken to her about this before now, she was more than a little out of sorts.

"We go where we've been ordered to go." Torbjorn spoke slowly as he settled a hand over his breast pocket and patted it. "As usual, it's not a place we want to see any closer, and when we get there, I don't expect anyone will be happy to see us. I understand this isn't how we usually do things, but I'm asking you to trust me. It won't make it any easier if you know what awaits us."

There was a single heartbeat of tension, then, to Ober and Tomza's amazement, the raucous trio of veterans exchanged looks before nodding their assent.

Torbjorn smiled at the three familiar faces staring at him resolutely. Fordwan Deorgar, the Eighth, and the whole bloody Holt'Dwan could think what they wanted. These were dwans among dwans, and nothing anyone could say would convince him otherwise.

"Fair enough. Let's not waste any more time. Bunk down and get what sleep you can. In four hours, we strike camp and get on with the business of this wretched errand."

CHAPTER TEN

"So, what did you really do?"

Ober gave a spluttering sigh as he adjusted his new cloak for the fifth time in the last hour, which was nearly as many times as Gromic had asked the question as the siblings took their turns walking behind the wagon. The wide dwarf stared intently as Ober took a second to check that his new weapons, a duabuw and a notched magsax, were still situated on his person and not catching on the travel mail he wore.

"We already answered that," Tomza called. Gromic frowned at both of them from the wagon's bed.

Tomza had almost panicked the first time the question had emerged from the dwarf's thick lips, but it had been clear it had come not from suspicion but gregarious curiosity. When they'd mentioned the charge of cowardice, Gromic's massive paws had dismissed the answer with a vapid flap, followed by the now-familiar line about Torbjorn refusing to take cowards into the shabr'dwan.

"You can forgive a dwarf for many sins," the broad shabr'dwan had declared sagely. "But if he's proven he's not willing to fight for himself and his comrades, there's not much he'll be good for out here."

Ober and Tomza supposed that was true, though they couldn't very well say it. For a time, Ober had distracted Gromic by asking him what "sin" he'd committed to earn his place among the less than illustrious shabr'dwan. Needing no further coaxing, the dwarf had told a tale about how he'd once served with Torbjorn after being seconded into the famed Sablestone Guard. During an event that Gromic was stoically evasive about, Torbjorn was displaced from his position as tweldwan and accused not just of disgrace but also treachery shortly afterward. Gromic was one of multiple members of the Sablestone Guard who had spoken in defense of Torbjorn and eventually in a protest that had ended violently.

"Well, Ondwan Glastuc knew it'd be too embarrassing to offer a dozen decorated dwans to Grimmoth," the stout dwarf had mumbled, a freshly lit pipe jutting from one corner of his mouth. "Then the Wheezers came back, and he had worse things to worry about. For nearly a year, we were stuck rotting in some soggy hole beneath Grayshelf until Lardwan Klaus had the bright idea of reviving the old custom of the shabr'dwan. Sent us off on our first mission, a nasty piece of work involving a grem uprising in the middle of a wheezer offensive. Half of us got sent to our clan on that one, but we got the job done. Even Glastuc couldn't argue with the results."

"He tried," Torbjorn called from the bench, which proved that the commander hadn't missed a bit of the conversation. "Klaus can be very convincing, though."

That had been a few miles ago. Gromic was pressing his question again, knowing his turn on the wagon would soon be up.

"Don't know what to tell you that I haven't already," Ober answered, looking up to see stains of yellow and orange creeping into the sky. "Must be heading toward the southern pickets by now, right?"

Gromic mirrored Ober's gaze, then shook his head bemusedly.

"You Vale-born and your sky." He chuckled, then took a long draw on his pipe. "You're not wrong, o' course, but I'd never look up at that mess to sort that out."

"I'm sure you felt the stones shuddering up your legs to chime it out on your bollocks." The dwarfess snorted. "You underlings and your earth-tingles."

Gromic's brows lowered, and he turned toward her. The siblings' expressions froze as they waited for a reaction. The big dwarf's blue eyes gleamed with a sullen heat before it melted into a mirth that bounced his wide belly in a counter-rhythm to the rocking wagon.

"Bwahaha, 'chiming bollocks!'" The stout dwarf guffawed. "That's a good one. Waelon, you hear that?"

The red-maned dwarf looked over with a frown. He was sitting on the opposite corner of the wagon bed with his legs dangling off.

"Your musical bollocks?" Waelon grunted as something flashed in the corner of his eye. "I'd think you'd be glad to know they're still there. Stones know it's been a long time since you've seen 'em."

"Too true, ha-ha," Gromic hooted, his eyes watering. "Might make me want to dance to the tune, eh?"

"Even better," Waelon declared solemnly. "You'll be using feet you haven't seen in nearly as long as your poor gravel-sack."

The barb made Gromic laugh until his body shook with merriment. In the face of such a wobbling comic onslaught, Waelon's grim facade cracked, and a crooked grin broke across his face. This was a sign that the siblings could safely partake of the camaraderie, and they joined in.

From the head of the wagon, Torbjorn smirked while the driver shook her head with a scowl. Their attention returned to the road, and they swore at the sudden appearance of a tall, thin figure in the middle of the way.

Haeda hauled back on the reins and clicked her tongue. Squeals of protests rose from the sow team, and it was all Torbjorn could do to keep from being thrown off the bench. Finally, the lead worcsvine came to a stop half a pace from a pair of finely crafted boots.

"What in Grimmoth's bloody name!" Gromic swore as he sidled off the wagon and joined Tomza and Ober on the ground.

Waelon had already hopped down, his crossbow at his shoulder as he moved to shelter at the forward corner of the wagon.

"Damned myrkling," the red-haired dwarf snarled as he eyed the striking figure. "Get your hands up, blade-ear."

Twice the height of any dwarf but weighing half as much, the lithe form could only belong to an elf, and from the deep, cool shades of his complexion, a svartalf. Flawless skin so deep a blue that it was nearly black shone in the dappled sun, but it was nothing compared to the sharp white teeth that flashed in ravenous greeting. The elf had a long saber hanging jauntily from his belt, and he wore fitted plate armor under a long, elegant coat whose tails almost touched the smartly rolled tops of his tall boots.

"Salutations," the svartalf called in a high, clear voice, seemingly not bothered by the crossbows and the half-dozen dwarvish scowls pointed his way. "Pleasure to meet you on this fine afternoon."

The elf's command of Dwarvish was exceptional. He had only a hint of the rolling lilt that usually marked his kind's pronunciation of the dwarven tongue.

"I said, get your hands up!" Waelon growled, his crossbow aimed to send a bolt ripping through the newcomer's unprotected face.

The elf met Waelon's eyes down the length of the cocked duabuw, his smile refusing to lose its brilliance.

"Like this?" the svartalf replied, one hand rising for a spritely wave at the dwarf. The other rested on the wire-wrapped hilt of his saber. "Is this what you are looking for, Master *Tozelchaun*?"

Waelon didn't answer, but his finger settled on the trigger as he matched his target's grin with an icy stare.

"Stand down," Torbjorn called. He got to his feet in the wagon. "We're still in dwarvish territory, after all. Damn it, stand down!"

Waelon swallowed a score of half-formed curses as his finger left the trigger. The aim of the duabuw gradually drifted earthward. Both elf and dwarf knew one twitch could send the crossbow snapping back to its previous position, but for the moment, Torbjorn's demands had their attention.

"Yes, sir." Waelon sniffed. Gromic and the siblings came around the wagon, duabuws directed where Waelon's was.

"Much appreciated," the svartalf remarked, taking the armed assembly in at a glance before focusing his carnelian gaze on Torbjorn. "I apologize for my sudden appearance, but I'm afraid I needed your immediate attention."

Torbjorn looked the elf up and down with arms crossed and brow lowered.

"Well, you've got it, sell-sword," the dwarvish commander replied coolly. "How about you get to the part where you tell me why needing my attention nearly turned you into hoof-jam beneath our sows?"

The svartalf threw back his head and gave a melodious chortle that earned deepening frowns from every dwarf present. As was commonly known, there was not a dwarf above or below the earth who would not suspect the laugh of an elf, no matter his origin.

"Well-spotted and quick to the point." The elf tittered, then launched into a rapid yet precise explanation. "I am Sir Utyrvaul

Urivianoc, and I am a retainer in service to Lady Banneret Tegwylivere Tivalinos and sworn to Lord Gwenmaelon Gwydarioc, who has pledged to aid your most honorable ondwan in your efforts to retake the valley. It is my lady's wish that I find aid quickly. Though I knew it was some distance to your camp, I was determined to see it done, so I set off through the wood.

"As I was striding along, I heard your jolly company's stout laughter and thought Rhiardis herself must have guided me to you. If you would kindly follow me, we can make for my mistress' position with all haste to aid her in this most important of tasks."

The dwarvish scowls were replaced by quizzical expressions, except for Waelon, who checked that Torbjorn wasn't giving him a surreptitious sign to shoot the elf. To his disappointment, no sign came, so he returned to attempting to bore a hole through Utyrvaul's face with his eyes.

Torbjorn cocked an eyebrow as he processed the harmonious cavalcade of words, then sucked at his teeth and gave the barest shake of his head.

"Seeing as we are in a hurry ourselves and you spent all those words to not tell me a whit of what you actually need, I'm going to have to pass," he explained with a perfunctory nod. "Best of luck to you and Lady Tegwwyl-ee-whatsit, though. Haeda, get us moving, please."

"Gladly, sir," Haeda replied as she gave a soft cluck and began to direct her team around the elf.

"Wait, comrades, please!" the svartling cried, springing back to place himself squarely in the path of the worcsvine. The pigs gave an irritated snuffle as they halted, and their protests were joined by four duabuws being leveled at the elf.

"Careful, Utee," Torbjorn warned. "I've got somewhere to be, and I'm not in the mood for games."

Utyrvaul raised both hands in placation, red eyes betraying less confidence with so many bolts aimed at his person.

"I can appreciate that, Master Dwarf, but please hear me out," the svartalf countered.

Torbjorn's voice, so rough and hard in comparison, ripped through the oncoming plea like a saw through silk. "I did, and you wasted my time, myrkling. Now get to explaining or get to stepping before I have four dwar—"

Torbjorn paused. He saw out of the corner of his eye that Haeda had removed her duabuw from under the bench and held it level with the elf.

"Sorry, make that *five* dwarfs who'll put enough steel in you that you'll piss wire."

A spasm of irritation slid over the svartalf's long face, but when Utyrvaul spoke, it was as composed as ever.

"My apologies. It is the urgency of the errand that caused me to misspeak. My lady is beset and needs aid. Brigands have—"

"You are sell-swords who can't even handle some uppity locals?" Torbjorn interjected, then continued in a steely tone, "So, either you're taking dwarf gold to prance about in armor, or you're lying to me. Either way, this sounds like a problem I can do without."

Torbjorn looked at Haeda, and the svartling gave a hiss of frustration.

"Name your price," the elf demanded, his pluck and good manners gone.

"Got any elf-draught?" Torbjorn asked, not bothering to hide the smirk hitching up one end of his mustache.

"You can't be serious!" Utyrvaul exclaimed. "By rights, you should aid us as your allies—"

"By rights, you shouldn't need my help," Torbjorn interrupted, sounding bored. "If this was a real fight, you'd be running to the southern pickets and raising an alarm at the watchtower. Since you were headed the opposite direction, I imagine you were hoping for a loose patrol or a batch of rangers to bamboozle into sorting out an internal squabble among you myrklings. I'll ask one more time and then be on my way. Whether you'll be breathing when I depart is entirely up to you."

"Your errand must be very important to extort *scienceren* from us," the svartalf replied archly. "That or you are one of the few truly clever members of your kind."

Torbjorn's smirk became a dark grin.

"Like I said, myrkling. I've got somewhere to be."

CHAPTER ELEVEN

"What do we want elf-draught for?"

Tomza's question was nearly swallowed by the rumble of the wagon as Haeda snapped the reins to coax more speed from her team. Utyrvaul had produced his sleek adyrclaf after the shabr'dwan commander had agreed on four measures of elf-draught, and now the long-legged reptile was bounding ahead of them. The svartalf looked as sure and comfortable atop the loping therapod as he did on his own two feet, which was an added irritation to the dwarfs who were trying to keep up in their wagon.

"It's not for us," Gromic shouted as he gripped the back of the bench as the wagon accelerated. "It's for the pigs."

"The pigs?" the siblings chorused. They were squatting in the back of the wagon, and they leaned forward as it mounted a rise in the road. Neither was certain that Haeda would stop if they fell off, which might not have been a bad thing. However, curiosity and a distaste for broken bones made them keen to stay onboard.

"I suppose it's not common knowledge," Gromic hollered over his shoulder. "But while elf spirits just make a dwarf act foolish, their effect on natural-born beasts is a sight to see. With a half-measure of elf-draught for each sow, we could maintain a sprint like this for near on a day."

When the wagon struck a patch of rough ground, neither saw that as a particularly good thing. The jarring impact made everyone's teeth clack, and Ober's duabuw had very nearly smashed his.

"Won't that kill the worcsvine?" Tomza asked as Ober fought to resituate his weapon without shooting himself or anyone else. "I mean, I doubt they can keep this up for much longer."

"I keep my girls fat and healthy," Haeda cried, pugnacity in her words. "They'll sleep for the better part of two days after a run like that, but it should get us a fair bit closer to the Fang's Nest. With a half-measure for each, we can make a trip of a few weeks in less than five days if the way's clear."

"Just seems like it would be dangerous to run at that speed," the younger dwarfess shot back. "And not just for the sows. How certain are we the way is clear?"

"Pigs and pathfinding are Haeda's business," Torbjorn called back, hoping to forestall more petulant crosstalk. "What you two need to worry about is staying close to Gromic and Waelon. I hope I don't need to tell you not to trust the myrklings as far as you could kick them with a sore toe, so nobody lets their guard down. They play games with us, you shoot first and ask questions later."

Ober, who'd finally settled the matter of his crossbow, frowned as he looked at the bobbing back of their elvish guide.

"How do we know when they're playing games with us, sir?"

"The same way you know when a myrkling's lying to you," Waelon growled, the heat in the words matching his fiery hair.

"How's that?" the young dwarf asked.

"His mouth's moving."

"The vile usurpers are just over this rise. We must strike quickly before they have time to organize themselves."

Torbjorn frowned. They'd branched away from the main forest road and followed a path that led into a craggy cut in the mountain's slope. Short, scrappy trees sprang up from ground, which was littered with scraggly bushes and loose scree as the cut jagged its way between humped shoulders of rock and the sparse soil. Plumes of black smoke rose from a spot hundreds of yards into the cut.

"I'm not going to rush in between those two lumps," Torbjorn remarked, pointing at the rough shoulders framing the passage before them. "That's as good a way to get pinned down and shot to pieces as any."

Utyrvaul's eyes followed the puffs of black smoke staining the darkening sky, and he ran a black tongue over his thin lips.

"Fine, but time is running out," he hissed, leaning down in the saddle to meet the wagon-mounted dwarf's eyes. "If my lady is dead, there will be no elf-draught for you, and the Holt'Dwan will be the worse off in more ways than one."

"Unlikely," Waelon growled. That drew a sharp look from the svartalf, but neither had time to continue the spat as Torbjorn took command.

"Simple right pincer seems the best option, with the wagon blocking the way out," the shabr'dwan commander instructed. "Gromic, take Tomza and head up the north shoulder. Waelon, you and young Ober take the south. Haeda and I'll creep up along the cut while you lot get into position overlooking the camp. No one looses a bolt until the wagon's within range of the enemy unless you've been spotted, and if that's the case, good luck to you. Utee, how are we going to know which myrklings we can shoot?"

Utyrvaul grimaced at the slur, but he replied with grim solemnity, "When I escaped, every member of my mistress' party was either dying or bound." The elf raised a hand to pat a barbed diamond embroidered on the left breast of his coat. "This is the sign of her house, always worn over the heart."

"What a great target," Waelon quipped. Torbjorn glared at the big dwarf.

"Focus, dwan," Torbjorn directed, his gaze lingering on Waelon for a moment before ranging around the rest of the company. "Aim for the ones still on their own two feet, and if that gets confusing, check for that bit of lace over the ol' blood pump. I want this done quick, sharp, and quiet if you please. Everyone understand?"

Not a dwarf spoke, though Torbjorn noted that Ober looked like he was doing his best to come up with a question. Mercifully, Utyrvaul piped up to break the young dwarf's concentration. Torbjorn motioned for his dwarfs to head out while he addressed the svartalf's question.

"Should I wait here?"

Waelon muttered something under his breath. Torbjorn didn't need to hear the words to get the gist of the deprecation.

"No, my good Sir Utee." The dwarf commander sighed. "You'll approach with us. If this whole thing goes sideways, I want to have the chance to put a bolt through your lying tongue before I die on elvish blades."

Utyrvaul didn't seem to like this answer, but he nodded stiffly before adjusting the pace of his adyrclaf to match the wagon as it rolled forward. The therapod snapped its jaws a few time, creating a quick staccato of pops, while the foremost sow brandished her tusks.

Torbjorn tried not to draw any conclusions from the display.

CHAPTER TWELVE

"Why do you hate elves so much?"

"Shut up," Waelon whispered in response to Ober's question. "Those blade-ears aren't just for show. Bastards can hear a heart beating at ten paces."

Ober's face scrunched. He very much doubted that was true, but it seemed like pointing that out was unlikely to yield any respect from the older, bigger dwarf. Instead, he focused on trying to be quieter as they made their way over the rough-hewn lump of earth. They were close enough to hear the crackle of the fire that was throwing up the sizable plumes of smoke. He supposed anything that hung around a blaze that large would struggle to hear much of anything, long pointed ears or not. Still, it was clear that he'd best follow Waelon's example as the dwarf was clearly an expert at this sort of thing.

Despite being considerably bigger and heavier, the dwarf seemed to know exactly where and how to step so that his broad boots made little sound and barely disturbed the vegetation or loose rock underfoot. Alternating between swiveling his gaze around their surroundings and making sure he stepped exactly where Waelon did proved to be taxing, yet Ober managed to keep pace. A light sweat broke out on his brow despite the cool air of the Vale, though.

For several moments they crept across the hills, careful to stay below the crest lest they paint their silhouettes against the deepening red of the sky. Thus, it was in gory light that Ober and Waelon came upon the svartling bonfire.

"Get down," Waelon hissed. He and Ober got on their bellies and crept to the crest of the hill.

Below, a dozen tall, armored elven shapes stood around a bonfire that was composed of heaped brush around the remains of several fine tents. When some of the charred tent poles writhed and gave thin, keening wails, Ober realized some were the stripped and smoldering bodies of unfortunate svartlings.

"Even to their own kind, elves are monsters," Waelon murmured at Ober's shoulder as he aimed his duabuw. "That's reason enough to hate 'em."

"But not the only reason?" Ober whispered as he mirrored the veteran dwarf's movements.

"Nope," the big dwarf muttered. "Not by a long shot."

The svartalfs standing around the fire were chatting. Some were holding mugs or goblets in their long hands while the agonized cries rose from the fire. Ober was certain he heard titters of high-pitched laughter amidst the crackling flames and rending wails, and his stomach turned. He'd grown up hearing that elves, whether the svartalfs from the eastern coastlands or the pale heathens here in Vale, were alien to dwarvish honor and values, but he'd never imagined that the divisions lay so deep.

It was not that dwarfs never fought or killed other dwarfs, but even the hated traitors offered to Grimmoth would have their hearts carved out on the Traitor Stone before both organ and corpse were offered to the vengeful god.

Remembering that he'd offered himself up for such a fate not long ago forced a shudder through Ober.

"Steady on," Waelon whispered, taking the young dwarf's trembling for nerves. "We won't shoot until Torbjorn's there."

Ober nodded but froze when he felt a hard hand on the back of his neck.

"And if you turn craven and try to run, I'll put a bolt through your spine," the big dwarf rasped.

Ober's heart hitched at the dire threat. He didn't doubt Waelon would execute it as precisely as he placed his steps, but even worse, deeper than his heart Ober felt something move—something within him, but not him. It couldn't be him—stirred fitfully in the sleep the mona root Tomza had been giving him caused. Whether in response to the threat or Ober's reaction to it, he felt it like the barest rumble from a deep well.

"We clear?" Waelon pressed, his grip on the edge of causing pain.

The rumbling inside him threatened to take the form of a primeval growl. He'd need to take another dose of the root soon. He was having to use it more often, but he did not allow himself to think about what that portended.

"I-I understand," Ober assured Waelon. He hated that the quaver in his voice would be interpreted as fear of the coming battle. The other dwarf did not know what he was even now battling to keep inside him. "I'm not going anywhere."

The grip about the young dwarf's neck vanished. A pair of svartalfs detached themselves from the gathering and moved toward the shadows at the rear of the camp. Dwarvish eyes, accustomed to changing quickly from light to dark, allowed the dwarfs on the crest to note that they were stumbling, which was out of character for the graceful creatures.

"Drunk at their atrocities," Waelon hissed.

The inebriated elves bent over something before hauling it upward. The light of the bonfire played across the face of a bound elf who was taller and more striking, even at this distance, than either of the captors. Elvish gender was not Ober's forte—

most dwarfs agreed that elves looked like children stretched to ridiculous proportions—but something in the trapped creature's movements spoke of feminine ferocity. When he caught the sharp ring of her voice, he was even more certain that this wasn't just any she-elf but likely the lady Utyrvaul was keen to save.

The she-elf's struggles drew the attention of the elves around the fire, some of whom raised their drinks with a cheer. All of them watched with rapt attention. It was apparently time for the main event.

"I think that's the lady," Ober hissed, nodding at the struggling figure being dragged toward the fire. "The one we're supposed to save."

"Maybe," Waelon growled, his flinty expression betraying not a whit of concern for her fate. "Torbjorn's still not here."

The bound svartalf managed to wrench free of one captor's grip. She used the increased mobility to pivot and snap a kick into the other warrior's knee. The elf gave a cry of surprise and staggered back, losing his grip, but before the she-elf could take advantage of the moment, the first captor leapt upon her, and she was wrestled to the ground in short order. More drinks rose in salute as melodious voices giggled over the roaring pyre.

The svartalf warrior who'd been kicked straightened and advanced on the pinned lady, unable to disguise the limp in his unsteady steps. When he reached the snarling captive, he rewarded her temerity by helping his compatriot haul her back to her feet, then gave her several sharp slaps with his gauntleted hand. Silvery elven blood flecked the metal glove. The cajoling of the assembled spectators caused the pair to resume hauling their captive toward the fire.

"If we don't do something, she's going to die," Ober pressed, adjusting his aim.

"Let her die," Waelon replied flatly. "One less hell-eyed myrkling doesn't bother me."

"But—" Whatever he was going to say was cut short when one

of the svartalfs dragging the she-elf twisted hard to one side and then fell to the ground, dragging the captive to her knees.

"Gromic, you softy," Waelon spat. He pressed his cheek to his crossbow's stock and loosed a bolt.

The other elf staggered back a step to paw at his throat with bloodied gauntlets before keeling over, a bolt sprouting from his throat.

Sabers and lances were brandished as drinking vessels hit the ground. Their melodious voices rose in defiance and challenge, changing from the music of songbirds to the shrieks of diving raptors. Long blades stained red by the firelight waved as they closed ranks, keen eyes searching.

That happened in a heartbeat. Ober was left scrambling to adjust his aim from the dead captors to the ring of wary svartalfs.

"Are you planning to shoot something today, meat?" Waelon growled as he finished his second pump on the duabuw lever. "We've got them on the ropes, but those longshanks charge us, and we're both dead!"

Ober squeezed the trigger and felt the kick of the stock as his ears registered the hissing whirs of the tightly wound pulleys. He blinked, knowing his shot had been "ugly," as venerable Fordwan Juulric would have termed it. The dwarvish officer responsible for Ober's training had insisted that they strive to make every shot precise and lethal. "Let humans and goblins fill the sky with shafts. A dwan with a worthy duabuw should know his target is dead before the poor wretch does. Clean kills with each trigger pull."

This one hadn't accomplished that.

The potent bolt had punched through plate and cloth to nestle in the splintered hip bone of an unfortunate svartalf, sending him screaming to the ground. One hand remained on his long-bladed spear while the other gripped at the stout shaft jutting from his pelvis.

"Oh, you're a mean one, meat." Waelon laughed as he raised

his duabuw for another shot. "Gave that myrkling a new codpiece!"

"I didn't mean to—" Ober's protest was cut off by another screech of pain when a shot from the opposite hill buried itself in the thigh of a second svartalf. The elf sank to one knee, leaning heavily on her saber as she screamed in a pitch so high that his dwarvish ears could barely register it.

"Shut up and shoot," Waelon snarled out the side of his mouth as he took aim at a high-helmed elf who was pointing at the other hill.

His duabuw whirred as the bolt flew from the string, and the helmeted svartalf lurched forward. Sparks flew from his armored skull, yet to Ober's amazement and Waelon's profane irritation, the elf staggered a step, then righted himself. The scored helmet swung their way for a quick hateful glare before the warrior returned to directing his fellows up the opposite hill.

"Damn svartsteel!" Waelon swore as he leapt to his feet, arms pumping mechanically at the lever. "Come on. They are still too many!"

Ober, torn between taking careful aim and joining Waelon, spoiled his second shot, which scudded across the dirt before burying its point a full five paces from its intended target. The svartalf he'd aimed at flourished his sword defiantly before following the rest of the warriors sprinting toward the other hill.

"Meat, move your arse if you want to save your sister!"

Ober needed no further encouragement, though he wasn't as proficient as Waelon at working the heavy lever for the crossbow while moving, much less running downhill. The big dwarf snapped off another shot as he bounded down the slope, which took an elf through the small of the back, and primed another shot as Ober trailed behind. The younger elf was fighting to keep his momentum from getting away from him as he worked on the second pump of the lever.

When a hurled javelin came within inches of his throat, things got complicated.

After the first volley, there were still ten or so svartalfs on their feet. Half a dozen were clambering up the hill while others wheeled to face the enemies bounding at their heels. Ober's feet struck level ground, and the elves loomed like elegant giants, impossibly long blades flashing. Fear flashed through his mind and threatened to freeze his limbs as the svartalfs sprang toward him, their long strides eating up the intervening ground. Their eyes were as bright with malice as they were unfathomably old, and they shone as they came for Ober's vital essence.

He was so small, so young, so weak. How could he hope to beat them face to face?

Juulric's words came to Ober's ears, but they were spoken in his own voice, echoed by that thing buried deep within him.

"Just do the next thing."

Ober finally finished the third pump of the lever. The svartalfs' eyes narrowed as they closed the distance. Then the duabuw's stock touched Ober's cheek and his eyes synchronized with the sighting peg. One elf warrior's mouth parted in a battle scream as his saber rose for a decapitating stroke.

The trigger gave under Ober's finger, and he heard the oddly comforting sounds of the weapon at work. The warrior's eyes widened as the bolt passed through his bared teeth to erupt from the back of his skull.

Like a spell had been lifted, time sped up. Ober realized he was in the middle of a fight, with a dead enemy at his feet and another coming for him. A she-elf whose spear had a leaf-bladed tip so long it could have been a sword was rushing toward him, weapon leveled at his heart.

There wasn't time to prime another shot. There wasn't time to do anything but try to stay alive.

Using the crossbow like a cudgel, he managed to bat aside the first thrust, and he drove hard against the second. The gleaming spearhead struck the stock and skidded up and over, and Ober caught the haft of the polearm. He shoved the deadly head away, but she answered the maneuver by spinning with impossible grace, the haft whipping with her. Ober had just enough time to appreciate the poise and speed of the creature before the steel-capped butt of the spear cracked against the side of his head.

Stars exploded in front of his eyes, and the world took on a quavering aquatic quality as he fought to gather himself. Instinct made him dive away from a slashing return swing that would have cleaved him from brow to teeth, but it was a clumsy lurch, and he lost his balance.

He lost his duabuw during the dive, but that was not his greatest concern.

"*A prone dwarf's a dead dwarf,*" Juulric roared in his ears from the sweaty, grueling days of Ober's training. "And get that magsax out already. You think it's hanging there to keep your danglers company?"

Ober's hand found the hilt, then he caught a flash of steel and rolled to avoid an impaling stab. His world narrowed to an instant-by-instant scramble to avoid the shrieking svartalf's spear blade while trying to decide whether to draw his weapon or get to his feet. Second by wearying second, he began to stand, only to abandon that in a desperate bid to get his magsax out. His breath came in ragged gasps.

He heard a dwarvish war cry whose words were lost to him as he rolled clear of another thrust.

Then came the sting of steel as the spear drove through his mail and burrowed into the underside of one outstretched arm. Ober gave a bark of pain, his curse half-formed as the elf drove the blade downward. Nearby, yet too far away to matter, someone screamed his name. Through watering eyes, he looked up to see the leering elvish face, sharp teeth displayed in a predator's mocking grin.

Searing pain radiated from the wound, and it stirred the thing he feared even more than elven steel. Ober felt the leviathan stirring in the depths of his flesh, and with all he was, he threw his will against it, the metal in his body forgotten. He felt the urge to change pressing against meat and bone, seeking to drive him into a shape he *would not take*. The prickling burn of bristles erupting across his flesh stole his focus as his bones buckled. His back arched, and he screamed in a voice that wasn't his or any dwarf's.

"No," he shrieked, pressing down with a strength of will he'd never before demonstrated. "Not now. *No!*"

Almost comically, he felt the mounting pressure grind to a halt just before he changed, and then with staggering swiftness, the presence shriveled. The presence retreated and retracted and sank into the depths of his flesh once more.

Gasping for air, Ober looked up to see his attacker staring at him with rapt attention, the voracious grin replaced by dread fascination. A musical elfin oath passed her lips as she studied his face.

Seizing the distraction, Ober kicked at the foot that was planted a little too close. The heavy kick buckled her delicate ankle with a gristly pop, and the she-elf pitched forward as her grip slid down the polished shaft of her spear.

The svartalf managed to catch herself before she fell on Ober by tightening her grip on her spear, then she adjusted her other foot. While she was fighting to keep her balance, Ober yanked his magsax free. The elf stiffened when the hardened tip of the blade punched through her padded jerkin into her tender flesh. The svartalf's teeth gnashed inches from Ober's face, but he tore the blade free and thrust it deeper. Her face twisted in a wordless scream as silvery blood bubbled from her mouth and the strength left her body.

The svartalf didn't fall so much as flop on top of Ober, her grace gone as her life blood pooled in her armpit. He watched as the bright light in her malicious eyes guttered and then went out, leaving blind red orbs in a lolling skull.

Panting, Ober tried to heave the svartalf to one side but realized he only had one arm available for the effort. The other was still impaled. The movement drew a fresh wave of pain, but it was colder and less immediate. He was relieved that the thing lurking within him paid it no heed as it sulked in petulant slumber.

Punching out with the hilt of the magsax, Ober managed to batter the svartalf corpse to one side. He was thinking about how to remove the spear pinning him to the ground when he sensed more than saw a presence looming over him. His grip tightened on the magsax, ready to make a desperate swipe, then a hard hand seized the spear shaft and wrenched it out before Ober knew what was happening. The world exploded in pain, and the thing inside him gave a warning rumble.

Ober tried to shore up his internal defenses as he was dragged off the ground. He settled on legs that felt gelatinous, his eyes pinched shut against pain and the thing threatening to awaken again.

"Steady now, lad," a familiar gruff voice exhorted as he convinced the thing to stay quiet. "Hold still, and we'll get you sorted until your sister can see to you."

Ober opened his eyes to see Torbjorn fashioning a rough bandage to bind his bleeding arm.

"Nothing fancy," Torbjorn rattled on as he tugged the binding tight, "but it'll do for now. Good work with that elf bi—"

The words died on Torbjorn's lips as he looked into Ober's eyes and caught the last trace of liquid black surrendering to pale gray. The commander's face showed his disbelief as the shabr'dwan tried to convince himself it was a trick of the light, then his expression hardened.

"We're going to talk about this," the commander warned, his voice cold and flat. "But first, I've got a debt to collect."

CHAPTER THIRTEEN

"A grand victory!"

Utyrvaul had recovered his exuberant and genteel demeanor in the wake of his mistress' rescue. As the shabr'dwans gathered around him and his liberated lady, the elven knight was all smiles.

His mistress, on the other hand, rose to her full and impressive height, exuding doggedly restrained wrath. Her eyes, so dark a red that they were nearly black in the firelight, flashed. She held herself with poise and dignity despite the swollen lacerations across her high cheeks and sharp jawline.

"Wouldn't you agree, mistress?" the svartalf coaxed as he sheathed the knife he'd used to part her bonds. "A timely and magnificent conquest."

Her head twisted viper-like toward her retainer.

"Very nearly too late," Lady Banneret Tegwylivere Tivalinos spat, fixing her retainer with a caustic glare. "I was on my way to the pyre."

Remarkably, the shorter svartalf did not wilt or even bristle at the recrimination but only smiled wider.

"I am very pleased to see that my lady has lost none of her

potent spirit." The elf chortled as though his mistress had just made a witty jest. "I'm certain our fortunes are soon to be reversed now that you can return to Lord Gwenmaelon Gwydarioc with word of vanquishing these base traitors."

The elf aristocrat uttered a few sharp words in her tongue, but Utyrvaul was unfazed.

"Oh, of course," he intoned with a deep bow and a gracious sweep of his arm toward the assembled dwarfs. "We will acknowledge the contributions of our good allies, and dwarven dignity being what it is, we would not want to embarrass them. They are such humble and dignified creatures, after all."

Torbjorn rolled his eyes. Gromic and Haeda exchanged wry glances, and Waelon spat on the ground. Behind the veterans, Tomza was tending Ober, his arm outstretched and his sleeve stripped away. Neither was paying much attention to the spectacle being put on by the pair of elves. They had other things on their minds.

"I appreciate the assistance you provided this fool," Tegwylivere assured Torbjorn, shooting another frosty look at her retainer. "I'm certain he didn't explain that if he had not run off with my steed, it would have been him bound and awaiting the pyre. That would have been fitting since he swore his life to my service, worthless though it is. At least you managed to bring the beast back in one piece."

"My only thought was to find aid as quickly as possible," Utyrvaul insisted with a deep bow as though he had just been given a compliment. "Overcome as we were, I knew our only hope lay in speed and a keen perception of those who would be willing to right a wrong most unjustly done."

Tegwylivere looked at Torbjorn with frustrated pleading. The commander held up his hands to indicate that his role in sorting out svartalf leadership matters was at an end. Lady Banneret gave a weary sigh and gingerly pinched the bridge of her long nose.

"What did you promise these fine dwarfs for their assistance?"

the svartalf aristocrat asked, her eyes closed as though to prepare for the blow. "At a glance, I can tell you didn't find actual soldiers, so I'm past hoping that this rescue will come without further cost besides my dignity."

The Bad Badgers stirred and muttered at the insult. Even Tomza tossed her a scowl as she finished bandaging her brother's arm. The svartalf didn't pay them any heed as she waited for Utyrvaul's reply.

"For their most courageous assistance in rescuing your person, these road-weary dwarfs have requested the meager boon of four full measures of *scienceren*."

Whatever Tegwylivere had been expecting, that was not it. Her dark eyes flew open, and her lips peeled back from her teeth. If she'd sprung on him and torn his throat out an instant later, none would have been shocked after the savage grimace that passed over her face, but pass it did. Her eyes shut again as though she was in pain, then she surveyed the sextet of dwarfs. Her face now wore an inscrutable mask, but her gaze lingered on the keen magsaxes and the freshly primed duabuws. Those implements of death had recently slaughtered her mutinous entourage to save her life, after all.

"I suppose that, given how very dire the circumstances were, you had no choice," she began, the words sliding from her lips in taut, curling syllables. "And I will honor the agreement you made as a sign of my gratitude. My retainer will see to the arrangements once we return to the Sufstan camp at—"

"Afraid not," Torbjorn interrupted, grinning into the elf's flashing eyes. "We'll take the elf-draught now if you please. As I explained to your retainer, we've places to be, and you've already cost us a longer detour than I'd hoped."

Lady Banneret Tegwylivere drew herself up at Torbjorn's brusque tone. Then she saw Waelon leaning forward, one hand resting on his axe. He'd used it on one of the traitors, and she'd seen his exultation as he hewed flesh and blood.

"I appreciate the situation," she cooed. "Yet, I cannot give what I do not have on my person. When I reach the Sufstan camp, I can reach out to my cousin, who will ensure that you receive your compensation—"

"Again, no." Torbjorn found nothing to smile about despite the svartalf's quivering nostrils. "First, Sufstan is in the opposite direction from where we are going. Second, the Sufstan camp is moving, and by the time you lot hoof it back to where the camp was, you'll have further to travel. Third, I don't make a habit of letting my debtors ride off with nothing but promises and miles between us."

Dwarf and elf locked eyes, and all present could feel the competition of wills crackling through the air.

"I cannot give something I do not possess," Tegwylivere reminded him with haughty patience. "Do what you will, commander, but even a dwarf can't squeeze blood from a stone."

Torbjorn's mouth curdled into a sour smile, but he gave no answer. The three veterans at his side let their hands trail toward their weapons. Tomza unlimbered her crossbow, and her brother's hand settled on his magsax.

"A dwarf never forgets a debt," Torbjorn warned as his smile faded. "We've also been known to charge interest."

Tegwylivere leaned forward, her face splitting into something that wasn't quite a smile but showed every sharp tooth.

"Well, we have that in common."

"My Lady Banneret," Torbjorn whispered. "Are you threatening me?"

The axe was in Waelon's hand, but there was a blur of movement from the svartalf's side.

"Oh, my good lady, how could we have forgotten?" Utyrvaul cried with a merry titter as he interposed himself between his mistress and the dwarfs. "You have the portion of *scienceren* you stowed just before Autyriel initiated his coup. Don't you remember that you saw to its safekeeping, along with some other treasures, while I sought to dissuade the usurper from his treachery? It must be around here somewhere."

The svartalf aristocrat held very still, refusing even to turn her head as her eyes darted toward her retainer. Her lips pressed into a grim line, then her face bloomed into a glassy grin.

"Yes, Utyrvaul, I recall now," she murmured through her rigid smile. "Thank you for reminding me."

Utyrvaul sketched a bow to his mistress and turned to the dwarfs to sketch a noticeably deeper bow.

"It is an understandable error after such a trying ordeal," the svartalf retainer offered with a wink. "I'm glad we could resolve this situation without further incident. Friendship is the rarest treasure in these troubled times."

"Quite." Torbjorn chuckled as he returned the wink and turned back to the raging she-elf. "Well, if you wouldn't mind fetching it then?"

Tegwylivere looked as though she would rather have faced the pyre again, but she gave a nod and turned toward the rear of the camp, where a small stand of squat trees clung to the rough soil.

"Utyrvaul, attend me," she hissed as she strode away.

"Always, mistress," Utyrvaul called, casting another wink at Torbjorn before hurrying after his mistress. As they strode away, the dwarfs heard Elvish hisses from the svartelf lady. Despite the verbal lashing, her retainer seemed as spritely as ever, dancing at her heels.

The elves were still within earshot when Waelon growled and spat upon the ground.

"I say we shoot them both and take the draught," the red-haired dwarf snarled as he shoved his axe back into his belt. "Wouldn't surprise me if the witch poisons the draught, leaving us with four dead pigs and no way to get where we need to."

Haeda's gaze sharpened at the mention of a threat to her beloved sows, but Torbjorn waved off the thought like it was a pesky midge.

"She's one of the more unpleasant myrklings I've met, but she's not stupid," the commander remarked. He twisted his head left, then right, eliciting a pop with each turn. "She knows we're suspicious, and if we check or test the draught, it wouldn't take much for her to earn a bolt in the head. Besides, do you want to spend the better part of a few hours hacking down trees and splitting them open?"

Tomza perked up at the mention of trees, and before Ober could silence her, she called to Torbjorn. "What's that about trees?"

The older dwarf looked at her over his shoulder, then his eyes shot to her brother. Tomza couldn't help noticing his suspicion, but his gaze also held deep weariness and for a second, a tinge of fear.

"Waelon." Torbjorn sighed. "Explain."

The big dwarf's gaze didn't leave the elves, who now stood at the edge of the firelight by the trees.

"Elf witchery," he growled. "Some of their kind, especially pureblood nobles, can speak to plants and bind them with spells. The thieving buggers stow plunder and whatnot in a tree or bush, and if you don't have the means to speak nice to it, the only way to get what they've hidden is hacking and uprooting."

"And there's little to no sign showing which one they stowed things in," Gromic added as he scraped out the bowl of his pipe. "If we didn't get lucky, we'd end up cutting down that whole copse to get the right tree."

"One more reason to hate the blade-eared thieves," Waelon snarled. "Every one of them is a filthy witch!"

Every veteran dwarf turned their head and spat.

Ober and Tomza exchanged looks, then lamely followed suit.

Tomza nodded stiffly, wiping a bit of spittle from her mouth as her gaze shifted to the elves. The lady and her retainer were engaged in an animated discussion in front of a scraggly, twisted fir.

"If you have to split them open, you might damage what's inside, right?" the dwarfess asked, narrowed eyes watching the bickering svartalfs.

Though it might only have been a trick of the light, it looked like Lady Tegwylivere was pointing one long finger at Utyrvaul while her other arm was buried to the shoulder in the tree.

"Worth the risk if you ask me," Waelon rumbled, a hand still resting on the axe on his belt. "Better than trying to deal with those cowardly, deceitful, treacherous—"

"No one asked for your opinion," Torbjorn asserted. "Let's stay focused."

"Looks like our friends could use that advice, sir," Haeda nodded at the elves. "Lady Spindle-leg there is spouting off more than a tea kettle in a blast furnace."

Torbjorn batted the air dismissively and waved toward the elves.

"That's just their way," he grumbled.

The air was rent by a piercing screech.

Every dwarf had their weapon in hand as they watched Lady Banneret Tegwylivere collapse to the ground, clutching at her throat. Utyrvaul stood over his stricken mistress, wagging the poignard he'd used to cut her bonds while he scooped up a sack that had fallen from the she-elf's hand. The retainer paused to take a peek inside the sack before drawing it onto his shoulder and striding away from the expiring svartalf aristocrat.

Over the fading crackles of the fire, the dwarfs could hear him singing a sprite ly tune.

"That's their way, all right," Gromic muttered. He went back to packing his pipe. Waelon gave a satisfied grunt, and Haeda and Torbjorn shook their heads. The siblings watch with dread fascination as Lady Banneret Tegwylivere Tivalinos stretched one bloody hand after Utyrvaul's retreating form, then collapsed. She did not move again.

Utyrvaul was cleaning his knife as he reached the dwarfs, his bright voice at odds with his words.

"Oh, most unfortunate fate, my friends. My Lady met with a most dreadful accident, and she is bound for the Halls of the Matron. But fear not, for she was able to retrieve your payment before disaster struck. With her last breath, she bid me give you not just four but eight measures for your efforts. It is a testament to her goodness that I can offer them to you freely, even though she will never receive your solemn thanks."

The dwarfs stood in stony silence, but as usual, the masterless retainer was unruffled. He slid his freshly cleaned blade into its sheath, then unslung the sack from his shoulder. Like everything about the svartalfs, it combined function and lavish decoration, silken sides emblazoned with gilt thread in the shape of the expired lady's device. Utyrvaul's hand plunged within, and a second later, it emerged with a crystal flask. Inside, a luminous green liquid bubbled and sloshed.

"I believe we are even." The elf held it out to Torbjorn, who nodded for Haeda to take the flask. The driver snatched it from the svartalf and unstoppered the flask to take a sniff of the fizzing emerald concoction. She nodded at the waiting Torbjorn, who in turn nodded at Utyrvaul.

"I suppose we are," the dwarf agreed, casting a sidelong look at the corpse near the tree line. "If anyone asks us, I won't lie about how your lady's accident involved your blade."

Utyrvaul laughed heartily as he bounced the sack. It jingled and clanked as he slung it over his shoulder.

"And why would you, Master Dwarf?" The svartalf twittered. "If the question came from one of my people, they'd hardly be surprised. If it came from one of yours? Well, let's be honest. What bother would it cause them if there was one less myrkling in the world?"

Again, Torbjorn produced that sour grin as he shook his head.

"You know, Utee, you're not wrong."

CHAPTER FOURTEEN

"I can't believe we just let that monster go."

Ober motioned for her to keep her voice down and leaned closer, a lump of treated mona root pressed into the hollow of one cheek.

"We've got bigger problems," he whispered, fighting the urge to eye their commander as their company set about making camp.

Torbjorn had had them clear out from the devastated svartalf camp, leaving Utyrvaul whistling to himself as he pranced among the dead, filching the odd bauble or trinket as he went. Haeda had stated her desire for the sow team to have a night of proper food and sleep before they made their long run on the elf-draught. To accommodate this, they'd traveled back to the main forest road and kept going in the dark past the southern pickets.

The square-stoned watchtowers, dotted with watchfires like burning eyes, sat upon the edges of the slopes like guards standing sentinel over the approach to a palace. At their closest, the dwarfs could hear sounds from within—the rattle of war harness and the clanks of sabatons on stone, and the deep-throated singing of dwans enjoying a meal and a drink together after their patrol. It was the sound of camaraderie, of community, which made it torturous to every shabr'dwan who passed in the night.

Not one of them spoke even after they'd passed beyond the reach of the songs. The next words were Torbjorn's order to make camp.

The siblings had paired off to set up the tents and had their heads pressed together in the near-dark at the edge of the wagon's lantern light. Ober's foreboding statement had Tomza sweeping her gaze around the group, but everyone seemed to be paying attention to their affairs or preparing to rest.

"What happened?" she hissed, the fate of the slain elf forgotten as she heard the fear in her brother's voice. "Did someone see something?"

"The commander," Ober murmured into her ear. "After the svartalf stabbed me, I nearly lost control. He saw the changes fading. I'm not sure if he knows what it means, but he promised we would talk about it after the business with the elves was done."

Tomza sucked in a breath. Both were certain the sound would draw attention, but neither dared look around. They hunkered down, acting as though they were wrestling out the canvas of the tent in the gloom. After a handful of seconds, Ober shuffled closer so he could speak in a whisper.

"What do we do? He's been on to us from the jump, and he's no fool."

Tomza swallowed hard, then glanced around again to confirm they were free of observation.

"We can run," the dwarfess suggested, barely mouthing the words. "No, not can; we *should* run."

Ober's body stiffened at the words, but his head remained bent toward the tangled canvas.

"No."

The word was spoken softly, but she felt the iron behind it.

She was more than familiar with that tone from him, and she hated it.

"We're clear of the pickets," she hissed, trying to catch his gaze. "We escape into the Valewood, move west, and—"

"No."

Neither harder nor louder than last time, but just as adamant and unshakable.

"Ober, please, listen to me," she pleaded. "This is our only chance. It's dark, everyone is tired, and we aren't in wight territory yet. Running now is our best shot of getting clear and starting over."

Starting over? The thought had not occurred to Ober. Having gone from bad to worse since the ruins in the glade, he had never conceived of a life outside of the Holt'Dwan. He was either going to be killed for what had happened to him and what he'd become, or he was going to spend the rest of his life hiding it from his brothers in arms and superiors. That had been the sum total of his future as he saw it.

Now that his sister had said it, he wondered why he hadn't considered it.

Start over? Turn his back on his family, his clan, his people, and all the oaths he'd sworn to them when he'd joined the Holt'Dwan? The family, clan, and people who had declared him unworthy of those oaths? Who would, if they know the truth, probably not even give him the ceremony of Grimmoth that was due even the most rank traitor? Who would put him down like...yes, like an animal and leave him to rot in some ditch, unburied and unmourned, except by his sister, who they would probably dispatch to assure no further corruption spread?

Why *not* start over? Why not find a place where his very existence would not be loathsome to those around him? Why not go where he could live without the constant threat of discovery? If not in the Ysgand Vale, there had to be somewhere else in the world.

"No."

The word tumbled from his tongue in his final answer. No, he could not run. He *would* not run.

"Ober," Gromic called in his bass voice. The young dwarf started. "Commander wants to see you."

Ober's stomach knotted and he thought the thing within him was trying to rise and cast its vote, but as he balanced on trembling knees, he felt a cold certainty that the betrayal was coming from his own flesh.

"Fresh Meat!" Gromic called again, and Ober heard his heavy footfalls approaching. "Can you hear me, lad?"

Ober told himself to straighten and say something. To do anything other than stand there and gape like a landed fish. Out of the corner of his eye, he saw Tomza's face pale, but she fought to keep her voice steady as she replied in his place.

"He's lost a lot of blood," she croaked around the lump in her throat. "Needs to rest. He's...he's not himself."

Ober couldn't see anything but Gromic's boots from where he crouched, head hanging. His mind screamed at him to *do* something.

"Hmmm, this don't look like what happens after a bleed," Gromic rumbled, then reached out a hand to the younger dwarf. "No, I know what this is."

Ober winced at the statement, feeling exposed and raw. Torbjorn must have told Gromic, a stalwart dwarf who would stand by his commander no matter what and defend him at all costs. Was that why Gromic reached for him even as he shivered and sweated? Was the hand about to seize him about the hair, dragging his head upward for a magsax to slide across his throat?

Ober was wrestling with those dark thoughts when a broad hand settled with surprising gentleness on his bowed back. The hand was warm and firm and exuded a reassuring strength that passed through Ober's shuddering frame.

"Got the war wobbles, eh, lad?" the hulking dwarf intoned

softly. "No shame in that, none at all. You looked death in the eye, and that's liable to affect even the sternest dwarf."

Neither sibling knew what to say, but Tomza's relief was palpable.

"W-war wobbles?" she stammered, her voice between laughter and tears. "What the hells is that?"

Ober looked up. Gromic's hand was still on his back. The stout dwarf looked at his sister, face twisting with thought.

"Nerves, but only comes after a proper hard fight," Gromic explained. "Leaves a dwan feeling like he can't breathe and he's not steady on his feet. Lots of times, his senses aren't working right either. Sometimes he's sick or kaks himself."

At the mention of kak, Gromic's gaze turned to Ober, quick to offer encouragement.

"Nothing to be ashamed of," he assured Ober emphatically. "I still get the wobbles myself after a particularly close one. Not often, but anyone who tells you they don't have 'em anymore? Well, there's something wrong with that dwarf."

Tomza saw Gromic's gaze dart to where Waelon was keeping watch, but Ober distracted her by standing. His face was hard to read at the edge of the lantern light, but there was grim determination stamped on his expression. It made her heart sink and her mouth fill with ash.

"I'm ready to go," he murmured, his voice thin but resolute as he looked Gromic in the eye. "Thank you, Gromic. I feel...better. You're a good dwan."

Gromic blinked, then slapped the younger dwarf on the back hard enough to stagger him.

"There's a Stone-boned dwan if ever I saw one. You're going to be all right, lad."

Tomza wanted to scream, *"No! No, he's not going to be all right!"*

Instead, she was mute and dry-eyed as her brother walked with Gromic toward Torbjorn and what was surely going to be the last moments of their lives.

"Sorry for the delay, sir."

Torbjorn made no immediate response as his dark eyes glimmered in the gloom.

"Lad had a bit of the war wobbles, I think," Gromic offered as he and Ober came to stand before the commander. "Shook it off like a proper dwan, but thought you should know, sir."

Ober stood before Torbjorn and met the commander's penetrating gaze as he'd said in the lardwan's tent not long ago. He felt empty, but whatever was left of him was made of sterner stuff than he'd imagined. Torbjorn, his formidable commander, was against him, but he would answer the questions put to him honestly despite knowing what the consequences would be.

The cards had been dealt, and the game was ending. He'd play his hand out and see what happened. It almost felt good to know that was the case.

"Much appreciated, Gromic," the commander stated curtly, ignoring the information about the war wobbles. "Go ahead and get everyone settled in, then get yourself some rest. Waelon's on first watch."

Ober's eyes wandered to the red-haired dwarf, who stood at the perimeter of the camp with his duabuw in hand. Waelon swept the dark woods around them, yet Torbjorn and Ober were never out of his peripheral vision. Ober imagined there was a simple explanation for that.

"Yes, sir," Gromic replied with a bob of his head, then looked warmly at Ober. "Good work today, lad. Did your clan proud."

Despite his improved mood, Ober could not force a reply. He nodded his acknowledgment.

Torbjorn and Ober were a fair way out of the camp, and there was a knot of trees at the young dwarf's back. The shabr'dwan commander wanted to ensure that if Ober ran, he'd have a hard time of it. With Waelon standing watch, Ober doubted he'd make it five steps before the red-haired dwarf put a bolt through his back.

Then things would get very interesting...or perhaps they wouldn't. That would be a relief.

Torbjorn's gaze bored into Ober, either looking for the truth or watching to see if the young dwarf's eyes would do what they had done before. It felt like with his superior stared at him for ages. Anxiety crept in, and when Torbjorn finally spoke, Ober started trembling.

"You've been hiding something from me," the commander stated, cold certainty in his voice. "Something that would explain why you were charged with cowardice. I've looked into your eyes and seen you fight, and I know you are no coward when it comes to a dwan's duty."

Ober wasn't certain he should speak since nothing had sounded like a question. He settled for nodding, glad to have time to master himself so his voice wouldn't squeak when he was called upon to answer.

"I think your sister knows about it, and her charge of cowardice was part of the cover-up," the shabr'dwan officer continued. "She must care for you very much or be scared of what might happen to you and her if the truth were known—or both—to keep this secret."

Again Ober nodded, feeling less likely to collapse.

"Hells, she might have a secret of her own." Torbjorn grunted. "Maybe it's tied in with yours, maybe not, but I think there is a good deal you two aren't telling me."

That was closer to a question, but since his sister had been mentioned, Ober was slow to respond with so much as a twitch of his head. He realized that his hesitation was an answer, and he cursed himself internally.

Torbjorn moved on to other matters.

"Regardless, what matters is that if something happens to you, she's liable to take it very personally." Torbjorn sighed heavily.

"So if I do anything to you she doesn't like, I lose the closest thing to medical we have out here, and my team is down two dwans instead of one. Do you see where this conundrum is leading, lad?"

At last, a question, but not the one he'd expected. The young dwarf's jaw dropped, and he stared at the commander, unsure he'd understood the question.

"Uh, I suppose not, sir."

Torbjorn nodded as though he'd expected that answer.

"I'll cut to the chase," The commander mopped his face with a scarred hand. "Whatever secret you have, do you have a handle on it?"

Ober's mouth swung open to divulge all manner of hidden truths. Then he realized that was not what he'd been asked. He closed his jaw with such force that his teeth gave a soft clack, and out of the corner of his eye, he saw Waelon twitch in their direction. Not wishing to give the violent dwarf further cause to pay attention to him, Ober held still and thought for a moment. Torbjorn stood in patient silence, but his eyes fixed on Ober's.

"I believe so, sir," Ober stated at last. "My sister has found ways to help. As long as she can gather herbs every few days, we should be fine."

Torbjorn was silent for a few heartbeats, then he nodded.

"I suppose, given that she tends all of us, that's easy to explain," he muttered, then frowned as he looked south. "What about going to Fang's Nest and then the Tooth? Change in climate, and if this assistance is from some plant, it could mean she won't have access to it. Does that change things?"

It was Ober's time to contemplate. He nodded as he offered an explanation.

"She knows we're going that way, so either she's confident she'll still be able to find everything she needs, or she believes she can store enough to be good for a while."

"How long is a while?" Torbjorn asked, his brows low and stormy over his glinting eyes.

"How far are we from the Tooth, sir?" Ober asked.

Torbjorn started to answer, only to stifle the words in his throat and splutter. He let out a long breath through his nose. When he looked up, something had changed. The unsureness and hard edges were gone from Ober's face, and his body radiated a fatigue that was beyond mere muscles and bones.

Torbjorn was tired to his soul. "I suppose we'll have to trust your sister." Ober watched him shake off the weariness through sheer force of will. "I imagine we've been doing it for a while without even knowing. It can't be helped, and so far, it's worked out."

Just before the last vestige of vulnerability was banished by the return of Torbjorn's commanding presence, Ober thought he saw something in his commander's eyes. A desperate, terrible calculation was taking place, something no good or sane dwarf should consider. Torbjorn must have hated to consider it. Ober didn't see what conclusion had been reached, but he couldn't help the dread mixed with pity he felt for his commander or his guilt. Torbjorn, whatever his reputation, was a good dwarf and a good commander in an impossible situation, one made all the more impossible by Ober's induction to the shabr'dwans.

"All right, lad, maybe I'm mad, but I'm trusting that you are telling the truth," the elder dwarf declared with an air of finality. "No need to talk about this with the others. You and your sister keep a lid on whatever it is you're hiding, and for the rest of this mission, I'll trust you to see it taken care of."

Ober heard no question, but he nodded before catching something that refused to be ignored.

"What about after the mission, sir?"

"We'll mine that shaft when and if we reach it." Torbjorn cleared his throat, then nodded toward camp. "First, we all need to get some rest so we can stay sharp for the next few days of rough riding. We'll be skirting close to the wheezers' holdings in Skadrun, and if we blunder into a patrol there, it won't matter what plants they have around Fang's Nest. Rest up, dwan. We've got a long road ahead."

Ober supposed it was practical, but Torbjorn's disinterest in his secret left the young dwarf confused and let down. He'd prepared to lay everything bare.

He hadn't been asked to share it, and he'd been told to go to bed.

"Move along, dwan," Torbjorn directed. "I need my beauty sleep too."

Ober's jaw clenched lest a torrent of words spill out of him.

"Yes, sir," he replied. "Good night, sir."

"Good night, lad." Torbjorn watched the young dwarf depart and saw him join his sister. The shabr'dwan was certain the two would spend some time debriefing before they slept, but as long as they kept it down, Torbjorn didn't care. He had other things on his mind.

He stared at nothing until a gravelly throat cleared at his shoulder. His head swung around and he saw Waelon, eyes locked on Ober and Tomza.

"Everything good, sir?" the big dwarf rasped.

Torbjorn frowned, then followed Waelon's gaze. The siblings were sliding into the tent, no doubt to hold their little conference.

"Nothing's been good for some time, Waelon." Torbjorn sighed. "And it doesn't look like it's going to get any better anytime soon."

Waelon frowned, not certain what to do with the answer and a little disappointed. He'd been prepared for the suspicious young dwarf to do something...unwise.

"Still," the shabr'dwan commander continued, having come to some conclusion in his troubled ponderings, "I've found the answer to a question that's been bothering me since I met with Klaus. I suppose that's something."

Waelon's brows lowered, and he turned to his leader.

"What's that, sir?"

Torbjorn's expression soured as he contemplated the question, then he shook his head and gave Waelon a weary grin.

"Not your burden to carry," he replied, clapping Waelon's strong shoulder. "Be thankful for that, deordwan. It's not something I'd wish on any of you. Now, I am tired, so I think I'll try to sleep a bit. You good for the first watch still?"

Torbjorn knew the answer before it passed the big dwarf's lips, but it was good to hear it.

"Yes, sir, ready and willing."

CHAPTER FIFTEEN

"This is bad for those poor animals."

Ober tried to answer, but his teeth clacked together as the wagon hit another hole in the road. He was certain he was only one or two impacts from permanent dental devastation.

Aside from his teeth, there was the matter of staying on the rattling wagon for the last few days of accelerated travel. Both siblings fell off a time or two during the first day of "draught-running," as Haeda had called it, so Gromic had fashioned a rope tether that bound them to the bench of the wagon. That might have seemed generous, but Ober had demonstrated before the end of the first day that there was just enough slack for him to be dragged behind the racing wagon if he pitched over.

After tumbling off and being dragged for the seconds it took for Waelon, Gromic, and Tomza to reel him in, Ober had been determined to keep his place. As a result, he'd been sore and exhausted for days. His skewered arm was showing remarkable signs of recovery despite his tribulations, though.

"Those pigs are not the first thing on my mind," he spat as he fought to keep his seat, knuckles whitening as he braced himself. "At least they have Haeda to look after them."

They'd gotten a late start the day after his conversation with Torbjorn. That was part of the reason none seemed eager to head into wight territory. The other reason was that Torbjorn and Waelon had set out at dawn and hadn't returned until near midday. Torbjorn informed them that they'd backtracked to the road near the picket tower in search of information.

Posing as a pair of enterprising prospectors, they'd hailed a passing patrol for word of the wights and their levies moving about the border. Parting with a few coins meant the fordwan leading the patrol was happy to share information about a goblin band and possibly a wight levy, though maybe an independent group of grem, moving westward. They were advised to hug the mountain shadows if they were foolhardy enough to go prospecting in the wilds between wight and dwarvish territory.

Torbjorn and Haeda had talked and decided whether or not to follow the fordwan's advice. In the end, Haeda stated that goblins heading west, most likely to Lake Blacmere, meant their best hope was to cut straight to Fang's Nest. Gromic and Waelon had expressed support for her plan since both held contempt for any threat goblins might pose. No one asked the siblings, so the decision was made. Despite this, Torbjorn delayed until the sky showed the blush of the sinking sun before they moved out.

Ober and Tomza, anxious that Torbjorn's deliberations had been on their account, were eager for things to get underway. They soon learned they would have been better off enjoying their last few hours of ease. Once the elven concoction was sprinkled into the worcsvines' mouths, the beasts had frothed and snapped their tusked jaws as their thick frames shivered with energy.

Haeda had only to give a soft cluck of her tongue, and the team sprang forward. The dwarfs could do little more than hold on for dear life. They'd carried on like this for six hours before pausing to allow Haeda to bark at the siblings to feed the snorting, snarling beasts a quick snack while Waelon and Gromic checked the wagon for signs of strain and effected maintenance and repairs as needed.

Once these tasks had been accomplished, with many profane oaths from Haeda, they'd launched again. Every third stop lasted a few hours to snatch some rest while the swine had a proper gorge and relieved themselves, then it was back to the grind.

This had gone on for four days.

They were drawing closer to a low tail of rock that sprang out of the mountain's spine. Other than the odd woodland creature that was quick to scuttle out of their clattering path, there were no other living things on the road to Fang's Nest. The last three times they'd stopped, no one had spoken. Everyone had carried out their duties in silence before dragging themselves onto the wagon again.

Tomza's grumble was the first time any of them had spoken in nearly a day. He wondered how that could be possible, but the wagon rattled again, and his jaw throbbed with an ache from the perpetual clenching, and he understood. How much longer could they keep this up?

An hour later, the first of the Fangs rose at the side of the road.

"First one," Haeda called in a hoarse voice, though the formation needed little introduction.

A spear of pale rock stabbed skyward, as thick around as a wagon wheel and so seamlessly rooted in the earth that it might have grown there like the trees that flanked it. Its white sides had been gnawed by time beyond mortal measure, but otherwise, it was free of the marks of living things. No moss clung to it, no graffiti stained it, and no tool marks had marred it.

Staring at the ghostly stone monument, stark amidst the green of a wood that had yet to feel autumn's bite, the siblings shuffled closer together. Whether their past experiences had left them superstitious or just sensitive, neither could look at the Fang without shivering. Nor could they look away.

"Welcome to wheezer-land," Gromic called over his shoulder as though he'd sensed their unease. "You two ever make it this far south with your division?"

Both shook their heads but remained silent as they rolled beneath the cold shadow of the Fang. Tomza gripped Ober's hand, which felt clammy, as though no comfort could dwell beneath the stone's shadow.

The wagon tore around another bend, and the bone-hued geolith was gone.

"Can a rock be...evil?" Ober asked. He felt stupid for letting the thought out, but when he peered at his sister, he saw that she understood.

"I wouldn't have said so until I saw that thing." She gulped and shuddered again. "And we are going to a nest of those things."

"Maybe it will get easier," Ober offered, though his face betrayed his doubts.

Tomza shook her head and squared her shoulders. "How long has it been since we could say things have gotten better?" she asked, frowning as the wagon gave a peculiar shudder.

"We've got to hit rock bottom at some point," her brother replied, grimacing at the wagon's shimmy. "What is going on?"

"Draught's run its course," Waelon muttered. "And so've the worcsvines."

The siblings realized the shuddering had been the gradual deceleration of the wagon, which was now unfamiliar. The team's sprint became a trot, and the grunting and wheezing of the sows rose in pitch and frequency.

"Bones and Stones," Haeda muttered, her shoulders drooping as the trot dropped to little more than a waddle. "That's it for them and for me."

"Well, we can't have you collapse here," Torbjorn stated as he hopped down from the bench. "Ober, Tomza, turn those swine loose, then see that Haeda's tucked in."

The driver, having been busy not just keeping her seat but

also directing the rushing swine, muttered several low curses and watched hollow-eyed as the siblings did as they were bidden with the pigs. The beasts tossed their heavy heads, and a few even snapped their jaws, but when the halters came off, they gratefully trundled into the trees. As they went, Tomza noticed how much thinner the beasts looked, their once-plump sides hanging in slack folds. The young dwarfess found it hard to believe the creatures had the strength to find food, but they had to. Their feed stores were gone.

"It seems cruel," Tomza muttered as she watched the last sow depart. "I understand it was better for us, but how can anyone think that wasn't awfully hard on the poor creatures?"

Ober, whose knee was still smarting from being clubbed by a sow's head as she departed, was less sympathetic.

"You can ask Haeda if you like," her brother whispered as they faced their second task.

Handling Haeda proved to be far more difficult than her sows had been.

First, they had to pry her stiff gloves off the reins, then her blood-crusted hands out of the gloves. The pain of this extrication roused the driver from her stupor, and she hurled verbal abuse at them. Helping her down from the bench drew more ire, which got worse when Tomza lost her grip on Haeda as they lowered her to the ground. The driver's elbow whacked the edge of the wagon, and her profane exclamations grew in intensity and pettiness.

"Ach! You whore-born bitch!" Haeda shrilled as a ravaged hand pawed her battered limb. "I hope your womb shrivels and your dugs dry up for that one."

"Charming, as always," Tomza grumbled as she righted herself and set about helping her brother lead her snarling ward toward a reasonable spot to make camp.

While the siblings were busy with Haeda, the rest of the Bad Badgers set about pushing the wagon off the road. While it was considerably lighter with the sow feed gone and absent the doughty dwarfs, the vehicle was cumbersome to shove between trees and over gnarled roots. A knot of underbrush snared the wagon while its rear wheels were still visible from the road, but a spectacular effort by Gromic and Waelon provided what was needed. The wagon cleared the tangle and was unloaded and left in a tight copse of trees.

Those tasked with managing the wagon found Haeda and the siblings without much effort. After they'd set the supplies from the wagon in a rough ring, Torbjorn took stock while Waelon loped off to secure the perimeter. Gromic saw to getting a small firepit dug and some kindling gathered.

"How's the hero of the hour?" Torbjorn asked as he came to where Tomza was examining Haeda's hands amidst a storm of venomous protest.

"This will need tending with salve and bandages, sir," Tomza reported, pointedly ignoring Haeda's tirade. "And we all need some rest to let our bodies recover."

"Never mind the...*ow!* The *infant*, sir," Haeda hissed between cries of pain as Tomza probed her raw digits. "Just a minute, and I'll be ready to go...*ah!* Stop that!"

Tomza's examination lasted a minute longer, though Ober could tell from his sister's face that she was done thirty seconds before she released the cantankerous driver's hands.

Torbjorn frowned as he contemplated Haeda's hands, then turned to Tomza.

"How long?" he asked.

Tomza looked up sharply, surprised to be asked. She almost answered but brought herself up short and studied her commander's expression. Was this a test? A trap where he would heavy-handedly impose his authority?

"I know we need to make haste, commander," she began in an even, thoughtfully paced cadence. "But I would suggest that since we will need to take watches, we don't set out until everyone has had at least a day of rest with food. Two if we can spare it."

"Don't listen to her," Haeda muttered, her eyes fluttering. "I'm fine. Besides, we...we..."

"We made great time, thanks to you and your team," Torbjorn told her, bending to settle a hand on the dwarfess' shoulder. "That means we can take some time to rest up."

Haeda quieted at his firm grip, and without so much as another curse, she was asleep before her head came to rest on the ground. Torbjorn allowed himself a small smile before raising his gaze to Tomza.

"Two days, then, but nobody settles in or goes foraging until Waelon's back with the all-clear," the commander instructed. "And you don't rest until her hands are tended to."

"Yes, sir." Tomza nodded, then went over to the crates to fetch what she'd need from their limited herb stores to make the salve. As she rummaged, she tasked her brother with fetching bandages.

When Waelon returned, he reported that goblins had been in the area a few days ago, but there was nothing fresh. Torbjorn gave Gromic the nod to start a fire, then raised his voice to address the Bad Badgers.

"We're going to rest here for two days, and then we're bound for Turoth's Tooth," he explained, seeming untouched by the fatigue that gripped the rest after their mad rush. "We're on foot from here on out, so in these two days, get your pack set for a good haul into the mountains. Anything we don't carry we'll bury beneath the wagon, but expect to be away for a good while."

For a time, there was no noise except Haeda's rhythmic snores and the muted sounds of the forest. None of them could complain about having two days of recovery time, but the mystery about what came after weighed on their minds. Torbjorn would have despised any commander who kept this from him, but his orders had been explicit, and on this rare occasion, he agreed with them.

"We're going up from Turoth's Tooth, then," Waelon rumbled, voice cold as his expression. "Toward Mount Onegdun."

"Aye." Torbjorn nodded. "I know you've all heard the stories…"

He paused and looked at the siblings, who looked lost.

"Well, everyone except you two Vale-born babes." The commander sighed. "But superstitions and tales to frighten children into shutting up around bedtime are not our business."

In everyone's eyes, he could see the question of what their business was on that gods-forsaken rock, but Torbjorn decided he wasn't going to give them the opportunity to ask it. They'd learn soon enough.

"Right. I'll take first watch while the rest of you see to things and then get some shuteye. Remember, we are in wight territory now. The fire stays low and the smoke limited, keep your eyes peeled and your ears open, and no one goes off on their own. We are officially in enemy territory."

CHAPTER SIXTEEN

"What the hell is this?"

Tomza awoke with a start to find Haeda in her tent, shaking filthy clothes in her face.

"Wh-what?" the young dwarfess stammered, blinking and yawning as she looked outside to see the sky gray with predawn light.

"This," the driver snarled, her bandaged mitts shoving the garments under Tomza's nose.

Tomza unwillingly inhaled a snoutful of stale sweat and arse. Her belly threatened to rebel.

"Ugh, stop and get out," the young dwarfess moaned. "I mend injuries, not do your laundry. Get out!"

The odiferous cloth was removed, and Tomza settled in for a little more sleep. Suddenly, the stink swallowed her head, and her world was overturned.

There was a brief sense of falling, then the dwarfess hit the ground hard enough to rattle her senses. For a moment, there was nothing but the noxious darkness of the soiled clothes as Tomza fought to get up. Her recovery was in no way aided by her head throbbing where it had struck the ground, nor by every breath being laden with choking stink. Somewhere beyond the suffocating snare around her head, a voice shouted furious words the young dwarfess couldn't make out.

The loamy earth beneath her fingers let her center her body and her mind. After that came anger.

Curses that were a match for anything the wagon driver had ever thought of spilled from Tomza's mouth as she came to her feet in a rush. The foul web of cloth flew off her head in a stiff wad and there stood Haeda, still spewing recriminations and threats from between her clenched teeth. Tomza's cot was upended on the ground, and the pile of fetid clothing lay atop her camp blanket. Just one more casualty of Haeda's outburst.

"...so help me, I'll do it!" Haeda hissed, pressing forward until she was nose to nose with Tomza. "You understand, bitch?"

For the first time, Tomza noticed that she had to bend down to look the driver in the eye. "What is wrong with you?" she snapped.

"Are you deaf as well as stupid?" the driver snarled. "You keep your hands off me, you hear? I don't need your grubby fingers pawing me, you needle-diddling deviant!"

Tomza blinked, wondering if she hadn't hit her head harder than she'd thought since nothing Haeda was saying made sense. The mention of fingers drew the dwarfess' eyes to the driver's bandaged fingers, where the recent violence had torn new lesions that wept red.

"Torbjorn told me to tend to your hands," Tomza shot back, nodding at the droplets forming on the outsides of the bandages. "Now I'm going to have to do it again because you've gone and broke everything open, you crusty old bint."

Haeda seemed to notice her bloody hands for the first time, glancing down before curling her fingers into crimson knots and glaring back up into Tomza's face.

"I don't give a kak about my hands," the driver rasped. "I'm talking about how you stripped me naked, pawed through my things, and groped me some more when you tugged new clothes on."

Tomza's gaze swung to the befouled clothes, then back to Haeda. She now understood what this was about, but it did nothing to make things less ridiculous.

"You can't be serious."

Haeda's guttural growl said otherwise.

"You were filthy. We all were," Tomza protested. She would have been laughing if she wasn't so angry. "I wasn't going to go to all that work to fix up your hands just to have you touching nasty clothes that could bring on infection."

Rather than ease the tension, the explanation inflamed the driver's ire.

"So, it was you!" she shrieked.

"Of course it was!" Tomza roared back. "I wasn't going to make Ober touch your leathery arse!"

The knife was in front of the young dwarfess' face in an instant.

"You ever touch me again, I'll gut you *and* your brother."

"Get out of my face," Tomza growled. "Or your hands are going to be the least of your problems."

"Just try it, you—"

Needing no further invitation, Tomza snapped a hand out and seized Haeda's wrist. The older dwarfess tried to twist free with surprising speed and strength, but the younger one held fast, and her square fingers bit deep between the bones of the wrist. The driver gave a screech of pain as Tomza shook the gripped arm like a terrier with a rat. A second later, the knife tumbled to the ground.

For her efforts, a bloody fist crashed into Tomza's face, then another. The third punch, she ducked as she bulled forward. The dwarfesses tumbled out of the tent, punching and kicking as they squirmed across the ground. Tomza was bigger, younger, and stronger and had a grip like iron, but Haeda was mean, quick, and hard of heart and head.

Flesh got bruised, eyes were gouged, and joints popped as Haeda's ravaged hands adorned both with smears of crimson.

Other voices rose around the pair, but neither had the time nor the attention for anything other than the fight.

Tomza's hands found Haeda's throat as bloody fists continued to pummel her face. Then there were hard hands on her, and she was hauled back. For half a second, she kept her grip on the older dwarfess, but something clubbed her extended arms, and she had no choice but to let go.

"I'll kill you," Haeda croaked. "I'll cut you from chin to cu—"

A broad open hand caught the driver across the face. The force of the blow spun Haeda around, and she fell to the ground, poleaxed. Tomza, gripped by two pairs of strong hands, looked up to see Torbjorn standing over Haeda. He was naked from the waist up, his dark hair and beard tangled and dripping. The livid scar tissue, once hidden by bandages, cut like a jagged bolt across his head from crown to brow.

"That's enough," the commander of the Bad Badgers growled in a low voice. "I don't care what this is about. It stops now."

Tomza realized she was still straining against the hands, which belonged to Gromic and Ober. With an effort, she relaxed the tension in her muscles, and the dwarfs loosened their tight hold. Despite that, Tomza couldn't look at Haeda's sprawled form with anything but loathing.

"She's crazy," the young dwarfess declared, not caring how raw and quavering her voice sounded. "Came into my tent and—"

Torbjorn's blazing gaze swung toward Tomza, and she felt her stomach drop and her throat tighten.

"Whatever this was about, it is over now," he pronounced with fatal surety. "We're miles deep in enemy territory and hardly through the first part of this mission. You are both going to bury this here and now, or by Grimmoth, I will bury you both."

Even the saltiest dwarfs would falter at the invocation of the ever-hungry demon-god, but more than the oath, his voice struck Tomza. Torbjorn Kinslayer *would* end them both if this wasn't over.

"Just keep her away from me," Tomza spat, retreating from the flaming eyes as Haeda got to her knees.

Torbjorn's voice rose in a laugh so cold and sharp it cut through her quivering anger and outrage.

"Not on your life, lass," the commander crowed. "You see her hands? That fresh cut over her eye? Those need tending, and you're just the ascedwan for the job. Do I make myself clear?"

Tomza swallowed her protests but continued to glare at Haeda.

"Yes, sir," she answered, throat tight and jaw clenched.

Torbjorn kept his glare on her for a second longer before turning to Haeda. She matched his gaze with a defiant glare of her own.

"If I hear one cross word or see you raise a finger against her…" Torbjorn warned. "Anything other than cooperation and respect—you heard me right, *respect*—gods damn me, I will tie your arse to the nearest tree and leave you there. I wonder what a band of grem with an axe to grind might do to a pretty little dwarf all gift wrapped for them a second time?"

Gromic drew a sharp breath. An expression of deeper hurt and hate than anything the young dwarfess had provoked flashed across Haeda's face.

"Do you understand?" Torbjorn asked, his voice suddenly heavy, every word burdensome.

"Yes, sir," Haeda choked out, spite thickening every syllable. "I understand."

For a moment, there was nothing but trembling silence. Even the forest held its breath. Then there was a soft rustle in the underbrush, and Waelon vaulted from between the trees to the edge of the camp.

"We've got company," he hissed, bloody axe in hand.

CHAPTER SEVENTEEN

"You're sure they're a levy troop?"

Torbjorn had thrown on his gambeson and field mail in short order and was just finishing with the leather laces on the sides. It was a far cry from the plated war kit most dwans wore, much less the Sablestone harness, but in this situation, he was glad for them. The blood glistening on Waelon's axe testified that they had minutes at the most.

"Don't know why humans put up with the smelly buggers," Waelon grumbled. "Spied five or six of 'em behind no less than a dozen goblins, all armed but not much in the way of armor. The humans weren't uniformed, so I'm thinking they're leftover from a conscription, or else a seasoned militia was drawn up to give the grems some spine. Hard to tell. You know how they all look."

Torbjorn did.

Few creatures matched the model of efficiency and quality of form that was the dwarvish body, but humans were an offense to any reasonable aesthetic. Looking like overgrown, poorly proportioned infants tottering on overly long legs, they combined the worst of elves and goblins, lacking grace or economy of movement.

Torbjorn remembered the first time he'd seen humans in the flesh. He'd nearly been sick at the sight of them, wobbling about on their ungainly limbs. To compound their perversely juvenile mobility, only one in a hundred could grow a proper beard, making age and experience hard to ascertain unless their hair had gone white. By then, most of the short-lived race were knocking on death's door.

He'd learned that those limbs made them faster on open ground than all but elves, and even without experience, they were stouter of body and heart than goblins. A dozen goblins were enough work for the six of them, especially with Haeda hardly able to hold a weapon, but add half a dozen humans, and Torbjorn didn't like their odds. Shooting drunken elves was one thing, but Waelon had had to dispatch one of their scouts, which spoke to them attempting to maintain military discipline.

"Any of them have a brass chain?" Torbjorn asked, holding his breath.

"Not that I saw." Waelon shook his head.

Torbjorn allowed himself to breathe again. It wasn't a guarantee, but their chances of the wights not discovering their presence would be far better if that were the case.

"How long have we got until they scent the corpse?" Torbjorn asked as he scooped up his helmet. "Is there any chance they'll pass this way without stumbling on us?"

Waelon looked back through the trees and sucked his teeth.

"If they haven't scented the death stink already, I'd be surprised, but I tucked the body under a fallen tree, so they might still be looking for him. Either way, they are going to be on their guard. Do you know any grem who's going to pass up a chance to avenge their kin?"

Torbjorn set about securing his helm. He supposed that was the goblins' one redeeming quality; in their own way, they understood responsibility and, therefore, vengeance.

"I suppose it's just as well." The commander sighed and

adjusted the helmet to accommodate the wound on his head. "We can't have anyone knowing what we're about. We'll just have to hope you're right about the brass chain. Then it's just a matter of making sure none of them leave here alive."

"Oh, is that all it is?" Gromic called as he stomped up to them, slinging a shield over his back. "A dozen grems at least, and six humans, all spoiling for a fight."

"You could always run away," the red-haired dwarf shot back as he checked his duabuw. "Not that you could run very far, but maybe you'll find a hill you can roll down to pick up momentum."

Gromic hefted his crossbow to his shoulder while rubbing his armored belly with a gauntleted hand.

"I'd just get stuck between the trees somewhere." He chuckled. "Besides, who's going to push you to keep your tally up if I toddle off?"

Waelon frowned as he let his rough fingers trail across the hatch marks etched on the stock of his duabuw.

"I suppose *someone* has to come in second." He grunted absently. "Though this time, it's your job to babysit the meat."

Ober raised his head. He had been checking that his magsax was clear to draw from the sheath. He shot the veteran dwarf an incredulous look.

"Babysit? Is that what you call it when you run off after elf scalps while I'm being stabbed?"

Waelon scowled, but Gromic gave a bark of laughter.

"Lad has a point," the wide dwarf snorted with a nod at the younger dwarf. "You can't blame your near-loss last time on him. You just have to face that if you hadn't finished that last myrkling with an axe to the back of the skull, your winning streak would have finally been broken."

Waelon had opened his mouth to protest when Torbjorn roused from his thoughts.

"We're not dividing up like last time," he began. "We've got a killing field to prep, and then we'll draw them in. Remember, not one of them can get out of here alive. Otherwise, they will bring others, and our trek to Turoth's Tooth will be near to impossible."

"Where are we going to find a killing field?" Tomza asked as she hurried to put the finishing touches on Haeda's mangled hands. "And how are we going to draw them in?"

Torbjorn's eyes lingered on the bloody bandages lying next to Haeda.

"Oh, don't you worry," he grinned wickedly. "Those are the easiest parts."

"You just had to say something, didn't you?"

"Don't you dare try to pin this on me," Tomza hissed. "And that sounded neither compliant nor respectful, so you'd best watch your tone."

Haeda's face twisted, but when she spat, it was into the stoked fire. She didn't bother to speak further.

The younger dwarfess was glad for the silence since her ears were straining to hear movement around them. She fought the urge to reach for her duabuw as she fed more bloody bandages into the campfire. The small plume of greasy smoke that emerged wasn't as bad as the smell of seared blood and scorched unguent that filled her nostrils.

The forest remained uncomfortably quiet as the sun neared its zenith. Tomza knew she was supposed to keep acting like she was tending Haeda's injuries, but her eyes strayed between the trunks of trees, expecting to see the glint of a goblin's lupine eyes, or worse, a human's towering form.

"Where are they?" Tomza muttered under her breath as she flicked more bandages into the fire. "I'm almost out of this stuff."

Haeda's face twisted and she restrained a sour comment, then her limbs stiffened, and her head inclined to point past Tomza's shoulder.

"We've got our first nibble," Haeda murmured. "Two grems sent out to sniff the bait."

Tomza's heart thundered in her chest, but her movements were sure. The uncertainty of waiting for the enemy to arrive was gone, and with it, her fear.

"Well, let's make sure they swallow it," she whispered, head down as one hand slid toward her crossbow.

"Wait," Haeda hissed and gripped her side as if she were in pain. "Too quick and you give it away. Let them make the first move."

Tomza froze, wondering if Haeda's dislike was strong enough to encourage her into doing something dangerously foolish. After all, the young dwarfess couldn't see the goblins behind her, and for all she knew, they were leveling their javelins to take her through the back. Admittedly, she trusted the mail hidden under her cloak to turn the best a grem could hurl at her, but to make them look like vagabonds and not soldiers, Torbjorn had forbidden her to don her helmet. A grem javelin in her skull or neck was not how she hoped to die, especially not so soon after escaping the prospect of the Deeping.

Tomza locked eyes with the driver, and to her surprise, she saw neither fear nor hatred. Despite her mock distress, Haeda's gaze was clear and confident, a dwarfess going about her business.

Tomza didn't reach for the duabuw lying under a seemingly cast-off pack.

"Holding still, pig!" a brittle voice a dozen paces from where Tomza knelt shouted. "Holding still, or sticking you we!"

Tomza looked over her shoulder to see a pair of goblins advancing with spears in their knobby hands. Their yellow eyes perched above flaring nostrils and a mouth full of jagged teeth. They wore a patchwork assembly of rough homespun and hides, with objects that might have been wolf teeth sewn here and there.

"Please," Haeda pleaded in a distressed quaver. "We don't want any trouble."

The goblins shuffled closer.

"Trouble no?" one squawked with an incredulous flash of teeth. "Murder why? Everywhere death smell!"

"It was an accident!" Haeda cried. "He surprised us, and I drew my knife. He stuck me before my friend took him from behind. She was just saving me!"

Tomza lowered her face to mimic regret and also to hide her surprise at the impressive performance the driver was putting on. If she hadn't known the truth, the dwarfess would have believed Haeda.

The goblins were less easily swayed.

"Lie filth!" one squealed as it advanced, spear shaking in its hands. "Kin-murder pig!"

Further epithets spilled from the grem's lips in its coarse tongue. Despite this, Tomza and Haeda were under no illusions as to the goblin's feelings on the matter. Some things transcended language.

From the tree line behind them came rustling and the snaps of branches. The vanguard's accusations were clearly drawing the others. Turning slowly on her knees, Tomza saw the gleams of more piss-colored eyes among the trees. What about the humans?

"This is it?" called a gravelly voice. "I thought you said it was a pack of dwarven rangers, not a couple of grubby prospectors."

The owner of the voice, a gaunt-faced man with a rakish scar over one eye, stepped out from behind a tree. Several more emerged as well, looking nearly as disappointed as their leader. A motley collection of axes hung at their sides or rested on their shoulders.

Their clothes included padded jerkins, leather breeches, and dappled cloaks, which were easy to lose track of in the woods. That marked them as woodsfolk, a group that dwelt in the south Vale. Tomza's family had done a brisk trade with them before the wights came, but unlike the weathered but genial people who came to her father's workshop, these men looked hungry and lean. Their leader's axe had a notched but shining blade, not unlike the gap-toothed sneer he trained on Haeda and Tomza.

"This lot's not worth the time," he spat, then called over his shoulder, "If we're late to the muster over this, you can bet I'll report the lot of you."

"Kin-murder!" several goblins shrilled as they clambered forward, though they were careful to give the men a wide berth. "Vengeance."

The scar-faced man turned a contemptuous eye on the grems, which Tomza counted as being closer to a score of goblins than a dozen.

"What do you think the marshal's going to do to you lot when we're days late, eh? Good luck with your vengeance then."

The goblins hissed and chittered amongst themselves at this prediction, giving Tomza a chance to do a quick head count. This had to be all of them, didn't it? Could she afford to wait for more to press in with them getting so close?

She felt as much as heard Haeda shift behind her, and the young dwarfess prayed the driver's aim would be true despite her damaged hands. A duabuw at this range would make a mess of her, armor or not.

"Enough," the leader shouted, and Tomza's attention returned to him. "Put some holes in the badgers, and let's get on our way. I don't want to be late."

Tomza's hand shifted beneath the concealing pack as she heard Haeda emit an icy whisper. "Afraid you're not going to make it, longshanks."

The *whir-crack* of the duabuw sounded in Tomza's ear as the bolt passed less than a foot from her neck. The dwarfess didn't allow that to distract her, nor the sight of the scarred human crumpling with a bolt up to its fletching in his chest. She drew her own crossbow, then sighted on the lead goblin and let fly. The missile tore cleanly through the spindly creature and had enough momentum to bury itself in the belly of another wretch behind it.

Tomza didn't celebrate her fine shot as she worked the lever on the crossbow. Human and goblin voices rose in outrage, and the mixed troop rushed forward.

Tomza could see that she wouldn't have time to ready another shot before they were on her in a flurry of stabbing and hacking. She and Haeda would be surrounded and torn to pieces, armor or no.

Then the ground, thick with leaf litter and vegetation, erupted close to the tree line. Tomza saw the glint of steel in the dappled sunlight and heard heavy feet rush toward the tableau.

The bootsteps were lost in a thunderous bellow.

"BAD BADGERS!"

CHAPTER EIGHTEEN

"I love it when they crunch!'"

Gromic's exultant cry sounded amidst the howl of battle as his boot descended on another staggering goblin. The grem, flattened by a sweep of the dwarf's shield, gave a gagging screech as its weedy bones snapped.

"Another good one," Gromic roared, casually swatting aside a pair of goblin thrusts.

Tomza kicked a goblin off her blade, snatched up its spear, and hurled it at a grem charging at Gromic. The crude implement flew true and took the goblin high in the chest. It spun and landed heavily, the spear's shaft quivering. Another pair of goblins darted around Gromic and made for Haeda.

"Gromic!" she bellowed. "Quit playing! You're letting them through!"

Spinning with surprising alacrity given his armored bulk, Gromic caught one goblin with a body check, but the other dodged past his stabbing magsax. With a club in each fist, the grem bounded toward Haeda as she frantically worked the duabuw's lever. Even with undamaged and unencumbered hands, it would have been a close thing. Haeda's efforts seemed as futile as they were desperate.

Tomza sprang forward, ducking a wild swing to ram her short sword into the goblin's chest. It managed to land a weak blow Tomza barely felt on her mailed shoulder, then tumbled back, retching dark ichor. Tomza tugged to free the blade, then spun to check on Haeda.

The driver gave Tomza a quick nod, then finished the third pump on the crossbow. A second to sight, and she added another human to her tally. This one had been exchanging frantic blows with Ober. The young dwarf raised his bloodied magsax in salute and turned to fend off a pair of goblins.

As glad as she was to see her brother safe, Tomza had problems of her own—a broad-shouldered human barreling her way. In the human's hands was a long-handled maul he swung with remarkable ease despite its obvious heft. Gromic was beset by a quartet of goblins that hammered and gouged at his armored form, so he would be of no help.

Tomza, with no shield and only her short-bladed magsax to defend herself, felt a rush of fear, but she buried it beneath her desperate need to survive. With a wild howl, she threw herself at the man, knowing her only chance lay in getting inside his guard.

Unfortunately, the woodsman knew that as well.

Rather than wind up for a crushing swing, he set his hands wide on the haft and used the length of wood like a quarterstaff. Her first swing notched the hard wood, but her following thrust was batted aside. In a quick reversal, he drove the butt of the maul into her chest. Her mail and gambeson took the worst of the blow, but with the man's weight behind it, the force sent her staggering back. Fighting for breath and shaking stars from her vision, Tomza had just enough wherewithal to see the oncoming maul descend toward her head.

Denying every instinct screaming at her to scramble back, the young dwarfess darted forward. The weighty head cratered the ground behind her after raking through her hair, but she was inside the man's long reach. Tightening her grip and bracing her other hand against the pommel, she drove the rigid blade of her magsax into the woodsman's belly. Steel punched through the dense fibers of the padded jerkin and buried itself in flesh until Tomza's hilt was stopped by his belt buckle.

Ignoring his wild scream, Tomza tried to tear the blade free, but hands wound around her throat, and she was hauled into the air. The woodsman, abandoning his heavy weapon, was intent on throttling her. Tomza gagged and retched, and her fists beat ineffectually on arms and a face like iron.

The dwarfess' world shrank as the corners of her vision darkened. The sharp pain in her throat was replaced by growing pressure, and she was sure her head was about to explode. She no longer had the strength and focus to clench her hands into fists, so she raked her fingernails across the huge face and its watery green eyes.

Her mind reduced to a foggy collection of instincts, she kicked out in a final desperate act of defiance.

Catch 'em in the danglers, she thought as she swung her foot forward with all her might.

Her foot struck something hard and metallic, not fleshy, and she tumbled to the ground. Tomza was sure she was dead, her soul returning to the beloved earth, but rather than welcoming her, the soil hurt her shoulder when she landed and rolled onto her back. She gave a retching cough, then realized she could breathe, and the pressure inside her skull was retreating.

She looked up to see the woodsman on his knees, clutching the hilt of her magsax, blood flowing down his chest. She realized what her fortunate kick had accomplished and smiled even as she retched up spittle and bile.

The man proved to be a tough nut. He gave a vitriolic snarl, clamped his hands on the hilt of the shortsword, and with a scream, he drew it out from his body. A blade slick with his lifeblood rose for a killing stroke as the human came at her, a pain-maddened scream tearing from his throat.

Tomza threw her hands out and tried to scramble crablike backward, but she touched the haft of the discarded maul. Her fingers closed around it, and with a snarl of exertion, she brought the weapon to bear.

The woodsman's swing was heavy but clumsy, and Tomza intercepted it with the maul's stout handle. Her parry staggered the human, and the young dwarfess scrambled to her feet. Setting her feet wide to leverage the heavy weapon, she checked his frantic thrust with the head of the maul.

Seeing her chance, Tomza swung the hammer over her head and brought it down. The blunt head buried itself in the ruined pulp of the man's head, and she let the weapon and the man tumble to the dirt.

The furious rush of battle abandoned her. Tomza bent double, hands on her knees, and she sucked air through her bruised throat.

When she looked around, she saw the ruined bodies of men and goblins scattered over the killing ground. Gromic and Torbjorn, blood-smeared and with the odd bit of vegetation still clinging to their armor, stalked among the dead and dying. Gromic offered a soft word here and there before his magsax descended. Torbjorn was a silent, stone-faced specter as he moved from one to another, his movements precise and mechanical. When they found a groping hand or a mewling voice, they stilled the owner with a quick thrust to the heart, clean and efficient.

Tomza straightened and searched for Ober, fresh fear gripping her heart. She didn't see his body among the felled, but neither did she see him in the camp or among the trees.

"Steady on," came a voice from behind her as the world threatened to spin. "Your brother's fine."

Tomza whirled to see Haeda shuffling toward her. Her hands

were dripping again, though otherwise, she was unharmed. The driver had clearly intuited Tomza's searching looks and saw the question in the younger dwarfess' eyes as she fought to croak out the question.

"He and Waelon took off after a pair of goblins," Haeda explained. "I imagine they'll be back any minute now. No grem's going to get away from Waelon."

Tomza's heart slowed, its hammering no longer a deafening roar. It wasn't what she wanted to hear since Ober was still in danger no matter what Haeda said, but knowing he hadn't fallen in the fierce fighting was a comfort.

"Thanks," she rasped, one hand rising to probe her throat gently. She knew there were things she could do to treat her injury, but her head was still muddled, and she couldn't remember what they were. She *was* desperately thirsty, and crushed throat or not, she needed a drink.

"Here." Haeda held out a waterskin. "Take small sips at first. Don't want you—"

Tomza, who'd seized the skin and begun gulping mouthfuls, pitched forward, gagging liquid. Water spewed from her mouth and nose as she fought to keep from pitching onto her hands and knees.

"To do that," Haeda finished with a sigh, then reached over to keep Tomza's thick braid from swinging into the effluence. Her other hand rubbed the young dwarfess' shoulders encouragingly.

"Easy now. Don't fight it. Just ride it out, then try to breathe."

Tomza might have gaped in shock at the tenderness in Haeda's voice and her thoughtful touch, but she was trying not to drown.

When the worst had passed, Haeda offered a rag without comment. Tomza took it with shaking hands. Mopping her face, the younger dwarfess tried to collect herself but found it was no easy thing. Her whole body felt off; her muscles trembled with tension, and her joints were loose and rubbery. She told herself this was neither her first fight nor her first time taking a life, but that didn't help. She reminded herself that she'd survived harder fights, though none which had brought her so close to death... except what had happened with Ober, but that had been...different.

"G-gromic t-talked ab-bout th-the war w-wobbles," Tomza stammered through hitching breaths. "W-wonder if-if thiss iss i-it."

Haeda nodded, and her hand tightened around Tomza's shoulder to draw her upright.

"Likely," the driver agreed, nodding to the waterskin clutched in Tomza's fist. "Slow, small sips. The worst'll pass soon."

Tomza nodded and complied. Haeda kept her arm around her until Gromic and Torbjorn shuffled over, their shields slung as they cleaned their blades.

"Twenty-six." Gromic chuckled, though he wasn't really amused, given the water beading in the corner of his eye. "Twenty-eight if you count the two Waelon and the lad are after. I'll have to tease Waelon about how off his count was. Off by double the number of grems and half the men. Hardly deordwan-level reconnaissance."

"Deordwan?" Tomza coughed, nearly throwing herself into another choking fit. "Waelon was one of the Dwarvish Rangers?"

The veteran dwarfs exchanged knowing smirks.

"We all used to be something else, you know," Torbjorn replied. "In fact, most dwans who receive the *honor* of becoming shabr'dwan had to climb high to fall so far."

"You didn't think we were common criminals, did you?" Haeda chortled as she nudged Tomza with an elbow. "I mean, who's going to work the Deeping if they all get to run around on suicide missions?"

That elicited a laugh from Gromic and Torbjorn. Tomza was not so befuddled that she didn't notice the fleeting look of pain in her commander's eyes. She didn't imagine any leader, even that of the Bad Badgers, enjoyed being reminded that their command was a death sentence.

"No, if not for that brother of his, Waelon would've been running his own band of rangers by now," Gromic rumbled as he wiped his eyes. "I'd take a whole charge of mounted wights on my arse over Waelon hunting me through these woods. Dwan's got a nose like a bloodhound and is more tenacious than a boar in rut."

"Only problem is, it doesn't seem like he can count," Haeda quipped, drawing another round of chuckles that were far freer than the last. Tomza wished she could join in, but the absence of her brother denied her attempt to relax.

"Shouldn't they be back by now?" she asked, happy to see that water and time had steadied and smoothed her voice. "You don't think they could've run into more levies, do you?"

The question quenched their mirth. Haeda and Gromic looked at their leader expectantly.

"Doubtful," Torbjorn replied, surveying the carnage. "There's nothing bigger than a forester's hovel for miles in any direction, so if these were heading west, they had to have come from one of the warrens on the eastern slope."

Torbjorn motioned toward the spine from which the nearby offshoot of the mountain descended.

"The grems have never been very populous here, mostly on account of the woodsmen," the commander of the Bad Badgers continued. "So, if this lot was worried about falling behind, it's likely they were following a much larger group. Probably the one that fordwan at the picket warned us about. If there's a force of that size mustering in the west under the wights, the wormholes in the east have to be near empty of anything resembling fighting strength. The only thing we need to make sure is that those runners don't catch up to the bigger levy. They'd send a pack after us for sure."

There was a rustle in the undergrowth, and the dwarfs spun, weapons in hand. Tomza held up the waterskin menacingly.

A familiar chorus of grunting snuffles preceded the arrival of the worcsvine that trundled between the trees. The sows swung their heads about, taking in the stench of the battle's aftermath, then with an affirming chorus of snorts, they set to devouring the corpses.

"Well, that spares us having to figure out how to hide them all," Gromic muttered as he sheathed his magsax. "Though I imagine we'll still have to gather the gear. Pigs can't eat metal, can they?"

Haeda and Tomza shot disbelieving glances at the dwarf. Torbjorn found something very important to stare at on a nearby tree.

"You're not serious, are you?" Tomza asked, noting the smile pricking the corners of Haeda's mouth.

"What?" Gromic huffed, arms crossing over his huge chest. "They eat just about everything else, don't they? It's a legitimate question."

CHAPTER NINETEEN

"So much for resting for a few days."

Tomza nodded along with her brother's grousing before casting a surreptitious glance to the left and right. Not long after Waelon and Ober had returned, hauling the goblin corpses behind them, Torbjorn had announced that they were moving out. Though the pigs and woodland scavengers would take care of the bodies and they could bury the discarded gear, he thought it foolhardy to hang about. They'd all groaned, but the process of striking camp had begun shortly afterward, allowing the siblings to make their own preparations.

"You see anybody watching?" Tomza whispered, her gaze returning to the bowl where a bit of mona root sat steeping in a fragrant concoction.

"Not that I can see," her brother answered after a quick look around. "Which reminds me, I wanted to talk to you about something."

Tomza raised a hand for silence while she retrieved a small flint knife from a hidden pouch on her belt. As Ober quieted, she lowered her hand and drew back her sleeve to reveal a collection of thin scabbed lines. Without a flinch, Tomza opened a hair-thin cut on her forearm, then pinched at the flesh to milk out a tracery of red. Tucking the blade away, she drew her fingers through the blood, then put her crimson fingertips into the concoction in the bowl.

The words, a collection of broken syllables paired with earnest intentions, hissed from her lips. Not for the first time, she wished she knew what she was invoking, but as with most of her life, her desires had little bearing on reality. She supposed she should be happy that she'd been able to learn this much.

The contents of the bowl stirred and gave off the scent of woodsmoke and seared sage. In the blink of an eye, there was nothing but thin ribbons of smoke curling off the mona root. Tomza picked up the root, ignoring its warm, pliable texture, and handed it to Ober. She then cleaned the bowl, which doubled as her camp crockery.

"That should last you until we get to the Tooth," she murmured, keeping her head down as she made to pack her things. "But you have to stay on top of it. No skipping doses because you can't feel it."

Ober had secreted the root in a pouch around his neck. He was lashing their disassembled cots together with spare twine when he began to mutter out the side of his mouth.

"I'll stay on it, but I've been thinking," he began, doing his best to ignore his sister's wince. "How long can we keep doing this? I mean, what's the long-term plan?"

Tomza bit back an angry reply as she shoved the rag-swaddled bowl into her pack. She was tired and her temper was short, but snapping at him wasn't going to do any good. She forced herself to take a slow breath before responding in her best long-suffering tone.

"We'll do what we have to do for as long as we have to do it," she replied, hating that she sounded like their mother yet finding comfort in the platitude. "Just like always. I don't have more of a plan than that right now, and that's probably for the best."

Ober paused in his work to look at her.

"How so?"

"Because if I were busy looking ahead, I wouldn't be paying attention to what needs doing now." She sighed as she checked to make sure her herbs were properly stored. "And that's the kind of mistake that gets us both killed."

"Yeah." Ober looked worried. "And the rest of the crew too, most likely."

Tomza shot a quizzical glance at him.

"'The crew?'" she asked.

"Yeah, the Bad Badgers," Ober replied as he hefted his handiwork over his shoulder. "Anything else you want to bury?"

Tomza frowned at her brother as she struggled to find words to express the confusion bubbling up inside of her. Aware that sharp words from her or Ober would get the attention of the others, she kept her tone even and disinterested.

"Since when did we become 'the crew?'"

"Well, I guess I called us that for lack of a better term." Ober shrugged. "Being as we aren't a proper division—Stones, not even enough for a forj—I figured it'd be best to call us a crew. Sort of like how when the schildwan organizes everyone into work teams when—"

"I understand the concept," Tomza interjected, heat creeping into her voice. "What I'm asking is when did *we* become part of this crew?"

Ober looked at her with the dumbfounded expression that had driven her to violence when they were children. She knew, perhaps better than any other, that her brother was not stupid—far from it—but sometimes... Sometimes she felt like she was beating her face bloody against his obtuseness.

"When did we throw our lot in with them instead of looking

out for ourselves?" she pressed, the words coming out low and angry. "When did you become a Bad Badger rather than just Ober the dwarf who got a raw deal?"

The young dwarf shuffled his burden around his shoulder, brows furrowed until they were like dusky clouds over his eyes.

"I don't know," he spluttered at last. "It seems like the rest of them caught an ill turn too, so it just makes sense. If anyone's going to understand, it's them, right?"

Tomza made a disgusted sound, but as she stole a glance at the Bad Badgers, she couldn't deny his logic. Gromic, a fordwan of the legendary Sablestone Guard, had come here out of loyalty to his commander. Waelon was here out of faithfulness to his brother, whose death he was still mourning. Torbjorn, who, for all his blistering discipline, had seen something of the truth Ober and Tomza were hiding, once in suspicion and once in evidence, but had chosen to spare them.

Even Haeda, despite her hysterical attack early, had shown care and camaraderie for Tomza after the battle, which she supposed was as close to an apology the salty dwarfess could manage at the moment.

The truth was that though she'd badly wanted to hold herself and her brother separate from them, the reality was that they were dwans like those she'd served with in the Sixth. Deeply flawed, yes, but they were fighters, and they were willing to put their lives on the line for their people, even if those people no longer thought them worthy of such an honor. What could be closer to her and Ober's experience than that?

"All right, I see what you mean," she began, her chest aching as she saw the hope budding in her little brother's eyes. "But the reality is that there's a lot we don't know about them, and even more importantly, there is a lot they don't know about us."

Ober opened his mouth to make an angry reply, but he remembered where they were and thought better of it. His mouth collapsed into a grim line, and as he turned to take the spare gear to the wagon, he growled at a volume only she could hear.

"Maybe, maybe not, but I know I can't keep doing this. Not forever."

CHAPTER TWENTY

"If you forget that we're in enemy territory and don't have a bloody clue where we're going, it's sort of pleasant, isn't it?"

For a time, no one bothered to answer Gromic as they moved along a small forest stream. True, their progress across the stone-punctured basin of Fang's Nest had been leisurely for the past few days, especially compared to the rabid draught run, but as they passed into the shadow of another pale Fang, everyone felt an uneasy chill. Waelon, walking at the head of their loose line, adjusted their path to avoid getting too close to the lithic lance, but all of them shuddered as the stillness endemic to the area thickened. They kept their heads down as they shuffled past, doing their best not to notice that their packs felt heavier and their feet moved slower until they cleared the Fang.

Gromic shuddered at the rear of the line. "All right, I could do without those creepy stones."

"What do you think they are for?" Ober asked as they trudged on. He tried to speak clearly despite the shaving of mona root in his cheek, though he was certain the others knew he regularly chewed the stuff. He was even more certain that none of them cared.

"Some say the grems make offerings at them," Haeda suggested as she slipped around a thorny bush. "Which others imagine the little wretches learned from the savagelings a long time ago. Some sort of heathen superstition about them being connected with old spirits in the Vale or something. Also, that's why there's no settlements in the area."

"Really?" Ober muttered, looking over his shoulder as though the Fang might be following them.

"Whatever the case," Torbjorn added, noting the young dwarf's reaction with curious concern, "the important thing is to remember that it is all heathen nonsense, meant to frighten the ignorant and the gullible."

"Maybe," Ober admitted, then pressed, "But where do you think they come from? They don't look like any stones I've seen in the Vale."

"Where does any stone come from?" Waelon grumbled from the head of the line. "Do you ask where the mountains come from?"

More than anyone else, Waelon seemed to hate the stones, though as usual, the terse dwarf refused to explain why.

"Well, I don't ask about the mountains because I know where they come from," Ober explained as he hopped over a knot of roots that had stretched out ages ago to enjoy the stream. "When the Shaper spun Eduna upon the World-Lathe, she grew hot, but her imperfections showed through so parts of her were soft and molten while others remained hard and cold. In time, the Shaper saw that she was riven to the core with imperfections, so he made to cast her away. She wept, and the Shaper's cold heart, for once warmed by her glow, was moved, and so he drew up those parts of her which were strongest to rise above the others an example to her weaker elements."

"And in those halls, the first mountains, he shaped creatures that would redeem Eduna," Tomza called. "So were the first dwarfs set to work in the first mountains, learning what lessons they could from them before spreading under and over stone to save Eduna."

The veteran dwarfs paused to stare at the pair, their expressions between amusement and confusion.

"Well, would you look at that?" Haeda chuckled. "Torbjorn fetched us a pair of priests."

"Our mother was a Rune-Caller, and our father was of the Engraver's Lodge," Tomza explained, not caring that her shoulders squared and her chest swelled at the honors she mentioned. "Not Priests of the Shaper, but they worked closely with the priest in our village, so we were taught the ancient truths before we could even walk."

As though the explanation broke some spell, the veterans nodded and gave knowing grunts. They resumed their march southward along the winding stream.

"I suppose it seems silly," Ober mused, "but growing up, I thought everyone knew the ancient truths. Maybe it was just our village, but it seemed like all the other children my age grew up hearing and reading the same things. We used to make fun of each other using the old stories, calling each other names like 'Mortung's Toe' or saying someone was 'as thick as Jaelshibburahx's name is long.'" He chuckled.

The young dwarf's laughter died when no one joined him. He looked over his shoulder for help from his sister, but Tomza, who'd thought his and his friends' little quips were stupid, shrugged. Clearing his throat nervously, then coughing out some of the mona root's juice, Ober put his head down and slipped into silence.

They marched mutely, each tending their thoughts. The sounds of the forest, muted compared to what one would expect in such untouched lands, wove around them, a soft rustle here or a murmur there, but frustratingly faint like the memory of a forest that had once dwelt there.

When Gromic at last spoke, though his words came soft and

low, many of them winced at their intensity, so unlike the wan ambiance that had crept over them.

"My ma never taught me the ancient truths," he stated matter-of-factly. "Not sure she could have if she'd wanted to. Old hag couldn't abide talk of anything that didn't lead to coin between her fingers, a bottle between her lips, or flesh between her legs."

Ober started at the frank description, but he saw that aside from Tomza raising an eyebrow, none of the others seemed shocked by his description.

"At least you knew the hag," Waelon called from the front. "Our ma took off while me and Raelon was thinking about growing our first whisker. Left us with our father, who was only hard to be around when he was drinking, which was only when he wasn't working. The day Raelon left to join the Holt'Dwan was the best day of our lives."

Ober, befuddled and feeling as though he shouldn't insult them with pity, scrambled to think of what he could say. For her part, Tomza saw the wheels turning in her brother's head and tried to get his attention to warn him off.

"Well, I suppose hard lives make hard dwans," Ober offered, which Tomza admitted wasn't too bad. "If it weren't for those challenges, you wouldn't be the most ferocious dwans I know."

To the young dwarf's relief, this drew approving nods from Gromic and Waelon, but before he could bask in his success, Haeda gave a wry chuckle.

"Then what's the commander's excuse?" she asked, nodding at the dwarf in front of her. "He's the hardest dwan any of us have ever even heard of, and he was born with the mountain under his heel."

Tomza was amazed.

"Really, sir?" she asked, then realized how she sounded. "Uh, I mean, that is, I uh, I didn't know you were noble-born, sir."

Torbjorn didn't respond, but he didn't have to since Haeda gave a low whistle.

"Not just noble-born, lass," the driver hissed conspiratorially as she tapped one side of her nose. "Commander Torbjorn's a Cyniburg, born and bred."

Ober and Tomza stopped so quickly that the other dwarfs protested.

"Royalty?" the siblings cried, nearly swallowing the word as they said it.

Torbjorn, shaking his head, shuffled around to look at each in turn.

"Not quite," he explained, his intonation that of a dwarf who'd had to repeat this until it had become a litany. "I'm from the clan of Cyniburg, but my grandfather is from an old branch that is never going to inherit unless every other Cyniburg drops dead, including the bastard-born."

"But you grew up on Mount Smarthdun in the Alrur's Palace?" Tomza asked. She continued at the slightest nod from Torbjorn. "Is it true that there is a room for each sacred metal? Do Glava's bones really hang over the grand hall? Is it true that the cellars really have fresh spring flowing through them even in the dead of winter? Is the Tollbur the Scholar's library as big as they—"

"Easy, lass," Torbjorn interrupted, one hand raised in surrender. He shot a look at Haeda, who was trying to hide a snicker. "You roll out all these questions, and I am liable to forget them, then we'll all lose focus."

Tomza bowed her head like a chastened child while rocking on her heels in eagerness. Torbjorn saw Haeda giving the young dwarfess a pitying look, so he heaved a sigh.

"Fine, but this is all I'm answering for now," the commander declared. "Yes, there is a room for all seven sacred metals, and yes, Glava the Jotun's skeleton still hangs over the grand hall, though I wish it didn't. Gave me nightmares as a child."

Gromic snorted, but a sharp look from Haeda quelled him so Torbjorn could conclude.

"As to Tollbur's Library, that I don't know since I was forbidden to visit it. When I was a wee one, I stayed up late reading old tomes, and half-asleep, I knocked over my lantern and subsequently burned up some of my father's books. One of them he had borrowed from Tollbur's collection. To keep the Clan Scribes from skinning me alive, my father swore I would never enter, much to my frustration. I liked to read in those days."

Tomza, who'd wanted to follow in her mother's footsteps as a Rune-Caller, could commiserate. Being so close to such a wealth of dwarvish history and knowledge and forbidden to partake was unconscionable.

"That's enough of story time," Torbjorn announced, then cleared his throat and adjusted his pack. "We need to pick up the pace."

The Bad Badgers muttered in assent and continued walking, their pace only marginally faster. That lasted until they encountered another Fang an hour later. Then their feet quickened to pass it. Each dwarf put their head down and pressed forward. None commented while within sight of the stone, but after such a brief time with naught but the menace of the sinister stone and their own thoughts, it seemed imperative to speak and dispel the specter of the monolith.

"Haeda," Ober called, "You never told us about your family."

Tomza winced in anticipation of a salty, sneering retort, but to her surprise, the driver chuckled and shrugged.

"Nothing much to tell." Haeda sighed. "No monster for a mother, nor living in palaces. I'm from Clan Folgrith in the Iron Stands, west and north of Grayshelf. Father's a wheelwright, Mother's a weaver. Neither is fond of the other, but me and my sisters didn't know that until we were grown, so they must have been doing something right. We always had enough, but there were no plans for an undermanse or a summer den over the Norling Sea."

"I've been to the Norling Sea," Waelon rumbled from the front. "You're not missing much."

"Maybe." Haeda nodded. "But all the same, I'd like to see it someday. Or at least, I would have liked to."

That grim reminder robbed the company of their conversational fervor for some time. They marched in silence until the shadows deepened between the boughs and the sky began to bruise in shades of dusk. When Torbjorn nodded at Waelon, they pressed on until the wee hour, aided by the gibbous moon. The forest, lit in silver and refreshingly cool, was idyllic until its serenity was interrupted by a Fang's puncturing presence.

This was the first time any of them had beheld one in the glow of the moon, and they shuffled together to stare in mute horror.

The pale stone shone, but thin, unsettling traceries of shadow were revealed by the cold light. What had seemed like the pitted weathering of countless years, the moon's glow revealed to be indentations of a sinister and intentional nature. The sigils scrawled across the stone were a mix of some ancient, blasphemous language and carnal pictograms. The combination was painful to look at yet difficult to look away from. Scenes of mass sacrifice and unnatural debaucheries were swaddled in script in a tongue that had been lost to the ages.

"Somehow, I'm not surprised," Gromic whispered. "I didn't know, but I expected it, you know what I mean?"

For a heartbeat, none spoke, but several nodded.

"Like, you didn't know why it was wrong when you looked at it before," Haeda murmured. "But now it all makes sense?"

Gromic swallowed as he nodded. His complexion looked like milk under the moon's glow.

"I studied a lot of different scripts with my mother," Tomza began, her tongue dry in her mouth. "We even had a book in Ælfar, with both savageling and svartalf dialects, but this is like nothing I've ever seen."

"I've seen it."

Their eyes, glinting like deep gems, turned toward Torbjorn, who seemed ignorant that he'd spoken. The company's collective question, no less immediate for not being asked aloud, hung in the air. Torbjorn, dark gaze lingering on the sinuous shapes, felt pressure mounting behind his eyes until they began to water. With a shuddering breath, he tore his eyes away and saw his company was watching him, pleas and demands in their expressions.

"Where'd you see it, sir?" Gromic asked.

Impossibly, the folded parchment in Torbjorn's pocket grew heavier and rougher, threatening to tug and chafe.

"On that chain around the bailiff's neck in Ipplen's Ford."

The air got cooler as the veterans of that encounter shared bitter glances. The siblings, sensing the change in the atmosphere if not understanding it, stood with eyes darting between their commander and the seasoned members of the Bad Badgers. The tension mounted, then Torbjorn blinked and cleared his throat.

It was a defeat even if none, not even their commander, could have explained how.

"We should get moving," Torbjorn growled, looking at Waelon. "Find us a good spot to make camp clear of that...thing."

CHAPTER TWENTY-ONE

"This isn't going well, Tweldwan."

Torbjorn didn't bother to correct Gromic's use of the title that had been stripped from him years ago. Gromic had learned not to use it around the others, but when it was just the two of them, the stout dwarf allowed himself the comfort of old trappings.

The former tweldwan and his former fordwan watched the supple light of predawn slide gently across the heavens. It was Gromic's watch, but Torbjorn, who hadn't been able to sleep, had risen to join him for a smoke when he'd heard the scrape of flint on steel. They stood in the chill morning air, pipes between their teeth, thin trails of smoke slithering upward.

"What do you mean?" the commander asked after turning a cottony puff loose.

Gromic fortified himself with a long, slow inhalation, careful to avoid the pipe bite, before letting out a long stream of smoke.

"You've never kept things from us before," the wide dwarf rumbled as he adjusted his stance, one arm resting on his round shield. "That's why we've always trusted you, even when things seemed mad and hopeless. A common dwan marches in the direction he's told, and nobody bothers to tell him why. You always knew we weren't common dwans."

Torbjorn's eyes reflected the cherry glow of his pipe as he drew his own long breath.

"What changed?" Gromic continued as he shuffled the pipe stem to the corner of his mouth. "What've we done to lose your trust? Or is this just about the new pair? Because in my estimation, that's starting them off on the wrong foot if you follow me."

Torbjorn made an abortive attempt to form a smoke ring before surrendering to a rough cough. Gromic was polite enough to keep his gaze roving outward while his commander composed himself.

"No," Torbjorn growled after a gulped breath. "It's not about you leathery buggers or the fresh meat. The truth is, at the start, it was about everyone else."

Gromic's curious blue eyes roved to his commander.

"Spies?" he snarled around the stem of his pipe. "Wheezer-friends?"

"Possibly," Torbjorn replied after another barked cough. "Though just as much other members of the Holt'Dwan. What we're doing might or might not be in accordance with the ondwan's wishes."

Gromic's lips pressed into a grim line as he nodded. With a critical eye, he assessed the bowl of his pipe and decided to nurse it a little longer with short, sharp inhalations. There was the faint crackle within the bowl, and he got in one last good draw before taking the pipe from his mouth.

"What *are* we doing, Tweldwan?" the stout dwarf asked as he tapped the upturned pipe on the rim of his shield. "What lies beyond Turoth's Tooth that the ondwan doesn't want us meddling with?"

Torbjorn watched the ashen leavings of Gromic's pipe spill on the ground, a single hot coal glowing as it tumbled onto the dew-dampened turf. It went out and disappeared amongst the wet blades of grass.

"You remember how this all started?" Torbjorn asked, taking his pipe in hand to wave before him.

"Should I wake the new lad up?" Gromic frowned, heavy brows knotting. "This sounds like one of those ancient truths questions."

Torbjorn smiled and settled a hand on Gromic's shoulder as he replaced his pipe. It was good to have a troop who was honest about his ignorance but not proud of it. Too often, it was one or the other.

"No, it's not that sort of question, Fordwan," the commander clarified with an affectionate squeeze. "I'm talking about the Wight Wars. Do you remember how those started?"

Gromic nodded as he reflexively disassembled and stored his pipe. "Well enough, despite being bottled up in Grayshelf." He sighed. "Word came back that the south was in chaos, the Vale full of armies of corpses as dwarvish homesteads were burned down."

Torbjorn nodded, remembering Klaus showing him the intelligence reports. Not just war bands but entire armies, professionally organized and coordinated, had sprung up literally overnight. Lands that had been pacified for years with only token garrisons had been swept away by columns of the marching dead. Even with refugees pouring in and word from a dwan in the south Vale, it had been difficult to comprehend the speed of the calamity.

Klaus, freshly made lardwan, had seen the opportunity, and only a few days later, he had broached the subject of reviving an old custom. Torbjorn's friend had always been like that. Was still like that.

Why else would they be here?

"Do you remember where they came from?" Torbjorn asked,

eyes not seeing the waking world as he walked through memories. "Where those armies of corpses had been hiding?"

Gromic shivered, which was all the confirmation Torbjorn needed.

"Beneath our very feet," the commander muttered. "We who were born in the heart of the mountains hadn't looked into the darkness beneath our boots as we marched across the valley. Even when the savagelings beat their chests over desecration and prophecies, we only saw the tumbled ruins jutting from the dirt as sources of stone for our fortresses."

The stout dwarf gaped at Torbjorn, then turned his eyes toward the south. Torbjorn knew that he had put things together, but he needed to let it run its course. After having it trapped within for days, it was now flowing out.

"Don't ask me how, but Klaus, the clever bastard, found one of their tombs in the cliffs over Turoth's Tomb. It was unopened, meaning that the wight within and his army haven't awoken. We're going to go take a look around, collect as much information as we can, and then hack Sleeping Beauty to pieces. That will ensure that the wight and its army never trouble the world."

Gromic looked away, fingers raking his beard.

"So, that's what Ipplen's Ford was for." He sighed. "An experiment in killing wights."

"We needed to know they could be taken down by anything less than artillery laced with baelgeld." Torbjorn nodded, then frowned at his pipe bowl, which had grown cold. "Raelon and Muri died to answer that question."

"Then why is the Sufstan moving back to Grayshelf?" the stout dwarf demanded. "We proved you can kill wheezers without baelgeld, and we're about to make sure no army pops on the eastern slope of the Vale. They should make the push before winter sets in."

"Ondwan Glastuc has served through two campaigns, and this third doesn't look to be going anywhere fast." The commander shrugged. "The old dwarf's looking to step down with what's left of his honor intact. Leave the business of the Ysgand Vale to a younger, hungrier commander who is willing to take risks, knowing he'll have the years to savor or recover from them, depending on how they turn out. Glastuc wants to go back to his clan and spend his days drinking with the old dwans and his evenings telling stories to wide-eyed great-grandchildren. I can't say that I blame him."

"That makes one of us." Gromic grunted. "Putting off retirement and restructuring a campaign to seize an advantage we haven't had in near to a decade…"

The stout dwarf's voice trailed off into a string of half-articulated curses.

"I've reason enough to hate Glastuc." Torbjorn sighed as he emptied his pipe bowl. "But I think, in this case, he's learned something we shabr'dwan learn not long after we sign up."

"What's that?" Gromic smirked sourly at the thought of signing up for the Bad Badgers.

"There's always another battle," Torbjorn stated, his eyes shuttered as he unscrewed the stem of his pipe. "Always another battle, another advantage to be seized, another position to be defended. Always one more."

Gromic frowned as he noted the strands of rosy dawn seeping into the sky.

"You make it sound like there's no end. What if we crush every wight to dust and retake the Vale?"

"No," the commander countered, opening his eyes. "It's never going to end. Not really. You heard the lad. The Shaper made us to fix the world, but the Holt'Dwan's purpose is to destroy, to kill, to ruin. True, we build, but just so we can win the next battle and launch the next attack. The workmen have taken their hammers to beat the farmers' plows into swords so they can buy another field and another workshop with blood."

Gromic swallowed heavily. It pained Torbjorn more than

words could express to see what glistened in the faithful dwan's eyes. He desperately wished he could have stilled the flow of words, but out they came, as cold and merciless as they were true.

"So, that's all a dwan is, Tweldwan?" Gromic murmured, his deep voice pained. "A spoke in the broken machine to fix the world?"

Torbjorn's shoulders sagged as he took a step away from his most loyal friend.

"Maybe, but maybe it wasn't always that way. I don't know. All I know is that to keep from being crushed by that machine, we have a job to do. It isn't glorious, and it might not be worth the bloody effort, but it's something to do on this Shaper-forsaken mudball."

"If you say so, sir," Gromic swallowed, a soft clicking sound coming from the back of his throat. "Should I rouse the camp?"

Torbjorn nodded, and the stout dwarf bent to pick up his shield.

"Might as well," the commander muttered. "Time to get this over with."

"So, we've just got to kill a wight? In his tomb? Surrounded by his army? Without a bloody, burning tavern to drop on top of him?"

Haeda's sarcasm wasn't unexpected. Torbjorn's revelation to the rest of the Bad Badgers was going as well as he'd expected.

"We don't know that the fire was what did it," Torbjorn stated, already knowing the response coming his way.

"Well, it didn't seem to like being on fire," Waelon growled, eyes flashing as though the memory had kindled the blaze's light. "But either way, that was a lower-order wight, a magistrate set over a pisspot using human conscripts to keep order. What are the odds this wheezer, a full lord with an army, is going to be as easy to destroy?"

"We don't know," Torbjorn admitted. "The one thing in our favor is that it seems to be dormant along with its army, which is why we have a slight chance to succeed."

The dwarfs sat in silence, considering what lay ahead. Their breakfast of fire-seared bacon and hardtack remained untouched.

"What if us trying to kill it wakes it up?" Tomza asked. "If we fail, it's not just a failure, but it also means another wight at the head of an army."

"Yes, that's possible," Torbjorn replied, rocking back on his heels. "Which is why Lardwan Klaus only sent us after he knew the Holt'Dwan was withdrawing to Grayshelf. Even if another army of the dead is raised by our failure, the distance will mean no force of any size will be able to move through the Vale quickly enough to catch the Holt'Dwan in camp. It's also late enough in the year that if they tried to make a serious press with multiple armies, they'd have a hard time doing it before winter sets in and everything slows to a crawl."

"Those goblins and woodsmen were going to a muster," Ober piped up, eyes wide with alarm. "Doesn't that suggest the wights are already planning to make a push? Maybe they've already woken our wight up, and that's why they're mustering?"

The veterans frowned, but none of them said the young dwarf was wrong.

"If a wight lord had risen near here, this place would be filled with clackers," Torbjorn countered with a shake of his head. "We'd have a lot more to worry about than scary writing on some rocks."

The veterans nodded slowly, surrendering to his opinion.

"Then what is the muster for?" Tomza asked.

"Like I said," Torbjorn replied with a gruff snort, his temper starting to show. "They're probably looking to press their luck at

Lake Blacmere, and if not, they might just be reinforcing wight positions across the boundaries across from the pickets in case the Sufstan tried to capitalize on the chaos at Ipplen's Ford. It doesn't matter since our mission is to the south and not the west."

The assembled dwarfs once more lapsed into a silence that was only broken by the scuffs of Gromic's boots as he kicked dirt on the campfire's embers. It didn't look like anyone would be looking for a second helping of bacon.

"Any other questions?" Torbjorn growled before tearing off a piece of bacon.

There seemed to be none, but then Haeda raised her gaze from her bowl. The swelling and bruises had finally healed and she'd had time to wash by the stream, so for the first time in many days, she looked like herself. Passably attractive by most races' standards and a striking beauty amongst her kind, she turned large emerald eyes on her commander that fixed him in place more surely than any enemy spear.

"Why'd you keep this from us, sir?"

The bacon turned to shoe leather in Torbjorn's mouth, but he forced it down with a heavy swallow of lukewarm stainleaf.

"Did you think we wouldn't follow you this far?"

The commander swore and spat, but the bitter taste clung to his mouth. First Gromic and now Haeda, thinking the fault was theirs. Taking the guilt of his obfuscation on their heads.

"No," he replied gruffly, forcing himself to hold the driver's stare. "I didn't doubt any of you for a second."

"Was it us?" Ober asked, remorse stamped on his open features.

"I said any of you, lad, and that includes you and your sister," Torbjorn rasped, feeling as though his breakfast was clinging to the back of his throat. "I knew from the moment we locked eyes that you were no coward and you were going to prove it. Your sister, Shaper save her, was determined to stick with you, so I never doubted either of you would come this far."

"Then why not tell us where we were going and why?" Tomza pressed with a quick glance at Haeda.

Torbjorn looked at the remains of his breakfast and fought the urge to throw it into the stream, along with his mug.

"At first, it was to make sure no word could reach the Holt'D-wan, for our sake and for Lardwan Klaus' sake," he began, a wry chuckle sliding free. "As you've already pointed out, it's a bit of a risk, possibly waking up another wight army, but I agreed with my old friend that it was worth it. Even if we fail, they can assume the wight and his army are awake, and it is better knowing that than having a hidden army that could spring up at any time."

There were a few nods, then more expectant looks that deepened the pit Torbjorn felt he was treading over.

"After that, well, it was easier not having to admit to you all that we were being sent to die again for no reason," Torbjorn croaked, fighting to control his voice. "A commander looks after his dwans; that's how it's supposed to be. He leads them into battle, leads them into death, but he makes sure it matters and every death counts for something. I suppose with each step we've taken southward, I've wondered if it's worth it and if that means I've betrayed you all by pretending it does."

Torbjorn wanted to say more, but the lump in his throat and what little composure he had left stopped him from continuing. He just sat, sullen and defeated, dark eyes boring into the remains of the campfire. As he stared into the spent and dirt-choked cinders, he let the shades of black and gray leach the color from his vision until everything seemed to be composed of black shapes and gray fog—a bleak vision to match his internal reality.

When a voice finally rose to breach the umbral shades, it was not Haeda's throaty timbre or Gromic's jovial basso, not even the youthful voices of Ober or Tomza.

"My brother's death meant something," Waelon declared with a voice like stones grinding together. "My brother's death meant Mori was avenged and the rest of us could see another day."

Torbjorn looked up, color seeping back into the world as he locked eyes with the fiery-haired dwarf.

"We wouldn't have been there if I hadn't led you there," Torbjorn hissed through clenched teeth. "Don't you see what I'm trying to say? I lead you on these missions with the assumption that they matter to the Holt'Dwan and the dwarvish people."

"That's never been why I went on these missions," Waelon replied with a shake of his head. "I only ever set off because of two things. First, my fool of a brother was going, and second, because a dwarf I loved like my brother and respected a hell of a lot more was going. That's why I went."

Torbjorn shook his head but couldn't find any words. It was all he could do to keep his eyes on the shabr'dwans.

"Fact is, Commander, none of us went on a single mission for the good of dwarfkind," Haeda explained. "We followed you because you were giving us a chance to do something besides be forgotten in some hole. That would have been enough, but you cared for us better than any leader we ever had, which only made us love you more. Really, what else could we do?"

Torbjorn looked at his Bad Badgers, wishing he could make them see he wasn't worthy of that loyalty or trust. However, it seemed "worthy" wasn't his to define.

"Comes down to this, sir," Gromic rumbled, with a nod to every dwarf present, even the new meat, who watched with shining eyes. "You have to be here, and we want to be where you are, so we're here. That's not going to change."

Torbjorn shook his head, coughed twice, and ran his thumb across the burn scar on his cheek as he drew a scrap of parchment from his coat.

"All right, then. I suppose we better get things moving, eh?"

CHAPTER TWENTY-TWO

"I'm glad we reached it early. I'd hate to see that thing in the moonlight."

None voiced their agreement, but it was still understood as the dwarfs emerged from the close-hemmed tree line that encircled Turoth's Tooth.

The only named Fang was distinguished not just by its size but also because it had pride of place. The stone, named after a monstrous wyrm of legend, was suitably dubbed for size alone. It was many times the size of any of the other Fangs, and the earthworks at the base of the megalith were properly serpentine.

Spirals and whorls carved deep to resist the shift and settle of centuries wound about the open ground. The furthest reaches of this flowing pattern reached within a few feet of the tree trunks that crowded close. The wizened trees formed a wall to keep Turoth's Tooth pinned against the gray cliffs of the Wyrmspines. Despite their vigil, none dared stretch a root to the riven ground marked by their ward, perhaps fearing its corruption might infect them.

If the other Fangs had spread a blanket over themselves, walking near the Tooth was like laboring under an oppressive sky. Its enormity gave off its own dark power, whispering in their minds with suggestions that if they didn't flee, they would never escape.

In answer, each shabr'dwan looked at Torbjorn, who in turn looked at the map.

"This way," he commanded, folding the parchment in half but keeping it at hand.

Heads bowed as they trudged onward, each was certain the polluted earth would turn against them at any second. At different points, they leapt across thin fissures or channels that had been carved into the earth, and at other points, they encountered trenches and were forced to scurry down one side and scramble up the other. A trench that lay beneath the shadow of the cliffs had sides steep enough to make the ascent challenging. When Gromic, the doughty anchor of their marching order, lost his footing and slid halfway back down, everyone expected to see him be gobbled up by the trench.

However, the Tooth seemed uninterested in the morsel, and with curses hissed between puffing breaths, Gromic reached Waelon's and Torbjorn's outstretched hands.

"Must've looked too big to chew," he gasped as he stood panting, seeing the gray slashes his sliding boots had rent in the earth. "Told you being this big comes in handy."

Waelon nodded and turned back to the cliff face as Torbjorn patted the stout dwarf's broad back.

"Maybe," Torbjorn muttered as he opened the map again. "But I don't think it will do you much good if you lose your grip on the next bit."

"I imagine" Gromic eyed the cliff warily.

"You Vale-born darlings do much mountaineering?" Waelon called as he fished out pitons and a hammer from his pack.

Ober and Tomza peered at the stone wall that reared overhead.

"I'll take that as a no." Waelon groaned as he looked at the company and evaluated everyone behind his glowering eyes.

"We shouldn't need all that," Torbjorn murmured distractedly as he alternated between studying the parchment and squinting at the cliff. "There is supposed to be a stair winding up to a cleft in the rock."

Waelon put down his climbing gear with a snort and frowned at the soaring stone buttress.

"I don't see it."

Haeda came to stand next to Torbjorn, who willingly proffered the map. She scoffed after glancing at it. "That's because you like doing things the hard way," the driver grumbled as her eyes darted between parchment and stone. "It's against your nature to find a solution that doesn't have you hitting something."

Waelon's brows knitted as he ran his fingers over the pitons and the hammer soothingly.

"It's not my fault most problems are more manageable with some steel driven through them."

"It's like he can't stand me being right." Haeda chuckled and winked at Tomza, who'd come over. "He's got to prove me very right."

The younger dwarfess was glancing at the map when Haeda gave a quick crow of victory, one hand stabbing at the parchment while the other gestured at the cliff face a few dozen paces from where they stood. There, on parchment and in stone, a bulge that looked like a knot in a tree served as the marker for the hidden stair.

Scuttling over, mindful of the trench yawning behind them, the dwarfs examined the staircase. It was so cunningly wrought that even the stone-canny eyes of dwarfs would not have seen it without standing directly in front of it.

"Dwarfs must've had a hand in this," Gromic muttered as they moved to the first stair. "I mean, look at that masonry. Turn your head to one side, and it disappears."

The other dwarfs nodded, but Tomza, who'd been the quickest to reach the stairs, called in a dour voice, "Well, they might have been made *by* dwarfs, but they weren't made *for* dwarfs."

To illustrate, she scrambled to mount the first step and was forced to give a little hop to get her shoulders over the lip. With a wriggle and a scrape of boots on stone, she managed to draw herself over, but it was far from a simple effort.

"Whoever used these as steps must've been as tall as an elf," she told her compatriots as she knelt on the first step. "Maybe taller."

As though summoned by the very word, a melodious howl cut through the air like a bodkin in flight.

"Savagelings!" Waelon snarled, yanking his duabuw off his shoulder.

"This far south?" Haeda asked, her dark brows knotting in confusion. "We haven't heard of a hunting pack below the Blacmere in years. The heathen buggers avoid the wheezers like a pestilence."

"Tell them that," Tomza called as she stood up and pointed at the edge of the trees. Following the young dwarfess' finger, they watched a score of tall, pale figures bound into sight. Even from this distance, the dwarfs could see the war paint daubed on their lean, muscular forms and the shine of bronze blades in their hands. Their feet hardly seemed to touch the ground as they sprang over the stitched earth beneath Turoth's Tooth, their destination as clear as their baying voices.

"Running bare-chested across open ground." Waelon chuckled darkly as he twisted his sighting peg to adjust for the arced trajectory. "I'd wager we can whittle them down to a quarter strength before they close, and if they don't break and run, we can finish the brave fools properly."

All eyes turned to Torbjorn, but a fresh howl rose across the entire tree line. Every dwarf, even Waelon, watched with slack faces as five score pale-skinned elves sprang from the woods. Not even the baying of an army of wolves on a moonless night would have frozen the blood like their combined battle song.

"That's not a bloody hunting pack." Gromic moaned, his gauntlet clanking against his helmeted brow. "It's an entire gods-damned war band."

The elven war cries rose in pitch and intensity, no less beautiful for how terrifying they were.

"Time to climb," Torbjorn bellowed, shoving Haeda and Ober toward the steps. "Let's go. Move your arses! Damn it all, I said, *MOVE!*"

The commands, delivered in the commander's best battlefield shout, broke the spell of horror laid over the dwarfs. Haeda was the first to reach Tomza's outstretched hand, and Ober was quick to provide a strong young knee to brace her. No sooner had the driver ascended than she and the younger dwarfess reached out to haul Ober over the lip, writhing and lurching.

Torbjorn turned back to see Waelon and Gromic rest their duabuws on the rims of the shields they'd planted in the ground. With as much hurry as one would expect from a pair of venerable dwans having a friendly shooting competition, the pair adjusted their sighting pegs and took aim.

"Enough of that," Torbjorn shouted over the thunder of the charging elves. "It's time to climb, lads."

There was a *whir-crack* as the first volley arced over the open ground. The savageling war band was shy two warriors a heartbeat later.

"Go on, sir," Gromic encouraged as he worked the lever of the crossbow. "We'll just be a minute. Waelon's got something he'd like to say to the savagelings."

"Several things," Waelon growled as the third pump clicked

home and he took aim. "I imagine this conversation might take us a bit. Don't bother waiting up."

Neither dwarf looked at him, but Torbjorn could see their grim resolution in their shoulders and hear it in their voices. He didn't bawl another order he knew they'd have another smarmy answer to. Instead, Torbjorn marched over and seized Waelon by the arm, spoiling his next shot, then spun him. The hardened dwarvish ranger managed to snarl half a curse before Torbjorn smashed his fist into the fiery-haired dwarf's mouth hard enough to rattle his teeth in his skull.

"You piss in my ear about following me out of love and respect, then pull this?" he growled. "You're following me, eh?"

Waelon blinked rapidly to clear the tears and stars from his eyes.

"Well, then you better listen when I give an order! Now, *move your arse!*"

To punctuate, he spun the dwarven ranger and gave him a sharp kick in the backside to send him toward the step.

"Take this with you!" Torbjorn hollered, wrenching Waelon's shield from the earth and tossing it after him. "A bloody deordwan should know better!"

Waelon shook his head to get rid of the lingering effects of Torbjorn's blow, then scooped up his shield and took the last shaky steps to Ober's outstretched hand.

Torbjorn turned toward Gromic and was thankful to see he had shouldered his crossbow and was tugging his shield from the dirt.

"On my way, sir," the veteran called. A grin broke out under his helmet. "On my way."

Torbjorn nodded and scooped up his own shield from where he'd left it, and they raced to the step.

"Get up there, dwans," Torbjorn shouted, slapping Gromic on the shoulder. "Get up and then haul me up."

"But sir…" Gromic swallowed, seeming ready to collapse as he stared up. "What if I fall?"

The elves hadn't slackened their pace, long and powerful limbs allowing them to leap cleanly over any earthen impediment beneath Turoth's Tooth. They'd probably covered half the distance while Tomza and Haeda had only just cleared the third step, hardly ten feet above where he stood.

"Then you kill us both!" Torbjorn shouted with a wild laugh, pressing his face against Gromic's. "Don't fall!"

CHAPTER TWENTY-THREE

"Come and get it, you blade-eared buggers!"

To reinforce his challenge, Gromic beat his magsax on the boss of his shield, raising a ringing din. In answer, the savagelings hurled javelins with barbed heads. One long-shafted dart shivered into the broad dwarf's helmet, but it troubled him as little as the others had when they tumbled from his shield. The seething war band fifty or sixty feet below snarled and gnashed their jagged teeth as they danced away from the spinning detritus.

Two steps lower than Gromic, the trio of javelin hurlers swept out leaf-bladed swords of bronze. Flashing amber eyes glared murder as muscles bunched beneath their milky skin.

"Is that all you got?" the stout dwarf bellowed at them. "No wonder you prancing periwinkle-painted pansies hide in trees and under shrubs. No stomach and no danglers for a real fight! Not a bloody one!"

The first of the savagelings, a warrior with pale hair and a body speckled in azure warpaint, sprang to the intervening step, blade outstretched. Cornsilk hair fluttering, the warrior made to cut Gromic's legs out from under him. Bronze sparked against iron as the dwarf's shield was interposed, sending the stroke into the stone.

Gromic leaned forward and delivered an overhand chop. The elf saw the stroke coming and raised a hand with a scream, only to see his hand tumbling down the steps before the magsax bit into his skull. The dwan yanked his blade out of the savageling's skull as his knees buckled. The dying warrior crumpled and rolled off the step.

The next two savagelings tried to be clever, the smaller making for the step while the taller vaulted catlike into the air, sailing over the intervening stone shelf to pounce the doughty dwarf.

"Incoming!" Gromic barked as he raised his shield overhead.

The tall elf's not inconsiderable weight came down on Gromic's upraised arm, but the dwarf heaved up and out and changed the pitch of the shield. The leaping elf spun screaming into the open air before plummeting, and Gromic twisted his hips to take a sword stroke on one armored leg. Swung with both hands and as much hateful fury as the elf could muster, Gromic took the blow with a grunt before stabbing down.

The elf's scream was interrupted by a foot of dwarvish steel punching through his throat and out the back of his neck. Gromic didn't even have to pull his blade free since the savageling slid limply back down the blade to flop bonelessly onto the stone step.

"We ready to move, sir?" Gromic called over his shoulder, hunkering behind his shield as another flurry of javelins were thrown by savagelings a few steps lower than their slain compatriots.

Torbjorn, sheltering behind the stout dwarf's armored vastness, used his teeth to tighten the bandage he'd fashioned around his hand. A sharp flint javelin and bad luck had seen him needing to tend to the wound before he slicked the stone steps with his blood until neither he nor Gromic could get a sure grip as they climbed. That and the bloody thing had hurt, a shard of flint having broken off to scrape and saw between the bones until he'd fished it out.

"Ready when you are," he snarled through the bloodied linen as he tried to snug it a little more.

"Well, not that I don't envy the scowl Waelon'll give me." Gromic chuckled as he swept his magsax down to knock a pair of clinging javelins off his shield. "But I'm thinking we're pressing our luck."

"Right you are," Torbjorn growled, bracing himself as he went to clamber up the next step. The pain in his hand convinced him there was still a piece of flint in there, but his grip held strong. Kicking and scrabbling, he managed to heave himself to the next step. Not pausing for a breath, he spun and held out his undamaged hand to Gromic.

"Come on, dwan!"

"I know, I know," the wide dwarf rumbled as he took his hand. "Move my arse!"

Torbjorn hauled, every muscle in his body taut and burning. He saw the danger too late. Springing like mountain goats up the steps, a pair of warriors, spears in hand, closed on them. Torbjorn wanted to scream a warning to Gromic, though it would do him little good as he dangled between steps. Every ounce of breath and energy went toward pulling him up.

The savagelings, seeing their opportunity, quickened their advance while their fellows shrieked encouragement. There was no time or chance to save Gromic from the spears speeding toward him.

"BAD BADGERS!"

A burning comet of a dwarf plunged from several steps above, smashing into the lead elf as he gained the step below Gromic. Dwarf and elf tangled, rolling and teetering at the edge before spinning back onto the step. Taken unaware but viper-quick, the savageling tried to force the haft of his spear under Waelon's snarling face as he kicked, hoping to hurl the dwarf up and over for a fatal plummet. In answer, the former ranger hacked with his axe, its bright smile parting the spear shaft before burying itself in the elf's breastbone. The savageling's back arched in pain, but Waelon put an end to that as he tore the axe free and sank a second blow into the side of the elf's head.

The second warrior was less quick to recover from the sudden appearance of the fiery dwarf, but the death of his comrade galvanized him. With a shriek, he thrust. Waelon twisted away on raw instinct, and the impaling point of the spear scraped across his mailed back. He wrapped a brawny arm around the spear haft and clamped down with a hard hand. The elf had one second to see Waelon's ferocious blood-tinged grin before the dwarf's powerful shoulders bunched and he was pitched off the stair by his own spear.

"Quit showing off and get up here," Gromic shouted, holding out a hand.

Waelon hurled the pilfered spear at the elves several steps below, not pausing to see if he'd claimed a third kill as he leapt and clambered to reach where Gromic knelt.

"Just couldn't leave me to it," Gromic growled as he hauled the big dwarf up beside him. "Not Waelon Elfhewer."

Waelon wore a broad grin as he cast an appraising eye over his shoulder.

"Couldn't let you have all the fun."

"If you two lovelies are done tickling each other," Torbjorn called from the next step up, "we've still got a mission to accomplish."

Gromic and Waelon saw a final stair butting up against a bulge in the stone. As they watched, Haeda and Tomza climbed the last step, then Haeda, with a wave of her hand, vanished into the cliff wall.

"Enough gawking," Torbjorn growled, unslinging his duabuw. "Get moving."

Despite the awkwardness of wielding the crossbow with his wounded hand, he managed to get a bolt primed and launch it down the stairs. It struck stone instead of flesh, but the savagelings who were creeping forward lurched back, their ascent arrested.

"Come on, sir," Gromic called, drawing Torbjorn's attention from wrangling his weapon. An armored mitt extended from the next step. Waelon was scrambling up to the step after that.

Torbjorn left off working the duabuw's lever and moved to seize the offered hand. Thus began a desperate coordinated effort to ascend before they died. Waelon, who was in the lead, would climb the next step before helping haul Gromic upward. The bulky dwarf was aided by Torbjorn's good hand pressing upward. Once the stout dwarf was secure on the step, he pulled Torbjorn up as Waelon ascended the next step.

Below, the savagelings were mustering their courage for another fierce press, but using their leap-frogging method, the dwarfs shrank the distance to the shelf where Ober stood, calling the trio onward as he knelt and sighted down his duabuw.

Believing their quarry would escape them filled the elves with a wild fury that tore from the throats of the war band. Their fellows' cries like spurs to a mount's flank, the savagelings upon the stairs rushed upward, some managing to clear two steps at a bound. A pair of front runners closed as Waelon climbed up next to Ober.

A *whirr-crack* sounded as Waelon bent to seize Gromic's reaching hand.

The first of the elves took Ober's bolt in his chest, lurching to one side as his legs buckled and blood flowed across his pointed chin. The second elf, arm raised to hurl a heavy spear, was knocked off-kilter by her collapsing companion. It was all she could do to keep from going for a fatal tumble.

"Get inside, lad," Gromic growled as he surged onto the ledge. "Not enough room, even with your girlish figure."

Before Ober could protest, Waelon hurled him toward the narrow seam in the cliff face. The former ranger spun to see a spear arcing just before it tore across his throat. He slapped a hand to the gushing wound as the other drew his blood-spattered axe, eyes locked on the leering elf who swept a sword from her hip.

Shrieking like an eagle plunging for the kill, the savageling lunged for Torbjorn's back, but Waelon's axe thrummed through the air and silenced the elf's war cry with a wet crunch.

Waelon tottered on the edge of the shelf, lifeblood welling between his fingers as he watched the dead elf spinning down the cliff face. He knew he was dead; he felt the cold creeping through his body as the world lost focus, but if he had been killed by a blade-ear, at least he returned the favor. He could almost see Raelon raising a cup in salute to the spiteful humor in it.

"As funny as any of his jokes," Waelon wheezed through the blood frothing on his lips. "And a dwan's death…"

He realized he didn't have the strength to keep his hand on his throat or his feet under him. His eyes rolled up as he pitched over the edge of the stone shelf.

CHAPTER TWENTY-FOUR

"*TOMZA!*"

Torbjorn's bellow was deafening in the confines of the stone passage.

"*Yes, sir?*" Tomza shouted, her voice faint in her ringing ears. She and Haeda had slid down the narrow corridor to give the others room to clamber in from the shelf, but she shuffled toward the figure silhouetted in the pale light from outside.

"Commander?" she asked as the figure resolved into her brother. "Ober, get out of my way!"

The young dwarf didn't argue as they struggled to let each other pass. In the intervening seconds, there was another demanding blast.

"*TOMZA!*" Torbjorn howled, wrath sharpening his tone. "*DAMN YOU! TOMZA!*"

The dwarfess slid free of her brother and staggered into as close to a run as she could manage in the tight confines. Up ahead, she could see a lumpy figure squatting at the mouth of the passage. Another few steps and she realized it was Torbjorn. He was kneeling over another dwarf laid across the floor.

"I'm here, sir," she wheezed as she skidded to a stop. She peered at the stricken dwarf. "I'm he... Stones preserve us!"

Waelon lay before her, his weathered face pale enough to be translucent except where blood had smeared across his lips and throat. She could see that blood had flowed freely down the dwarf's chest, but the flow was slackening. Torbjorn was trying to drag the burly dwarf into the passage with his good hand. His bandaged mitt was clamped over the torn throat.

"Stones aren't going to save him," Torbjorn growled, stealing a glance at her as he left off trying to drag Waelon in. "You are. Now, get to it."

Tomza froze. There was too much blood. She was choking on the smell, and the only thought she could manage was, *Too late*. Even if she'd been trained as a battle barber, there would be little she could do to save Waelon, so much blood had been lost. Even if she were practiced in the art of needlecraft and had every resource at her disposal, Waelon had lost so much blood that he would linger only a little longer before his body finally surrendered. As it was, there was nothing she could do.

Nothing, except without conscious thought, her hand strayed to the flint knife tucked into her belt.

"Now, lass!" Torbjorn cried, his voice strong despite the note of pleading. "Do something or tell me what to do, but don't just stand there."

Tomza looked at Waelon's slack face, then to her kneeling commander. Doubts and fears screamed from every corner of her mind, but Torbjorn looked up at her, his dark eyes asking in a way his voice could not. The look silenced every protest, and her mind was shut up.

"Just remember you asked me to do something," she growled as she dove onto her knees across from Torbjorn, flint blade in hand. "Remember that."

"What?" Torbjorn snarled, his eyes taking in the blade with confusion.

"Move your hand," Tomza instructed, the other hand groping within her pack and emerging with sharp-smelling herbs crushed in her fist. "Now."

Torbjorn blinked and obeyed, dragging his blood-sodden hand away from the wound while trailing a mix of his and Waelon's blood across the stone. Tomza, her movements sure and swift, pressed the crushed herbs into the wound, then swept the flint across her clenched knuckles. When the mashed plants were stained by both Waelon and Tomza's blood, she intoned the syllables. Despite never having tried this working, each rippling sound came out as she'd always known it would.

"Shaper's Hand." Torbjorn gulped, his eyes bulging. "What is this?"

The young dwarfess bent to the wound. The smell of burned honey rose in curling wisps. Tomza felt power flow through her body and into Waelon. The hurt was deep, the situation dire, but the energies she felt welling up within her... She'd never truly understood the concept of infinity until she'd pressed herself into this working

"Torbjorn," Gromic called from the shelf as his shield deflected a score of javelins. "About to get crowded out here, sir."

Tomza, her gray eyes shining with a pale light in the shadows of the passage, met Torbjorn's horrified gaze.

"Only a little longer," she hissed, although her mouth didn't move. "Just a little more time."

Her voice seemed to come from everywhere, even inside Torbjorn's skull. Smothering a shudder, Torbjorn nodded.

"H-hold them, Gromic," the commander stammered. "For Waelon and all our lives, you hold them back."

"Yes, sir," Gromic growled, then his voice boomed out like a deep-throated bell. "Come on then, you naughty little bastards. Uncle Gromy's goin' to give you a paddlin' before I pitch your red arses back to your mums downstairs. Don't be shy! Come on, now! *WHO'S FIRST?*"

The screams of the elves rose outside the mouth of the passage, but within, Torbjorn could only watch in silence. The air seemed to crawl around Tomza's outstretched arm, and the light in the dwarfess' eyes illuminated her features, picking out the lines of wonder and strain that deepened with the smell of scalding sugar.

There was a heart-rending shriek from the shelf, and it descended rapidly into the baying of the savagelings. Gromic launched more challenges as he threw more elves down the stairs or into the open air.

Tomza felt the working come to its culmination, the power beginning to retract from her. In its wake, she felt hollow and weary in a way that she'd never felt before. Something heavier than exhaustion or despair sank into her bones. She saw color returning to Waelon's face, then his eyes fluttering open, but she felt cold and worn. She knew she should be thrilled and elated, not just for completing the work but for saving the life of a good dwan, yet it was like trying to coax a fire out of long-cold ashes.

The only thing that might warm her heart and spirit was to touch that power again and feel it flowing through her, but the thought filled her with icy dread. Her breathing was heavy, but her skin was cold. Tomza slid back onto her haunches as she looked at Torbjorn.

The commander stared at her and then at Waelon, who was looking up from the stone floor as though he had just woken from a nap.

"Some fool burning honey cakes?" the red-haired dwarf rumbled as he sniffed the air. "Waste o' sweets."

Torbjorn's gaze swung to the young dwarfess, wonder and disgust warring on his features. Tomza might have been hurt if she could have felt anything, but she only nodded as she climbed to her feet. The hand that had been filled with herbs trailed a fine curtain of ash as she raised it for leverage against the wall.

"We should move deeper," she stated and took her own advice with leaden feet.

Torbjorn stared after her, his stomach knotting as it tried to follow his heart into his throat.

"Torbjorn?" Waelon scowled at him before popping up on his elbows as he looked around. "Why am I laying down?"

Torbjorn shook his head violently, then spun toward the shelf.

"Gromic!" he shouted. "Time to withdraw."

"I'm not going to complain," the stout dwarf snarled as he shrugged a blade stroke up and over his rounded helm. "Buggers don't seem to know when to quit. One second, sir."

Gromic rammed his gore-coated blade into an elf belly as Torbjorn helped drag the still-befuddled Waelon to his feet.

"You sure Tub of Guts will fit?" Waelon asked, frowning at the narrow passage.

"He'll make a good plug if he gets stuck." Torbjorn laughed, his voice more brittle than usual. "Either way, we're moving deeper in to give him a shot at it."

Waelon nodded as he began to shuffle, then his hand settled on his belt.

"Where's my axe?" he asked, turning back to the passage's mouth.

"In some elf-bint a hundred feet below," Torbjorn snarled, and he shoved Waelon down the corridor. "Now get moving, or it's going to get a *lot* more cramped in here."

Gromic's voice boomed behind them.

"Make a hole and make it wide, lads!"

As it turned out, Gromic did not get stuck, and the savagelings *did* know when to quit.

The passage widened a few dozen paces in. Once the armored bulk of the broad dwarf bulled through the bottleneck, Haeda and Ober fired back up the passage. The elves who'd entered the passage had nowhere to go, and with hardly a cry or a wail, their limp forms collapsed to the floor. There were a few more attempts, but it didn't take many salvos before the passage was choked with corpses. Some of the bolts passed through one elf's chest to stick fast in another.

As the savagelings withdrew, allowed at Torbjorn's order to drag back their wounded to the shelf, the dwarfs took stock of things.

"We're down to less than half our bolts, sir," Haeda reported, eyes glinting in the shadows. The only light came from the passage mouth. "We should distribute them evenly among the crew."

Torbjorn stared up the tunnel, then peered down the passage into the darkness. The passage had widened, but none of them had gone more than a few strides from the end of the bottleneck. Dwarvish eyes were good in low light, but even they could not see in absolute darkness, and none felt like striding off into the dark, where a pit might open up, or worse, a wight attack.

The commander's eyes caught the light playing across Tomza's face as she leaned on the stock of her duabuw. He wondered what else he had to fear in the dark. He'd told himself that what he'd glimpsed in Ober's eyes could be put to work in the task of slaying the wight, but how did he justify that to himself, much less the others? It was only a matter of time.

"We've only got enough food and water for two days of fighting," Haeda went on, ignorant of Torbjorn's perplexity. "And that's if we really tighten our belts and portion things out evenly. Some dipped a little deeper into their rations than others."

Torbjorn's head bobbed in acknowledgment. He was only half-listening, but the last comment drew his eyes to Gromic, though not for the matter of rations. The stout dwarf was standing against the wall, savoring the chance to catch his breath after the excitement. As the commander studied him, he tracked the gleam of his eyes beneath his helmet. The dwarf's gaze was fixed on Waelon, who stood a few feet away. The red-maned dwarf was running a large, rough hand around his neck, pawing at his throat and bloodied mail like he'd lost something and was trying to recall where he'd left it.

When Torbjorn climbed onto the shelf, he'd seen Waelon, throat rent open, about to tumble into the open air. He had managed to snare the dwarf's belt, but he would have gone over with the big dwarf if Gromic had not put his weighty might to work and anchored both Waelon and commander.

After they'd reeled Waelon in, Gromic had seen the blood. In his efforts, he'd gotten a fair amount of it on him as he'd helped Torbjorn move Waelon to the opening in the cliff before more elves had required him to stand as a bulwark on the shelf. He was a veteran like Torbjorn, so Gromic would not be taken in by any lie Torbjorn could fabricate. He'd seen what the commander had seen—a dwarf ready to be reunited with his clan—but now, not only was Waelon alive, but he was standing on his own two feet without a scratch to explain why he was covered in his own blood.

"Torbjorn?" Haeda pressed, her voice making it clear this wasn't the first time she'd tried to get his attention. "Sir, are you all right?"

The dwarf commander mopped his face as he looked at the driver. Then, the question finally understood, he nodded quickly as his bloodied nails raked his scarred cheek.

"I'm fine," he lied, then made a show of squinting into the dark. "Let's get some lights up. We need to take stock of the place if we're going to hold it long enough to see our mission through."

Haeda nodded, but even in the shadowed corridor, he could see the doubtful frown on her face.

"Aye, sir," she replied, then turned to dole out instructions to Ober and Tomza. Ober was standing beside his sister, silent but clearly worried. He nodded acknowledgment of the orders, but he was slow to comply until Tomza whispered something and squeezed his arm.

Torbjorn found himself wondering what madness had driven him to bring the two youths along. He clenched his teeth, angry that he was letting his frayed nerves distract him. He didn't need regrets or to second-guess himself. He had to sort things out. By a miracle or a curse, he still had his full command with him, and if they were going to finish their mission, much less survive, he had to keep them from tearing themselves apart.

"Waelon, keep watch for our pointy-eared friends," Torbjorn instructed as he moved to Gromic's side, not waiting to see if Waelon complied. That was how he would have treated the ex-ranger before, so that was how he acted now. As he reached his former fordwan, Torbjorn let out a sigh of relief. His eye caught Waelon hefting his duabuw and moving eagerly to his task.

"Have any spare tobacco?" the commander asked in a low voice. Gromic didn't respond, and he repeated the request with a little more force. "Gromic, I need smoke to clear my head. Do you have any tobacco?"

The stout dwarf started and turned from staring at Waelon, one hand reaching for his tobacco pouch. He blinked at Torbjorn.

"One moment, sir," Gromic muttered, taking off his bloody gauntlets to fumble with the leather wallet. "I'm a bit out of sorts. Not sure what's got me all turned about."

The pair heard the strike of steel on flint, and the flashes like miniature lightning bolts stabbed through the dark to vanish just as suddenly.

"I understand," Torbjorn murmured softly, retrieving his pipe. "But keep your voice down."

Gromic paused in his groping to nod, then managed to open the pouch.

"Here you are, sir," he whispered, leaning forward as he extended the open pouch. "To tell you the truth, sir, I know just what has my beard in a knot."

The flashes of light behind them ended, and a faint but growing glow gnawed at the edges of the blackness.

"Steady with that," they heard Haeda growl in the darkness. "Took you too long to get it. Don't want to have to start over."

A lantern shutter's hinge creaked, and the glow quickened its assault.

"So do I," Torbjorn answered and took out a pinch of leaf, which he pressed into his pipe's bowl with a practiced hand. "Knowing more about what happened with our dear, nearly departed friend will not make you feel any better. Might be wiser to let it rest—you know, until things settle down."

Gromic grunted noncommittally, the bemused lines of his face becoming visible as the light brightened. He rummaged a little more, found one of his last matches, and struck it on the wall before offering it to his commander.

"Thank you." Torbjorn fitted the pipe between his teeth and leaned forward.

"I'm not going to tell you how to go about things, sir," Gromic murmured, forcing his hand to move in a steady circle to give his commander a good charring light before the true light. "But remember what happened the last time you thought it was best to keep things from the crew."

Torbjorn frowned, barely avoiding a tongue bite as he drew a sharp breath.

"Crew?" the commander muttered. "You're not the only one to use that word. Haeda just used it. When did we become a crew?"

Gromic's brow furrowed, eyes a flash of blue as the pipe glowed. He didn't answer until he'd dropped the match and ground it out under his boot.

"Think it was Ober, sir. Lad used it to describe us, and it seems to have stuck. That's to be expected, I suppose. Every new Bad Badger's going to bring something that helps the group change and grow. I don't see any harm in it."

Torbjorn leaned back to puff on his pipe.

"No, I don't suppose there's anything wrong with that, and I think you're right, Gromic. I think I've learned my lesson about keeping secrets."

White smoke curled toward the stone ceiling, now revealed to possess an inset spine buttressed against the walls. Like the steps outside, it was fine work, showing precise craftsmanship while using the natural grain of the stone. It would be the pride of any dwarvish mason worthy of the name. Torbjorn supposed there were enough mysteries ahead that he didn't need to bring any more with him.

"Thank you for reminding me." He puffed on his pipe. "You're a better dwarf than I deserve."

There was enough light in the passage to see Gromic blush and slide his eyes sideways. "Proud to serve, Tweldwan," he muttered. "And glad you trust me."

Torbjorn's hand settled on Gromic's shoulder.

"Always, Fordwan. Always."

The stout dwarf's eyes met Torbjorn's, and the commander saw pride and satisfaction that matched the smile lurking beneath Gromic's heavy blond beard.

"Well, let's get on with it, then," Torbjorn muttered, releasing Gromic's shoulder. "Before the—"

"We've got company," Waelon snarled from the passage's bottleneck.

Gromic couldn't suppress his belly laugh as Torbjorn's eyes rolled up in search of absent deliverance.

"Never fails," he grumbled, unslinging his duabuw, pipe still clamped in his teeth as he looked over his shoulder. "Haeda, you and the babes poke around down the corridor, but don't go far in case things get interesting on this end."

"Something off about this one," Waelon called over Haeda's acknowledgment of her orders. "Just one, and he's moving funny."

Torbjorn cocked an eyebrow and turned around. Waelon hadn't shot the elf upon seeing the silhouetted form, which was strange, and the report caught the commander's attention. He moved to join Waelon at the narrowing of the passage, squinting at the figure silhouetted in the daylight beyond.

They were as tall as an elf and proportioned correctly, but the agility and litheness present in every movement their kind made were absent. The figure shuffled awkwardly, its arms not moving from its sides as it advanced a few more halting steps into the passage.

From the shelf beyond the corridor's portal, sharp savageling voices snarled commands. The shambling figure paused and twisted, and the awkward movement confirmed Torbjorn's suspicion that the creature was bound. They gave a snarled reply in a similar but distinctly different Ælfar dialect.

Torbjorn frowned when the voice struck him as familiar.

"Do you want us to shoot you now and save you the trouble of arguing with the savages?" the commander called down the passage.

"I would appreciate it if you did not," came the reply. The voice was rougher than usual but instantly recognizable.

"Utyrvaul?"

CHAPTER TWENTY-FIVE

"While I wish we were meeting under better circumstances, I can't deny that I am quite happy to see you all."

Despite Torbjorn's innate assumption that everything a myrkling said was a lie, he believed the svartalf this time. The elf stood in the corridor, wrists tied behind his back and feet hobbled. His once-immaculate armored coat was a bedraggled mess, but a huge sharp-toothed smile spread across his face.

"I'm still not sure how I feel about this whole turn of events," Torbjorn admitted. He was crouching next to Waelon. "Though I'm awfully curious how you happened to find your way into this predicament."

"Absolutely understandable, my good dwarf," Utyrvaul called, shuffling forward another few steps. "It would be easiest if we simply called it an unfortunate string of circumstances, of no fault of my own, mind you, but I imagine you will not be satisfied with that answer, will you?"

Torbjorn's stony silence was answer enough.

"Yes, quite," the svartalf declared as though reading the dwarf's thoughts. "Well, after the ill-fated business with my former Lady Banneret, I rode off to report to Lord Gwenmaelon

Gwydarioc, who was supposed to be conducting reconnaissance patrols along the Blacmere. Well, I thought to avoid misunderstandings about why I was in possession of some of my deceased lady's effects, so I ended up skirting south of the pickets and made for the Blacmere when I discovered what was happening."

A cry of savageling Ælfar sounded from the mouth of the passage, and Utyrvaul paused in his recitation to bark a few phrases in his more sibilant svartalf dialect.

"Sorry about that. My leash holders are eager for news of our progress." Utyrvaul sniffed and returned to his tale with gusto. "Anyway, with a spritely adyrclaf under me, I made good time to the lake, but that only meant I was relegated to the experience of trying to avoid a running battle between wight forces and coordinated war bands of my distant elven cousins.

"It seems that the wosealfs, what you dwarfs call savagelings, had come creeping along from their holdouts further north and were trying to use Blacmere and her waterways to move into wight territory. I'd have been happy to let them sort it out among themselves, of course, but it seems Lord Gwenmaelon was tasked with keeping tabs on the situation. He being the rapacious opportunist he is, I was soon swept up in an ill-timed raid on a supply line that left me separated from my party and running for my life from both my bestial cousins and the living dead. So I fled south, dodging levies mustering to support the wights in what was clearly becoming a three-sided battle."

Torbjorn snorted at hearing Utyrvaul speak disdainfully about anyone being a "rapacious opportunist" but didn't interrupt. Assuming they made it out of this alive, this would all need to be shared with Klaus back at Grayshelf. It also made him happy to know that the levies being mustered were to deal with a series of expanding skirmishes between wights, the savagelings, and myrkling mercenaries rather than a plan to press into dwarvish holdings as the Sufstan Holt'Dwan withdrew.

"So that's where our woodsman and grems were headed,"

Waelon muttered, coming to the same conclusion as Torbjorn. "Almost feel bad about killing them if all they were doing was heading off to kill elves."

Torbjorn motioned for silence, but it was too late. Utyrvaul paused his tale and crept a few steps closer. Torbjorn thought he caught the gleam of the svartalf's red eyes. Even Torbjorn, a mountain-born dwarf who was accustomed to things emerging out of the darkness, found that discomfiting.

When the svartalf spoke again, it was still in his high, cordial tone, so out of place with the shambling, burning-eyed thing that crept toward them.

"I assume that is the fiery-haired dwarf who so very eagerly put down the traitors, though I imagine their treachery was only a pretense for his violence."

"Right on both counts," Waelon spat. "Now, you want to get to the point before you get much closer. My finger gets itchy around elves, you see, so the closer you get, the less certain I am that I won't make a terrible mistake."

The savagelings called out in sharp voices, a few of their heads poking around the mouth of the passage from the shelf.

"Your friends seem to be getting a bit anxious," Torbjorn observed. "Sure you don't need to hustle back and put them at ease?"

Utyrvaul tittered, then called over his shoulder in Ælfar before turning around and spoking in a low, rushed voice.

"They've reason to be nervous. I think they realize that using a captive as a translator and negotiator is not the best strategy, but you seem to have wedged yourselves firmly in their way."

"Now we are getting closer to something I care about," Torbjorn growled. "What are they doing here?"

Utyrvaul twisted around to look back the way he'd come.

"I think I'm just clear of a javelin throw," he hissed. "If you promise not to shoot me when I run forward, I swear I'll tell you everything they've told and everything I've learned since they took me captive."

The elf voices behind called out more sharply, and a savageling detached itself from the passage entrance. Utyrvaul's gaze swung back toward the dwarfs, and his voice pressed in more urgent and pleading

"Do we have a deal?"

The svartalf was a snake, but he could provide valuable information. Also, if there was some negotiating to do with the savagelings, he'd rather have the myrkling dancing on his string rather than on the savagelings'.

"Better run, elf," Torbjorn called. "You've got ten seconds to get down here before we do a little more bolt-scrubbing downrange."

Utyrvaul didn't need further encouragement; he began a hobbled gallop down the passage. The savageling in the passage behind him snarled and started after the escaping prisoner with a dirk flashing in his hand.

As ever, the speed of the wild elves was frightening. In a heartbeat or two, the distance between the bound svartalf and his captor shrank to a few strides, and the dwarfs could see the arm raised for a quick cast.

"Down, elf," Waelon called a half-second before the duabuw whirred.

Utyrvaul, eyes bulging in terror, threw himself to the side as Waelon's bolt ripped by. The svartalf rebounded off the wall of the passage, then hit the floor hard with no hands to catch him. He was far better off than his pursuer, who clawed feebly at the bolt jutting from his chest as he crumpled. The myrkling flopped and wriggled as Torbjorn stepped into the tunnel and seized Utyrvaul by his collar.

"Much obliged," the svartalf remarked without a hint of gratitude as he was dragged out of the bottleneck. More savageling warriors had moved into the passage, but once Torbjorn was out of the way, Waelon and Gromic sent enough bolts downrange to force those still alive to scurry back to the shelf to fume and scheme about their next move.

"Second time in my life I've killed elves to save an elf," Waelon grumbled as he checked his crossbow's magazine. "And each time, you're around, myrkling. You are the worst kind of bad luck."

Utyrvaul scooted like an inchworm over to Torbjorn's feet, then sat up and shot the leader a smile.

"Oh, believe me, I'm not immune to this cloud of misfortune which hangs about me," he assured them, nodding at his hobbled legs. "I would be happy to share my travails and tales of woe from these past several days, but first I would appreciate you liberating me from these bonds since they are most uncomfortable."

Gromic and Waelon looked at Torbjorn, who gave Utyrvaul a very cool once-over.

"Not to be cruel, but I think they'll stay on until you've finished explaining why you're here, why the savagelings are here, and how we got caught up in all this."

From deeper in the stony chamber came a voice. Torbjorn spied one of the lanterns bobbing toward them.

"Is this really necessary among such battle-bound brothers as we?" the svartalf lamented, his head lolling back to rest against the stone. "Fine. If you insist, I will resume my tale, albeit under duress. Perhaps that will add zest to the story."

Torbjorn rolled his eyes. Haeda entered the chamber and called, "Torbjorn."

"I'm here," he replied over his shoulder, then frowned at the miserable elf at his feet. "It would go a lot quicker and you'd potentially get out of those bonds a lot faster if you stopped the bellyaching and the dramatic flourishes."

Utyrvaul rolled his head away from the dwarf commander, although his crimson eyes still squinted in his direction.

"Dramatic flourishes?" The svartalf scoffed. "What you take as embellishment is only the honest truth that I, as an honored knight of the Lord Gwenmaelon Gwydarioc—"

"The rapacious opportunist," Torbjorn interjected as his arms crossed over his chest.

"One and the same," Utyrvaul affirmed without losing a beat. "As one of his knights, I am bound to always speak truthfully. Part of speaking the truth is speaking in full so no lie of omission may be inferred from my silence."

"Torbjorn!" Haeda called insistently.

"Haeda, I'm right here," he shouted, unable to keep the irritation out of his voice. He gazed mildly at Utyrvaul. "All I'm hearing is your dainty mouth flapping but nothing like an answer to my questions. Maybe I should toss you back to the savagelings since they seem to appreciate your tongue so much."

To illustrate the point, Torbjorn reached down to seize the svartalf's collar, but Utyrvaul twisted away sharply, teeth bared. It seemed for a moment that the myrkling might snap at the dwarf's fingers, but on seeing the dark look leveled on him, the elf's grimace bloomed into a smile.

"I don't think we need to bother with such displays," Utyrvaul replied softly. "Which question would you like answered first, dear comrade?"

Torbjorn heard the scuff of boots and the warm light of a lantern spilled around him, but the prospect of getting answers had his attention.

"Why are the savagelings here?"

Utyrvaul sighed, then nodded down the corridor that led deeper into the mountain.

"They've come to destroy whatever is kept here," the svartalf stated. "Apparently, there is a prophecy—new or old, I don't know since the wosealf have a dire prophecy about every other day and every cave or old tree in this valley and seem to come up with new ones constantly. The point is that they thought this particular prophecy was so important that half a dozen war bands came together to attack the wights to make sure another war band could slip through and see the deed done."

The commander of the Bad Badgers stared at the svartalf, trying to process the information. Its immensity made his stomach twist, and his head felt as though it might float toward the ceiling.

"Torbjorn," Haeda hissed at his shoulder, interrupting the sensations he was experiencing. "I need to show you something."

He could tell from her tone that she was serious, but the incredible implications of Utyrvaul's revelation left him distracted. He waved for her to wait as he scowled at Utyrvaul with open suspicion.

"If they're here to destroy it, why attack us?" Torbjorn demanded. "There's no love lost between our races, but we're both fighting the wights. We're on the same side in this."

Utyrvaul's face indicated that he couldn't believe the dwarf would ask such a stupid question. The commander had to make an effort not to punch him.

Finally, the svartalf heaved a sigh. "Well, I'm not certain I know the exact reason for the decision," he began in an innocent voice. "But it might have to do with you sharing a certain family resemblance with the last batch who ignored elvish prophecies and went and woke the wights up."

Waelon and Gromic growled at the gently delivered barb, but they could not refute the statement. It wasn't openly spoken about, but any dwarf who'd served in the Ysgand Vale had heard the rumor that the wights had arisen because greedy dwarfs broke into their tombs after the savageling shamans and chieftains had issued dire warnings. Even if it wasn't true, the wild elves below believed it. It also explained why, despite their inordinate losses without any real success, they continued their efforts. They had a lot more riding on this than the scalps of six sweaty dwarfs.

"All right, fair enough," Torbjorn murmured, and he raked a

hand through his beard. "But we don't have to fight about this. No one else has to die. If we could convince them we're on the same side and get them not to kill us, we could kill this wight together. Everyone could walk away a winner."

Torbjorn looked at Gromic and Waelon, who were watching him intently. "This changes everything."

"So does this."

Torbjorn spun to the driver. Haeda wore thick veils of cobwebs. One look at her face told him something was very wrong.

"What?" Torbjorn asked, his heart beginning to slide up to his throat again. "What happened?"

Haeda, eyes blazing green fire, jerked her head toward the recesses she'd emerged from.

"You need to come see this."

CHAPTER TWENTY-SIX

"Watch your step."

Haeda's warning came none too soon. The stone floor in front of Torbjorn's feet fell away into a yawning chasm.

"Stones and Bones," he hissed, pausing to allow his muscles to relax and his heart to start beating again. "A little more warning if you please."

Haeda didn't respond but slowed her pace as she led him over what seemed to be a stone bridge stretching over a canyon. Torbjorn forced himself to focus on moving exactly where and how she moved as she trudged ahead, lantern held overhead.

"Not bottomless," she explained after they took ten or twelve strides more. "If you hold still and stay quiet, you can hear that there's water running down there, but I wouldn't count on it flowing into the open anytime soon."

The thought of tumbling into the icy black waters, only to be sucked down into the suffocating darkness that wound beneath the Wyrmspines, made him shiver. Dwarfs were creatures of the earth, the domain given to them by the Shaper, so to die by drowning within that earth would be the ultimate cruel irony. He'd rather be cooked alive on a goblin's pyre or butchered for the savagelings' cannibal rites than drown in an underground river.

He could hope that a spark from his charred body would catch a goblin's greasy hair on fire or his cantankerous meat would choke a gluttonous elf, but in that dark water, there was no such hope. His body would be borne to who knew what pit or pool.

Yet, for all these grim thoughts, he knew that wasn't why Haeda had come to get him. He'd been forced to leave Waelon and Gromic guarding the entrance, with Utyrvaul underfoot. She wouldn't have dragged him through long, silent chambers where graven pillars held up the walls and cold, blurred faces on faded bas reliefs watched them pass. There must be something worse at the end of this little excursion.

"I thought I told you not to go very far," Torbjorn grumbled as he stole a glance over Haeda's shoulder and saw the end of the footbridge was near.

"We didn't think we had," Haeda replied as she stepped off the bridge. "There's something strange about this place. We thought we'd only ventured a little farther and we'd pause. We could hear you and the lads talking like you were just a stone's throw away, so we'd go a little deeper and pause, then hear you lot yammering, and go on a little more. That was how we ended up here."

Haeda hefted her lantern high. The commander looked around and whistled. They were in a palatial courtyard with twisted sigil-encrusted pillars that stretched to the roof. Tiles spiraled out in a bewildering pattern that could only be appreciated from a bat's-eye view. Scattered between the pillars were elegant benches and divans of black marble that were sized for beings taller and more powerfully built than elves or men.

Torbjorn struggled to imagine what sort of creatures could sit comfortably on the oversize furnishings. The courtyard was not unlike the one that sprawled outside the grand hall in Alrur's Palace. Dignitaries loitered there with court officials as they waited for the hall to be opened and the King's Court to be in session.

Even this, as wondrous and ominous as it was, was not why she'd dragged him back here.

They moved through the courtyard, their boots scuffing on the tiles or crunching when they found an area where time had taken its relentless toll. The air was thick and close, and Torbjorn's mouth got dry, although he was sweating. If asked, the commander would have said the place was sinister rather than peculiar.

He felt watched and unwelcome, and he fought the urge to look over his shoulder for eyes glinting at the edge of the light or strain his ears for hushed footsteps. They reached a huge doorway set into a wall of flat black basalt. The stone that formed the door frame was akin to the black marble that the furniture behind them was crafted of, but its seams were raw gold, which was instantly apparent to dwarven eyes. Like the other stonework in this place, it had been shaped by a master. It seemed like the rock had been molded like clay by careful hands rather than felt the bite of chisels and rasps.

The enormous doorway was draped in the same cobwebs that shrouded Haeda, but he now saw they were the remains of a vast curtain. The age-chewed silk that hung over the portal clung to the dwarfs in streamers as Haeda led Torbjorn through the curtain.

Beyond the portal was a seemingly endless flight of steps, and atop it were two points of light that must be Ober's and Tomza's lanterns. He and Haeda made for the stairs, which were also dark stone, except rather than twisting seams of gold, Torbjorn saw whorls of crimson like someone had stirred in molten rubies.

As they climbed, Torbjorn ceased counting the steps and eventually ceased caring if he'd ever reach the top. The sense of a hostile, alien awareness mounted, yet for all his discomfort, he knew in his bones that whatever lay at the top would be worse.

Eventually, the steps ended, and he staggered up the last one to see Ober and Tomza and their lanterns. Their expressions were almost embarrassed, and they seized on his appearance as an excuse not to look behind them.

The only other thing on the platform besides the dwarfs was a long, low rectangular box that had been placed on a dais of jet-black stone half its size. To Torbjorn, it looked like it was composed of frozen smoke, but as he shuffled forward, he realized it was glass or crystal that had grown dingy with time.

There was something within the long box—a figure whose dimensions seemed wrong. Torbjorn stepped closer, his heart hammering in his ears.

"I'm sorry, sir." Ober gulped as the commander stepped past. "I just can't. Well, I won't, sir."

"Neither will I, sir," Tomza added, and her voice sounded weary and drawn. "I just won't."

Neither of them looked at him when they spoke, though he sensed that had more to do with making sure they didn't look at what was in the box. They held their posts, clutching the rings on their lanterns, but they would not move closer. Haeda, lantern held before her in a steady hand, approached with him, then held the light over the time-fogged case.

The events that had brought him to this moment threatened to overpower him. He wanted to retreat. He was certain that if he looked within, he would see something that would un-dwarf him. The premonition was as real as if he'd seen it carved on a wall.

To gaze upon it was to be ruined; he knew that. It would be the end of all things.

The unyielding force within him drove him to look.

The figure within that murky box was a human child.

In size, she was at the age when human females reached maturity, but her features made her look much younger. Her strong but slender shape was clothed in a raw silk gown, and her face was serene and untroubled. Torbjorn, who had no children of his own, much less tended human young, was sure this girl was barely a decade old. He was uncertain about her ethnicity.

Her skin was the palest copper, and her features, while striking and noble, were not like anything he'd seen from the various humans he'd encountered in a century as a dwan. Even more unusual was her hair. While her brows were thin dark lines on her lovely face, the equally dark hair that spilled over her shoulders was streaked with a rich blue. Torbjorn knew that some females, even among his kind, dyed their hair, but when he studied hers, he knew it was natural. Sable and azure, it was her crowning mantle.

"I don't understand," Torbjorn rumbled as he wrenched his gaze from the child to glare at Haeda. "Where is the wight?"

"If there is one here, it's her," the driver answered, then nodded at the opposite wall. "This is all we found. No side passages along the way, no other chambers. Everything leads straight here to her. Then there's a wall of solid rock."

Torbjorn scowled at the blank black wall as though it was personally thwarting him.

"This can't be it." Confusion and frustration mounted inside him. "Where are the armies of dead soldiers? Where's the dead wight lord on his throne? This is a child, a human girl. We didn't come here for this!"

"No." Haeda sighed, and a burden tumbled off her shoulders. "No, we didn't."

Ober and Tomza relaxed and gazed hopefully at their commander, eyes shining with relief.

"So, we're not going to kill her?" Ober almost sobbed. "Oh, Shaper be praised!"

Tomza didn't speak, but glittering trails coursed down her cheeks as she took one hitching breath after another.

"Kill her?" Torbjorn snarled, his confusion mixing with outrage. "What the hell are you talking about? I came here to smash a wheezer to bits, not desecrate a child's tomb! What's wrong with you?"

His voice seemed blasphemously loud to his ears, but he didn't care. The mission had been turned upside-down, and everyone around him was acting mad. That did nothing to help him recover from his shock.

"It's not a tomb," Haeda murmured, nodding at the translucent casket.

"What?" Torbjorn shook his head. "This place is ancient. She can't be—"

Behind the dull crystal, the child shivered and rolled onto her side as though refusing to wake. Torbjorn gaped, hardly daring to breathe, as her dark lashes fluttered open. The child stared at him with eyes of burnished gold.

CHAPTER TWENTY-SEVEN

"I know this won't be a popular option, but I still think we should kill her. Hear me out...*ufh!*"

The kick propelled Utyrvaul across the floor, and he lay gasping for breath.

"I've got a counter-argument on the other foot, too," Gromic growled as he loomed over the svartalf. "In case you wanted to make your case from another angle."

The myrkling shook his head vigorously as he fought to keep air moving in and out. "No, I've stated my case. Carry on, please. I'll just lay here, collecting my, uh, thoughts."

"Gromic, quit playing with the elf," Waelon called. "We need to sort this kak out."

The red-haired dwarf was manning his post at the bottleneck in the passage, watching for savagelings as the sunlight outside deepened from orange to scarlet. Despite his vigil, he couldn't keep from letting his eyes stray to the peculiar creature with Haeda's arm and cloak thrown over her shoulders. The child looked from face to face, golden eyes flashing with interest or confusion. She'd yet to utter a sound.

The dwarfs were anything but silent.

"It doesn't make sense to me." Haeda shook her head. Her hand gently but inescapably clasped the girl's shoulder. "Why would they want to kill a child?"

"A prophecy," Ober offered with a shrug. "That's what Torbjorn told us the elf said."

Haeda didn't bother to voice how nonsensical that seemed to her.

"Why they want to kill her doesn't matter," Tomza replied. The color and strength had returned to her face and voice. "How are we going to get everyone out of here alive?"

"You're telling me you can't use your witchery for that?" Gromic had stomped back to the crew after depositing the svartling against the wall.

Conversation halted, and every eye swung to the broad dwarf, then to Tomza, whose face had lost its color again.

"I-I don't know what you're t-talking about," Tomza stammered limply.

"Too late for that, lass," Gromic growled. "I don't know what you did, but Waelon was on his way to his clan when Torbjorn and I hauled him inside, and now he's as hale and fit as he ever was. I may not be an ascedwan, but I've served long enough to know that not even needlework could do that, nor any herb, either."

Waelon's hand strayed to his throat, fingers massaging a spot where he was sure something was missing, along with his memory of what had happened after he'd hauled Gromic onto the last step. It was like a gap where a tooth had been, and his mind was working it to conjure what had once been there.

"What did you do to me?" the big dwarf asked, his voice flat but not hard. The former ranger was too confused to be angry.

Every eye turned to Tomza, who stood quivering, gaze darting from face to face in panic. She wanted to flee, though whether into the forbidding darkness or onto the shelf outside, she wasn't certain. Yet, that uncertainty isn't what held her in place but rather the voice that rose in that trembling silence.

"She saved your life," Torbjorn declared, first looking at Waelon and then meeting every other dwarf's gaze. "I'm not sure what she did, but whatever it was, it saved Waelon's life, and that's enough for me."

Tomza tried and failed to smother the sobs that wracked her frame.

"I-I learned it from books m-my m-mother kept," the dwarfess confessed, her face awash in tears. "I w-was j-just curious at first, but th-then it h-helped folks. It's just h-healing, n-nothing else. I'm s-so—"

"You used it to save a good dwarf's life," Torbjorn interrupted as he took her trembling hand. "That's enough for me. You hear me, lass?"

Tomza fell silent and nodded, fighting to regain control of her breathing. Ober moved alongside her, and she sank against him for support.

"But, sir," Haeda pressed, her face knotting with confusion. "Dwarfs are forbidden magic unless it's the baelgeld, and even then only—"

"Haeda, most everything you've done since becoming a Bad Badger has been forbidden," Torbjorn interjected, his voice gentle but firm. "It's the irony of our lives that breaking the rules of our people is what got us here and being ready and able to keep breaking those rules is what kept us out of the Deeping. A shabr'dwan doesn't get to pick which tool to use. That right was taken away from all of us. We use what we've got to do what we can."

One hand rose to settle on Tomza's shoulder, and Torbjorn pointed at Waelon with the other. "And this dwan used what she knew to save that dwan's life. Like I said, that's enough for me. We clear?"

Haeda stood rigidly for a moment, then looked at Waelon before meeting Tomza's eyes levelly.

"Yes, sir." the driver nodded at the younger dwarfess. "That's good enough for me, too."

Tomza nodded back and straightened, though Ober's arm remained about her shoulders.

"Anyone else have a comment to make on this?" Torbjorn asked. He turned to Gromic, who sighed and shook his head, and then to Waelon.

"I've something to say," Waelon rasped, meeting Tomza's glistening gray eyes. "Thank you, lass. I was not ready to return to my clan just yet."

His dark eyes swung to the girl standing under Haeda's arm, and he gave her a playful wink that drew a cocked head and a crooked smile from the child. "Not when things have gotten so interesting."

That drew every dwarf's attention back to the matter at hand.

"Interesting indeed," Torbjorn growled. He squinted at the sky at the end of the passage, in which bruised-looking clouds were visible. The savagelings had apparently vanished, but the commander knew that only meant the elves were planning something. Though the dwarfs had dubbed the wosealfs savages, Torbjorn was not fool enough to think they weren't as cunning and ingenious as their svartalf cousins. Considering what they'd invested and lost in this endeavor, they would not just throw up their hands and leave. When moved by their unfathomable superstitions, the wild elves were as implacable as any dwarf.

"I'm willing to bet those sharp-eared savages will make another push once the sun goes down." He gestured at the stiffening bodies scattered across the floor. "I imagine they'll creep to the edge of our lanterns' light and clear out the dead as quietly as they can so they can try to push through again."

"They pack in that close, and we'll spit two or three to a shot."

Waelon chuckled and patted the stock of his duabuw. "Might even beat my record of four elves with one shot."

"Even if every shot killed three elves, we wouldn't have enough bolts to put down half of them," Haeda reminded everyone. "And once we're out of ammunition, their numbers will count for a lot more."

"Not if we keep 'em pinned here." Gromic slapped the walls on either side of the narrow passage. "Taking shifts, we could hold this for a long time. I'm betting their spirits break long before we or the stone do."

"I'm not certain you're giving my cousins enough credit," Utyrvaul called from his spot against the wall. "But even given your optimistic evaluation of your position and dim view of those fellows outside, you are still talking about days of fighting. That presents its own problems."

"If it's a question of rations, we can all tighten our belts," Gromic rumbled pugnaciously.

"Oh, I don't doubt *that* for a second, my svelte fellow," the svartalf replied wryly before looking at Torbjorn. "The issue is that although the war band was able to slip quickly down the Blacmere's channels and navigate the tangled Mereseep, they weren't invisible. I was bound in the bottom of one of their boats, but I'm certain we passed the outer pickets of Cer'Ren. The only reason they didn't send out forces to stop them was that the bulk of their garrison was fighting at the Blacmere. Word will have gotten back by now."

The crew looked grim.

"The wights are coming." Torbjorn spoke as if every word was made of lead. "And they'll be bringing an army of the dead, along with living conscripts, to crush the war band and hunt down every last warrior. They can't have stray savageling hunting packs harassing their vassals all winter."

Utyrvaul nodded, although his long, narrow face bore an exaggerated frown.

"I'm afraid you are correct," the svartalf stated with what sounded like genuine sympathy. "So you see, it's not just a matter of outlasting my cousins. You have to break them or elude them before the wights arrive and kill us all."

"Well, 'elude' is out," Waelon grumbled, though one might have thought he was happy to say it. "They're camped in front of the only way out, and it's a long climb down even if they're not waiting on the stairs. We'll be spotted, and they'll be on us in one shake of a svartalf's dangler."

"Oh, they'll show up much quicker than that," Utyrvaul declared confidently. "Trust me."

Waelon looked disgusted as the myrkling waggled his eyebrows.

"What about trying to go up the cliff rather than down?" Tomza asked.

"Same problem," Waelon told her, grateful for the distraction. "We'll be even slower going up, and even if they take a break, they'll see what we're doing and come up to drag us all back down and cut us to ribbons. Like I said, eluding is not an option."

"Then we're back to breakin' 'em." Gromic pursed his lips in thought. "Which means we kill or maim a lot of 'em in short order. That's where I'm stumped. I know me and Waelon can handle a couple of elves at a time, especially with our backs to good stone, but it'd still take time. One bad bit o' luck, and the whole thing goes tits-up."

"Not to mention, how are we going to keep *her* safe through all this?" Haeda worried, drawing the child closer. "If those murderous bastards are looking for her, there's no guarantee we can keep them from getting to her if we get into a fight where it's more than one on one."

The dwans thought, their eyes downcast. Torbjorn alternated between staring at the child and looking at Ober.

The young dwarf was wracking his brains for ideas, and when

he saw his commander's eyes on him, he shared his half-formed thought.

"Could we, uh, fashion a trap?" he asked, losing his momentum after the second word. "Or something like that."

Gromic didn't bother raising his eyes as he shook his head dismissively.

"Don't have the time, tools, materials, or dwarfs for anything on the scale we'd need. Nice try, though, lad."

Ober nodded appreciatively, but his shoulders slumped. He realized Torbjorn was still staring at him. "Yes, sir?"

Torbjorn closed his as he drew a deep breath, then looked at Ober levelly.

"Today's the day for revelations, lad. No reason to take yours to the grave if it might be the one to save us."

Ober's eyes bulged as every dwarf swung their gaze to him. He wanted to scream, shout, or roar, but all he managed was a deflated sigh. "Well, kak."

CHAPTER TWENTY-EIGHT

"Dwarven military science has always eluded me, but this does beat all."

The dwarfs around the svartalf didn't bother to respond as they checked their gear for the final time.

They'd relocated en masse to the chamber where the bridge spanned the lightless waters. On the far side of the bridge in the giants' courtyard, Gromic, Waelon, and Haeda stood beside the svartelf. The mute girl waited on a high stone bench Haeda had hoisted her onto a dozen paces away with Haeda's lantern beside her. Gromic's and Waelon's lanterns were on the ground before them as they checked their weapons and adjusted their armor.

As the dwarfs had entered, or in some cases, re-entered, the bridge chamber, the last light of the sun died outside. As they got ready to fight, the carved pillars in the courtyard began to emit a pale blue/green light. The spectral glow lit everything except the platform across the bridge.

The dwarfs, suspicious of unexpected occurrences, had frozen with their weapons in their hands when the columns lit up. After several heartbeats passed without incident, they'd decided it was part of the arcane construction that made the place so peculiar.

Once the shock had worn off, Torbjorn had acknowledged that Alrur's palace had alchemical wonders that produced similar effects at the king's request, which was only made when visiting dignitaries had to be impressed.

"Keep your lanterns lit and close," the commander had instructed. "No telling if that witch light will stay on, and the last thing we need is to be isolated by darkness."

The trio of veterans stood on the far side of the bridge with Utyrvaul, who had been allowed to collect weapons from the dead after they'd cut off his bonds. No one had forgotten the "accident" that had befallen his deceased mistress, but for the time being, the svartalf had firmly cast his lot with the Bad Badgers. He now stood beside the veteran dwarfs, chattering in his amiable fashion as he laid out the collection of javelins and spears he'd gathered from the dead. A leaf-bladed sword of burnished copper hung at his belt, another acquisition from his former captors.

"I'm not saying your commander doesn't know his business." Utyrvaul tested the heft of a pair of javelins. "But I fail to see how placing one of your warriors alone across the bridge serves a purpose. If we needed bait to lure the enemy toward our position, that would be one thing, but the enemy will come for us very soon in any case."

Three sets of dwarven eyes regarded the elf icily, which prompted the irrepressible myrkling to set aside his javelins and gesture expansively at the bridge.

"It seems like a waste, is all I am saying."

"You were sitting right there when Ober admitted to being a vildergaest, weren't you?" Haeda asked, her hand hovering over the magazine of her duabuw.

"Yes, I remember that term being tossed about a bit," Utyrvaul mused, tapping his chin pensively. "I also remember that announcement was of dread significance to you all since the young female dwarf, the one you say is a witch, looked like she was ready to burst into tears. The young fellow looked uncertain about making the confession, but I'm afraid I have no idea what it means. Does it have something to do with your kind's inexplicably prudish ideas about magic?"

The dwarfs exchanged looks, then Waelon and Haeda glanced pleadingly at Gromic. The stout dwarf scowled at them and shook his head, but their beseeching faces grew insistent as the svartling prattled about the dwarfs' "stunted views on magic endemic" and his theory that it might "tangentially be related to diet." Gromic rolled his eyes with an exasperated splutter, then cleared his throat forcefully to get the myrkling's attention.

"All right, here's the ore on vildergaests, and it's only connected with magic transgenitaly."

Haeda and Waelon stifled groans at Gromic's initial attempt at intellectual discourse. Utyrvaul's eyes glittered with cruel mirth.

"Truly, I am in the presence of a savant!" The svartalf chortled. "I've been pronouncing tangentially wrong all this time."

Gromic, sensing the mockery, left off honing his magsax to wag the keen point under Utyrvaul's nose.

"Do you want an answer or to keep on being an ass?"

The svartalf's nose crinkled as though he were about to sneeze, and he took a smooth step backward as he shook his head.

"No, no. My apologies for interrupting. Please continue. I hang on every word."

Gromic frowned and wondered how great a loss it would be to pitch one elf over the rail to see how long he screamed on the way down. Then his eye strayed to his commander on the far side of the bridge, and he told himself to behave…for now.

"A vildergaest," Gromic told him, "is any poor sod who's encountered with a wild spirit that left him or her permanently changed. Sometimes they are called spirit-ridden because of how the thing comes over the poor bugger. You blade-ears *have* heard of spirits, right?"

"Yes, my large-nosed, whiskery friend," the svartalf replied. "I'm curious about the exact nature of the spirit. Is it a possessing demon that will allow him to summon a thunderous blast of sorcerous power? I can see the advantage of having the youth at the front to unleash his fury before the demon consumes him from within if that is the case."

Gromic shook his head.

"No, no. You got it all wrong. It's not a demon, though to be fair, most dwarfs would rather have one of those than what the poor lad's got. Like you said, a demon's going to chew you up quick, and then it's over. Some say the spirit can actually help vildergaests live longer, but they don't get any less dangerous in old age."

Utyrvaul, having selected his first javelin for the upcoming battle and grown bored with the conversation, waved his hand dismissively.

"Yes, yes. Well, I'm sure it will be fascinating to watch, but I do hope those other two hurry. I can't imagine it will be much longer before my erstwhile captors arrive, and I'd hate for them to get caught up in...whatever the young dwarf is going to do."

Across the bridge, Torbjorn was equally cognizant of their shrinking timeline. He spoke to Ober in a calm and encouraging manner.

"You just do what you can, lad," the commander intoned. "Try to direct it at their side, but no matter what happens, we understand you're doing your best. None of this would've been possible without what you're about to do."

Torbjorn remembered what he'd glimpsed after the battle with the svartalfs, and his stomach tightened.

"But if you could keep it on this side of the bridge, we'd be much obliged," he added, then regretted it.

Ober nodded, his honest features showing his fear and doubt, but he sounded confident as he looked his commander in the eye.

"I will, sir, and, uh, thank you, sir. Thank you for believing in me and giving me this chance. And also, thank you for sticking up for Tomza. That couldn't have been easy."

Torbjorn was embarrassed to receive gratitude from one he was asking so much of but expressing that would make Ober uncomfortable. "It was a good deal easier than having to bury another of my Bad Badgers." He gave Tomza, who was standing beside her brother, a nod and a smile. "I'll leave you to it, but don't dawdle, lass. Those bastards are coming. I can feel it."

With that, Torbjorn scuttled across the bridge, refusing to offer a farewell.

"Well, I suppose this is it." Tomza sighed and looked her brother over, willing herself to stay strong. She'd shed enough tears today. Ober needed her to be strong and believe in him.

Yet, with all his weapons and armor removed, wearing only trousers and a tunic that was too big for him, he still reminded her of the rascally little brother who used to follow her around. She forced herself to see only his handsome beard and the layers of heavy muscle on his frame, but noticing those differences only made his features look younger.

He was still her little brother, and nothing would change that.

Although she exercised her considerable will, tears welled in her eyes. She clamped them shut and leaned forward to press her forehead to his like she had in the dark days after the wights had taken their home and family from them. In those days, they'd had only each other, and they'd leaned in to support and be supported. That had been a balm to their broken hearts.

Eyes shut, heads and hearts connected, brother and sister stood together.

"I'm scared," Ober whispered.

"Me too," Tomza replied.

"What if I lose control?" he croaked. "What if it's like the last time?"

"It won't be," Tomza murmured. "This time, you're going to ride the beast, not be ridden. Say it, Ober. Tell that thing inside you that you are Ober Draulson of Clan Jaln, and you are doing the riding tonight. *Say it, Ober!*"

"I am Ober Draulson," Ober began, his voice shaking. "Of C-clan Jaln, and I'll be the one riding tonight."

From a distant corridor came the echoes of sharp voices intent on blood and death.

"Louder, Ober," Tomza hissed, nose to nose with her brother. "Wake the beast up! You're ready to ride!"

Ober nodded, and there was a ripple beneath his skin.

"I am Ober Draulson of Clan Jaln!" he growled. His voice thickened and got raspier with each word. "I'm the one riding tonight!"

Footsteps like war drums pounded in the darkness behind Ober.

"Louder!" his sister cried, her hands seizing the sides of his head as bristles broke out in jagged patches. "Let Grimmoth himself hear you and fear."

Ober's head snapped back as he roared loud enough to shame the thunder in the tempest.

"*I AM OBER DRAULSON OF CLAN JALN, AND I'VE COME TO RIDE!*"

His dark eyes snapped open to see Tomza's tearful but fierce smile.

"Give 'em hell, little brother," she whispered as she tore back across the bridge.

CHAPTER TWENTY-NINE

The savagelings came at him in waves.

Their pale bodies crested like foam on the waves, bearing razor-edged detritus. They hacked, pierced, and sliced as they crashed down on him. The onslaught might have worked moments before when he was just a dwarf, a small but sturdy son of a race born of the mountains.

But now? Now he *was* a mountain.

That thing inside him had risen, and for once, it did not defy his will but acted in concert with it. With unity came power. His body stretched and swelled, refusing to be hindered by petty mortal constraints. When he stood, he was several feet taller, and dark, bristling fur rippled across his muscle-corded limbs. He both was and was not Ober of Clan Jaln. When he saw the first wave stream toward him, he opened his jaws to loose a roar that was also a laugh.

He raised his sickle-nailed hand and scattered the wave with a single swipe. As foam parted at the swipe of a hand, so did their pale bodies. All the jagged weapons they tried to use to kill him bounced off his pelt like thrown sand, so beneath his notice that they drew another thunderous laugh. He shook the viscous remains of the first wave off his paw.

"*MORE!*" he roared in a voice that belonged to the storm as well as that hungry thing in the woods whose heavy claws were feared by one and all. "*MORE!*"

Like the ocean, another wave came. This one was thicker with cresting foam, its detritus gleaming with eager confidence in its drive to hew and gouge.

This is what he wanted.

Arms raised, he plunged into the wave, paws raking left and right. He snapped at those who came at him, and pieces of their fragile forms splattered around him while his maw filled with the salty and sweet taste of the fluid that sustained them. Rich and metallic, it slid down his throat and filled his nostrils.

"*MORE!*" he howled ecstatically.

Like the ocean, more waves came.

The Bad Badgers and Utyrvaul were prepared to aid Ober as he unleashed the wild spirit that had inhabited him after the fateful patrol. Ober, with Tomza supplying additional details, told them that upon stumbling across an ancient ritual site, their fordwan had commanded the dwans under his command to deface, desecrate, and destroy the site, lest it be used for any further "heathen nonsense."

Ober had not been long from his initial training. While his mother had taught him that all writings and people could offer insight, if not wisdom, he knew that when he joined the Holt'D-wan, he would be required to do things he might not understand or like. He'd done as he was told and hewed down a ring of sacred saplings, then smashed the little votive pots that had swung from their tender branches. Seeing that the others were hard at work, he tried to yank out the roots of the saplings he'd hacked down. It was hard work since, though they were young, the plants had grown deep into soil made rich and welcoming by sacrifices. They eventually came free, their sap running hot and thick like congealing blood.

Among one of the knots of roots, he found an idol, a ludicrous caricature of ursine fury wrought from baked clay. Frustrated by his hard labor, he'd spat on the snarling face and crushed the figure in his hands. The shards bit deep into his flesh, and the clay softened when his blood touched it. A moment later, Ober was no longer the sole occupant of his body.

The changes did not happen at once, and their gradual nature allowed Ober's sister to plumb her knowledge of occultic herblore and hedge wisdom to help him. She came up with a treatment using mona root to keep the worst at bay.

During the savagelings' ambush, the siblings realized they'd had no concept of what "the worst" meant in terms of Ober's condition.

At present, the young dwarf's comrades in arms stood before the bridge, struck dumb when they caught a glimpse of his truth.

The dwarfs had intended to fire bolts at the savagelings, but as they watched the furious ursine, they realized their aid would be like spitting into a flood. The savagelings attacked again and again, each time in greater numbers. Each time Ober, or what possessed Ober, greeted them with a roar that was as terrifying as it was exuberant. Massive humped shoulders rolling, he bounded toward them, rasping laughter bubbling up as the elves screamed their hatred and defiance and thrust their bared blades at him.

The savagelings' weapons dug but found no purchase as long forelimbs tipped with claws longer than a magsax's blade raked left and right. Those who encountered those limbs had their bones snapped and shattered and were hurtled away from the collision. The more fortunate were those touched by the gleaming claws since their bodies came apart and they died instantly.

Any who escaped the initial onslaught intact, which was rare, were caught by his return strokes. Any who survived either fled back the way they'd come or leapt, mad with terror, into the darkness that yawned on either side of the bridge.

"I knew it would be bad." Gromic gulped. "But I don't think I could ever have understood if I hadn't seen it with my own eyes."

Torbjorn nodded but said nothing. Haeda and Tomza had looked away, and Waelon looked pale and sickly, his duabuw held limply in his hands.

Only the svartalf seemed unfazed, but his attempts to engage the dwarfs in conversation about the spectacle were summarily ignored. He might have lamented witnessing such a unique experience with such poor company, but he was relieved of this thought when a wosealf managed to slip past the meatgrinder that was Ober and bounded across the bridge toward them.

"Allow me!" the svartalf cried. He hefted his javelin, then let fly with an expert cast.

The savageling took the flint-tipped missile in through his bare chest, then his feet tangled, and he pitched off the bridge with a piteous wail. The wail died several seconds before a splash echoed from the waters below.

"Not to worry, not to worry." Utyrvaul chortled as he selected another javelin. "All in a day's work." The dwarfs, still captivated by seeing Ober's wrathful spirit unleashed, didn't notice the elf's actions. They were even less aware of him pouting at being ignored. "Let's just remember this when we are talking about who contributed what to this occasion, shall we?"

It was unclear how long the carnage lasted. Ober raised his gore-smeared muzzle when there was no fresh crop of savagelings to slaughter.

At the edge of the light created by the glowing pillars, the last few attackers stood quaking at the sight of their fellows' brutalized remains. A tall she-elf with skin like alabaster and a shorn scalp upon which sat an antlered crown strode out of the pitiful handful of horror-blasted survivors. In her hand was a staff from which dangled sharp-toothed totems and fetishes, and atop the staff was a hunk of amber the size of a fist.

She threw back her head and sang a resplendent dirge. Her voice cut through the blood-drowned stupor that gripped the dwarfs, and they shivered as they recognized the spirit of the cry, even if the words were unknown to them.

The dwarfs were not the only ones who heard her. The hellish bearlike creature who was also Ober loped toward them with frightening speed. If the savagelings had ceased to come to him, he would go to them.

The she-elf leapt gazelle-like toward the exit without ceasing her song. Some of those who stood with her followed suit, but others, their spirits broken or their minds numb with horror, stood unmoving. A moment later, none remained.

The savagelings had broken and fled.

The dwarfs across the bridge watched Ober warily. Even Tomza understood how precarious the situation was. Was the spirit appeased, or was its appetite only whetted? Would it come across the bridge, which was barely wide enough for a single dwarf, much less a creature of its size? If it did brave the crossing, what, if anything, could the Bad Badgers do?

All these questions found their answer in the low, chuffing groan that rose from the ursine shape as it dropped to the floor in the remains of the bloodbath, laid its head on its paws, and began to snore.

"Is it… I mean, is *he* safe?" Torbjorn asked.

With a sound like dawn breaking after a terrible storm, Tomza laughed. "*Yes!* He did it. Look!"

The instruction was not necessary. As the dwarfs stared, the mountain of bear shrank, and its fur was drawn within. In a few more heartbeats, there was only a very bloody and very naked young dwarf, snoring contentedly.

CHAPTER THIRTY

"What did she say?"

There had been so little conversation since their rapid flight that it took Utyrvaul a moment to realize he was being addressed.

"I'm sorry, what was that, Commander?" the svartalf asked, more to buy time than because he hadn't heard the question. The elf was still learning about this peculiar band of dwarfs, and though he prided himself on his ability to talk to anyone about nearly anything, given the state of things, he thought it best to be cautious.

"The she-elf with crown," Torbjorn repeated. He stood just out of earshot of those circled around the small campfire. "What was she saying before she left?"

Utyrvaul frowned and scanned the figures huddled around the meager flames. His eyes settled on the child seated snuggly between Gromic and Haeda. She watched the dwarfs with youth's enduring focus, drinking in every word and expression. She was clearly learning about them, despite not having spoken a word.

Why would she speak when she had no need to?

The dwarfs fed her, kept her safe, and carried her when she grew tired of marching beside them. They had even created a cloak for her by cutting strips from their own cloaks.

Utyrvaul was not confused by the little darling's muteness, unlike Haeda, who doted on her. Words were weapons, and one who brandished his weapon without need was a greater fool than one who carried no weapon. The svartalf knew the game, and for the time being, he was enjoying it. No need to spoil the fun by being overly forthcoming.

"Oh, uh, the wosealf wise one?" he muttered as though trying to recall who they were talking about. "She did screech something before beating a hasty retreat, didn't she? Hmmm. I was not paying attention at the time."

Torbjorn let out a long steaming breath through his nostrils. The nights were getting colder, but they had to be careful about their fire, even with the child to think of. They'd cleared out of Turoth's Tooth and returned to the Wyrmspines before the wights and their army arrived. From their elevated vantage point, they had been able to see that the wight had brought a considerable force. Immaculate lines of cadaverous soldiers in armor had trudged through Fang's Nest while levies of humans and goblins and even a few turncoat savageling hunting parties loped behind like hounds at the heels of their masters.

Astride a huge steed as leathery and cankerous as any of the soldiers was the wight lord. He looked tall, menacing, and terrible, even from atop a ridge.

"Enough games, elf," Torbjorn growled, then winced. This discussion was not meant for other ears. "Just tell me what she said."

The svartalf smiled innocently at the dwarf. "Oh, Commander, you know how those heathen savagelings are. I can't remember her exact words, but they were something like you've doomed us all, then a bit about despair. She finished by calling down curses on all our heads. You know, typical barbaric excess."

Torbjorn nodded without a word, but his dark eyes succinctly declared his suspicion.

"I'm sorry I can't remember more," Utyrvaul continued. "Perhaps in time, I will, but I don't think it's very important. After all, Commander, you made your choice, and there's no going back now, is there?"

Torbjorn frowned at the golden-eyed child sitting at the fire with his dwans—his crew. They still didn't know her name, but she fit in perfectly, as mad as that sounded when he thought about it. He tried to avoid thinking these days since it reminded him that there would be questions asked and explanations required. As his eyes roved around the campfire, he wasn't sure what he was going to say.

Everywhere he looked, there were questions, whether it was Ober, or Tomza, or...or the girl.

They were his responsibility now, and he would have to answer for them, even if he didn't know what those answers were.

"I suppose you're right." He sighed, his breath streaming out of his mouth like the smoke he wished he could draw from his pipe.

"There's no going back now."

AUTHOR NOTES - AARON D. SCHNEIDER

WRITTEN JANUARY 3, 2022

Dear Reader,

We're off on a new adventure, and to say that I'm excited to see where it goes is an understatement. With six books planned, we've just begun to plunge our hands into the muddy and brutal morass of the Wight Wars in the Ysgand Vale, and who knows what we'll dig up when everything's said and done? More secrets and schemes than a svartalf has teeth, I'm sure. All things in God's good time, dear reader.

In the meantime, there are other things on the horizon.

I'm continuing to learn the ins and outs of this whole writing gig, much of it under the tutelage of the great folks at LMBPN, especially Mike. I also have a lovely Canadian expatriate who is also a constant source of wisdom and friendship. Altogether, I am very blessed and also very busy. Working with some fantastic folks at Inbound Horizons at the time of writing this, I'm days from launching a new website and trying to expand the reach and accessibility of my work while still writing feverishly. The website will hopefully not just function as an opportunity to market books but also give you a chance to get to know me a little better as I'll be trying to put up an article every few weeks concerning my thoughts about writing, literature, history, mythology, and whatever else catches my fancy. With improvements and revisions coming to my social media presence, this should allow me more chances to interact with you, Dear Reader, though let's all agree to be gentle with each other, at least in the beginning.

Otherwise, we continue to soldier on in the not-so-old US of A, with me being thankful for walks about the frozen pond near my home. To be honest, I could do with a bit more snow, but the air's stayed brisk enough that I can trundle about comfortably. Occasionally the fluctuating weather causes my abused ankle to act up, but then I just take up my boar's head walking stick and trudge along. I don't think I appreciated the full meaning of calling a regular walk a "constitutional" until I became a professional adult (or at least got good enough at pretending to be one to trick myself). The constitutional isn't just about your muscles or your heart rate or all of that wonderful stuff, but it's also about getting out and experiencing the world, even if it is the world you know. It's almost like something touched on by the song "What About Everything" by Carbon Leaf. Sometimes I need to get out and out of my own head to breathe fresh air and have the world breathe over me, and nothing works better for that than a walk on a cold day.

I'm already dreading the departure of the cold in a few months, knowing the heat and the sweat will drive my thoughts inward again when I take those walks. I don't mind sweat so much, especially when it mixes with the ring of iron, the smell of chalk, and the scuff of mat and gloves, but that's not for walking under these trees or around this pond, and that is still about pressing in, not clearing out.

So I suppose I should just go enjoy it while I can. Sounds like I'm heading out for a walk, but I won't be far. Hopefully, we'll see each other soon.

Until then, Godspeed, Dear Reader.

Sincere Regards,
Aaron D. Schneider

AUTHOR NOTES - MICHAEL ANDERLE

WRITTEN JULY 14, 2021

Thank you for not only reading this book but these author notes as well!

I'm presently in Roma (Rome), sitting on a train leaving for Florence to visit an Airbnb on a converted farm.

No restaurants, no easy taxi, but lots of green vistas.

OMG, PIZZA

I'm a huge fan of pizza. So much that I felt going to Italy was going to be my version of Nirvana on Earth, like back in 2018 when we came to Rome the first time as a family.

Nirvana became purgatory when I couldn't find any pepperoni pizza. Like, they didn't even know what the hell I was talking about (pepperoni), and their suggestions consigned me to Pizza Hell.

On this trip, I found Pizza Diavola, and I've made it through until...*the Train Trip.*

Roma Termini, to be exact, and Pizza Heaven.

Save a little time if you are going to the train station in Rome to visit this restaurant (and stomach room.)

The food is on the third level (lots of choices, including Five Guys for you hamburger fans). All you have to do is go up the escalator (stairs, elevator...your choice) and look almost straight ahead (a little to your left). There is what looks like a sandwich place. RIGHT BEHIND that and to the right is a little pizza place.

Thank me when you have your pizza. Their Pizza Diavola is divine.

It's Summer...

So, you can tell that Aaron wrote his author notes a LONG time ago, and I'm writing mine right as we release this series! It's about ninety degrees outside the train as we go through the Italian countryside (and EVERY tunnel in the country blocks my wifi).

Not that I'm complaining...much.

Italy and Dwarfs

Off in the distance is a hill (maybe four hundred feet high?) that has a small town perched on the top. The buildings were all built on top of each other, crowding together like a bunch of lemmings. To my very untrained eye, it looks to be about three to five hundred years old.

I have no idea if anyone still lives there, but if they don't, it would make a hell of a fun place to check out.

This is the country our beloved dwarfs in the story would find themselves in. Few roads, lots of trees, and high adventure.

As our ass-kicking guys move forward, why not join us for another fight?

Talk to you in the next book!

Ad Aeternitatem,

Michael Anderle

>MORE STORIES with Michael newsletter HERE: https://michael.beehiiv.com/

CONNECT WITH THE AUTHORS

Connect with Aaron Schneider

Website:
https://www.aarondschneider.com/

Email List:
https://www.aarondschneider.com/free-short-story-download-the-tops-tails-of-dreams/

Facebook:
https://www.facebook.com/authoraarondschneider/

Instagram:
https://www.instagram.com/aarond.schneider/

TikTok
https://www.tiktok.com/@aarondschneiderauthor?lang=en

Amazon:
https://www.amazon.com/Aaron-D-Schneider/e/B07H8WZ2HT/

Connect with Michael Anderle and sign up for his email list here:

Website: http://lmbpn.com

Email List: http://lmbpn.com/email/

https://www.facebook.com/LMBPNPublishing

https://twitter.com/MichaelAnderle

https://www.instagram.com/lmbpn_publishing/

https://www.bookbub.com/authors/michael-anderle

OTHER BOOKS BY AARON D. SCHNEIDER

The Warring Realm Series

War-Born

War-Torn

War-Sworn

Rings of the Inconquo

(with A.L. Knorr)

Born of Metal (Book 1)

Metal Guardian (Book 2)

Metal Angel (Book 3)

World's First Wizard

(with Michael Anderle)

Witchmarked (Book 1)

Sorcerybound (Book 2)

Wizardborn (Book 3)

The Outcast Royal Series

(with Michael Anderle)

Circle In The Deep (Book 1)

Voice On The Wind (Book 2)

Doom Under The Shadow (Book 3)

Join Aaron's Email List

https://www.aarondschneider.com/free-short-story-download-the-tops-tails-of-dreams/

BOOKS BY MICHAEL ANDERLE

Sign up for the LMBPN email list to be notified of new releases and special deals!

https://lmbpn.com/email/

For a complete list of books by Michael Anderle, please visit:

www.lmbpn.com/ma-books/

www.ingramcontent.com/pod-product-compliance
Lightning Source LLC
LaVergne TN
LVHW041757060526
838201LV00046B/1030